WHEN OUR HAVEN BURNED

To Buell,

For your mentorship and always balancing fun and service.

[signature]

WHEN OUR HAVEN BURNED

TYLER HEGGANS

NEW DEGREE PRESS

WHEN OUR HAVEN BURNED

ISBN	978-1-63730-842-4	*Paperback*
	978-1-63730-908-7	*Kindle Ebook*
	978-1-63730-944-5	*Ebook*

For what matters in life is not whether we receive a round of applause; what matters is whether we have the courage to venture forth despite the uncertainty of acclaim.

A GENTLEMAN IN MOSCOW, *AMOR TOWLES*

CONTENTS

For those with the audacity to dream
and the courage to create;
you are the ones who carry the flame

CHARACTER GUIDE

Aldrix Sterling—CEO of Sterling Energies

Alfred Sterling—Father of Aldrix; Previous CEO of Sterling Energies

Branson Wellsworth—Father of Liam; Previous CEO of Onyx Bank; Lord of Wellsworth Associates

Liam Wellsworth—CEO of Onyx Bank; Heir of Wellsworth Associates

Apollo—Aldrix Sterling's Personal Guard; Wellsworth Associate

John Hadley—Executive Assistant of Aldrix Sterling

Emerald Silva—Mayor; "Droughtie"

Amelie—Emerald's Friend and Chief of Staff

Ezra—Ex-prisoner; EMT; a childhood friend of Nick and Lucas

Meg—Ezra's EMT Partner

Sam—Morning Prison Guard

Jazer—Evening Prison Guard

Mariah Coleman—Ezra's Mom

Ray Coleman—Ezra's Dad

Suzuka Maamoun—Scientist; Activist; Partner of Lucas

Lucas Maamoun—Software Engineer; Partner of Suzuka; a childhood friend of Nick and Ezra

Sierra Maamoun—Daughter of Lucas and Suzuka

Anna—Colleague of Lucas

Nick Myelin—Engineer at Sterling Energies; Caretaker of Aunt Stacie; a childhood friend of Lucas and Ezra

Aunt Stacie—Nick's aunt

James (Jamie) Myelin—Brother of Nick

Rodrigo Martinez—Engineer at Sterling Energies; Father of Lucia; Colleague of Nick

Lucia Martinez—Daughter of Rodrigo; Oceanographer; Reporter at the *Chronicle*

HAVEN

Circa 1998

For just a moment, it was beautiful.

Slices of floating orange light pierced through a haze as if they were fireflies in the depths of a magical wood. Fragments of light danced amongst the posters lining the walls. Still, under the weight of sleep, Emerald's young eyes began to focus on the dazzling shadows of gold prancing across the bedroom.

Then the roof collapsed around her, the heat, unlike anything she'd ever known.

The glamour tore violently away as the swirling plumes swept under the door, invading the eight-year-old's lungs.

Soot pummeled her as heat radiated across the room.

Scrambling out of bed, she fell hard onto the floor.

The raging fire drowned out her cries for her parents. Her mind raced, trying to see past the pitch-black smoke.

Emerald stumbled through the haze toward the window. Her room became a disorienting maze, leading her to trip on the nightstand and careen to the ground.

Her knee pulsed in pain, blood seeping through her pajamas as her lungs cried out for breath. Flickers of orange climbed closer, the wind fanning the flames through the opening above.

Throwing herself to her feet, Emerald reached out for the window. Her hands found the smooth glass, hope blossoming within her as she desperately pulled upward.

It wouldn't budge. The pit in her stomach grew greater as the fire scorched her skin.

She lunged at the window, attempting to shatter a path to safety. She kicked, fought, and battered the glass, but nothing worked. Her blows grew weaker, the heat ripping at her back.

Finally, the window caved inward, shards throwing themselves across her face. The flames flared, branding her neck as she cried out again.

Hands reached through the window, pulling her onto the grass below. Her mother's face was plastered with a fear Emerald had never seen before.

Despite the blood dripping down her mother's hand, she barely winced as she scooped Emerald into her arms.

Emerald held on fiercely and briefly closed her eyes, wishing she could return to peaceful dreams.

She soon turned her gaze back to the reality in front of her, watching the ash fall like darkened snow upon the vast meadows, the only place she'd ever known.

Through tearstained eyes, Emerald watched as her home was engulfed in flames.

A CITY BY THE SEA

There once was a city by the sea, where the streets hummed with power and the fish swam free.

And on a ridge overlooking their home, a trio met on a meadow of stone.

All came for the power they felt they were owed, none of them knowing how events would unfold.

While trading threats in voices low, they weighed the future of those down below.

As nightfall reigned, only one walked away, the others defeated as the tree branches swayed.

PART I

1

SEEKING REVENGE

Present Day, Circa 2025

Ezra can't sleep tonight.

Drip. Drip. Drip.

The leaks flow into a melody, a lullaby of despair.

When the morning dawns, two guards in matching gray uniforms will appear at his door. One will remove a keycard from a slit in the back of his vest. The other will heft the bars open before both men escort Ezra to the entrance of Fort Laurent Correctional Compound. Another officer will be waiting with his confiscated belongings and carelessly thrust them into Ezra's chest. Then, the guard will step aside, and he will walk out into the dawn.

Ezra knows precisely where his first stop will be. Though, he fears he no longer has a pulse on the outside world—nothing to guide him other than his own vengeance.

He stares blankly at the ceiling as the moonlight bounces off leaking pipes above his cell. The drops fall as if in slow motion as the starlight glimmers off each one. As they patter to the ground and the minuscule droplets disperse, Ezra feels a soft tickle on his toes. He tries to count the beats of this aquatic song, but eventually, the sounds just fade into the background noise of the storm raging in his mind.

After spending ten years in prison, Ezra doesn't know what to expect of the other side of the barbed wire gates.

He repositions himself on his cot, the scar on his abdomen stretching. Nature's nightlight illuminates the cinder blocks around him.

He has been patient for a full decade. All so he might see tomorrow and take his revenge. With the visualization of the morning in his mind, Ezra finally allows himself to drift off to sleep.

In the morning, long before dawn, the guards unlock Ezra's cell and lead him unceremoniously to the door.

Without even a nod of recognition, he is tossed from one wolves' den and into another.

As he takes his first steps past the concrete walls, paralysis grips him.

Looking around, he sees there is no one to usher him home. No obligations he must fulfill, no rules, no commands, nothing but his freedom, and it is entirely overwhelming. Even though he knows exactly what he wants to do today, exactly who he wants to track down, he struggles to take even two steps.

For a moment, he surveys the world around him. It is still dark, the sun not yet piercing the horizon. But he looks to the gas station a few yards away and the elongated cars passing by, their headlights illuminating the world around him.

He saw this scene thousands of times whenever he looked out the windows of the prison, but he'd never noticed the smallest details that have changed.

He never noticed how the taxi's advertisements were a tad bit too bright. Screens replace the plastic he'd known.

Around the street corner, there is a small park with a small meadow. He bends down to feel the dew resting on the blades and realizes how much he's forgotten what nature felt like. How calming the trees are in comparison to the concrete yard.

The neighborhood he walks through is full of burnt-out brick bungalows and pock-marked sidewalks. Patchy front lawns and boarded windows adorn the many abandoned homes.

He is alone on the streets as he wanders aimlessly, hoping to find a subway entrance while attempting to take in the innumerable novelties around him.

At each intersection, there is an opportunity for him to turn, a chance for him to change course, but all he does is walk straight.

Cars with bashed bumpers and replaced doors pass by, the drivers sitting low in their seats. When the animated walking symbol flashes, Ezra pauses, still not trusting that he does not need to receive verbal confirmation that he may cross. No one will order him to turn left or go straight.

He hasn't made a single choice for himself in years. Now every decision is his, and he's terrified he'll make the wrong ones.

There are strangers everywhere, but he does not dare speak to them or even look them in the eye.

He feels he should warn them. Tell them he's a dangerous criminal, or, at least, that's the only thing he's been called for the past several years.

His anonymity is odd, the fact that no one seems to be fleeing his presence or trembling as he strides down the street.

Finally, Ezra happens upon a large metro sign and follows it underground.

The world shakes around him as noises echo and people rush on and off platforms.

Again, he stops, taking in the complete chaos of the world he'd forgotten. He tries to make sense of it, find some semblance of order or patterns, but he doesn't find anything.

Nothing except the map. He stares at it hopelessly, looking for a single stop, but not knowing where to start.

He traces his finger across the board like a child, trying to pinpoint the direction he should go. He used to ride the metro every day. How had he understood something so convoluted?

Apparently, he's loitering too long, the station attendant beginning to side-eye him.

At least knowing when a guy is staring you down behind your back is still a relevant skill on the outside.

To his relief, his finger finds his station, and he runs to find the train he needs.

The once vibrant city of his memory is now menacing.

The streets are exactly as he remembers, and yet Ezra feels as though every person walking the street is a threat.

The brightness of the lights seems hostile. He tries to calm himself as he exits the metro, but it seems after years in a pressure cooker, his survival instincts aren't turning off so easily.

He takes in everything from the sleek screens the crowds stare at as they walk by to the piercing way the neon signs reflect off the glass towers above him.

He makes it to his destination, feeling as though everything around him means to exude fear. The skyscrapers rise into the overcast sky, enclosing around him. He waits on the street corner.

He observes everyone coming in and out of the carved stone entryways.

Despite the shared anonymity of the city crowds, Ezra knows he stands out. His reflection gleams off the sides of the polished buildings around him, the haggard image of his ripped hoodie and worn jeans painfully clear.

The handbags draw close, and the stares pierce him. The guards stationed beside the enclaves of wealth wield semiautomatic machine guns with transparent magazines. They look him up and down.

Ezra does his best to still the nerves. It's not like he's trying to break into the gilded cages. He's had his fill of that.

He only waits for a particular individual to walk through the square.

Knowing it might take time, he ignores the scrutiny and sits on the street corner, stomach rumbling as he realizes he hasn't eaten.

His anger drives his patience as he systematically surveils every face that exits the pristine lobbies of Renlen Boulevard.

An hour passes without anything.

Two hours go by, and Ezra still waits in the predawn darkness. The bustle of the city comes awake, but his target is still nowhere to be found.

Well into the third hour of vigilance, he sees his target exiting the building in a dark suit, golden tie, and slicked-back hair.

The man walks down the sidewalk, holding himself as if he owns the city.

Seconds afterward, another man exits the building, his large stature and lumbering gait guarding the other man's back.

Ezra pauses momentarily but then begins his approach nonetheless.

He doesn't care about the guard. He doesn't care about the consequences.

He follows the pair down the sidewalk, hatred filling his mind as he nears the man responsible for the loss of his life. His imprisonment for nothing other than being in the wrong place at the wrong time.

As Ezra inches ever closer, he pictures the man's bloodied face with satisfaction.

Now only a few feet behind him, Ezra thinks of how he would smile as the prison gates shut in front of him once more. How satisfied he would feel as long as his target's life was ended or equally as miserable.

Adrenaline courses through him, his focus laser-sharp and directed squarely at the back of his target.

Only steps away, Ezra raises his hand, ready to push past the guard and throw the slimy man in the suit to the ground, but suddenly the target makes an abrupt turn toward the curb, and a black sedan rolls up to whisk the city's wealthiest man away.

Ezra then realizes the face in the suit is too young. It only hits him now how smooth his gait is. The man's hair lacks gray on his temples.

The face is the same. The same self-confident smirk and sense of invincibility.

His arm still raised, Ezra watches Aldrix Sterling's tinted window as the vehicle speeds away.

The chase over, Ezra begins to see his surroundings once more and notices the guards who had begun to encircle him, fingers on their safeties.

The sun has just begun to pierce the horizon, and he feels exposed in the morning light.

Ezra turns back toward the metro, surprised.

His anger still swells. Both generations have earned his hatred.

It doesn't matter whether it is the father or the son. Alfred Sterling may have ruined his life, but Aldrix nearly ended it.

Under the shadow of Sterling Tower, Ezra schemes his next shot at revenge.

2

ISN'T HE HELPING?

Tap. Tap. Tap. On the seventy-fifth floor of his building, Aldrix Sterling startles as someone raps on his door in quick succession, almost spilling his coffee onto the opulent carpeting.

Irritated but carefully setting down his morning cappuccino, he orders the visitor in.

John Hadley, his meticulously groomed secretary, enters the room. He looks the part in a gray suit and lined blue tie.

Apollo, his personal guard, shuts the door behind John, his ever-vigilant eyes turning back to scan the hallway.

John begins in his usual dull tone, "Good morning, sir."

Aldrix barely reacts to the words, continuing his work. For all of his brilliance, John isn't quite the most engaging company.

He also has the vexing habit of starting Aldrix's mornings with a rash of negative news.

He strides across the room, places a freshly printed newspaper on the desk, and continues, "Sir, I wanted to ensure you were aware of today's front-page publication in the *Chronicle*. I believe you'll find it quite—"

"Yes, John, I'm aware 'the good residents of this fine city' haven't been thrilled with me recently. That is not news," Sterling cuts in curtly.

"Yes, sir," John responds. "It's just the rage seems to have exceeded the normal parameters, sir. Maybe the company should reconsider—"

"No," Sterling states unwaveringly. "The pipeline is an excellent initiative for the company and will pay dividends well into the future. I don't care if a few bums off the street think they're savvier about my own company than I am. My board unanimously agreed on this decision, and that is nothing short of a miracle."

John pipes back in, "Understood, sir. It's just that, support for Alteryn—"

"I'll take care of Alteryn, John. That's my job. I don't need you telling me about that self-righteous group of hippies!"

As a heavy silence fills the room, Aldrix's blood pressure begins to return to healthy levels.

John's lips wordlessly stammer for a second before finally settling on, "Thank you for the education, sir. I will be right outside at my desk if you need anything, per usual."

As casually as he can, but failing miserably, John slinks out of the room.

Turning his back to the door and staring out the window of Sterling Tower to the luminous streets below, Aldrix releases a sigh.

As the third Sterling man to direct this company, he is the first to encounter such issues. His father and grandfather were never asked to be 'environmentally conscious.' They didn't have renewable energy start-ups popping up like weeds.

Why does it matter where the energy comes from? Why does the media always have to present his faults instead of the jobs he creates and the raving reviews from his employees? Why can't they catch him during one of his CEO floor tours, showing how he respects those lowest in his organization?

If it weren't for Sterling Energies, the same people who protest outside his gates would be unable to read to their children by lamplight. What would the masses do if they were suddenly unable to fire up the stove whenever they wanted? If the heating suddenly died in the brutal heart of winter? And God forbid if they were unable to charge their smartphones! Would the millions of souls below finally appreciate him then?

Aldrix Sterling isn't dumb. He's seen the data. He knows the climate is being changed. Though he doubts his company's actions would really matter if his competitors across the nation don't change as well. He wonders why the people in the streets don't go bother them. *Why does he always have to be the one they pick on?*

From this height, no humans are visible, simply the energy that they so ungratefully take for granted. Among the clouds, Aldrix Sterling poses a single question to an empty room: *Isn't he helping?*

3

FALSE VICTORY

Emerald thought she was ready, but the stage curtains open to blinding light and a wave of shouting.

"Madam Mayor!"

"Mayor-elect!"

"How did you pull off such an upset? Do you think your gender played a role in your election?"

"Madam Mayor-elect! What will your first one-hundred days look like?"

"Do you feel qualified as the youngest person to hold this office?"

"How are you going to celebrate?"

"Madam Silva, what will you do about the Sterling protests? Will that be a factor in your proposed clean energy policy?"

The cameras click rapidly, their flashes adding to the chaos around her.

Stepping up to the podium, eyes still adjusting to the bombardment of light, she says, "I... Um..."

"Mayor Silva!"

The press assails Emerald with questions, each voice trying to drown out the others.

"Ma'am, how do you really expect to lead a city you weren't born in?"

Flash

Years ago, alone in an empty hole-in-the-wall storefront, Emerald stood in absolute awe.

The overhead floodlights burst to life. *Kachunk. Hmm.*

All of her colleagues went home after work leaving the greenhouses of the conservation center for homes filled with families and roommates. Emerald was single and lived alone. Nothing awaited her except tempting Nutella breadsticks.

Every night, she walked with everyone to the metro, then took the line the opposite way. She walked through thinning crowds in the snow, or the rain, or whatever crazy hailstorm the city decided to drop on her. She made her way far from the city lights to a small neighborhood with cracked concrete and flickering neon lights, her fingers gripping her keys and mace as shadows passed by.

Emerald heaved open the cast iron door, entered her tiny office, and turned the lock. The walls were bare except for experimental campaign posters, her only workspace a rickety desk. She reviewed resumes and reached out to university students, hoping for volunteers. She read dozens of articles and watched all the coverage she could find about the other candidates.

Then there was the writing. Scribbling out policies that she'd love to see. Policies that could save the earth and the economy and make people happier.

Well, she thought. She didn't know if any of it would work. That's why she typed away and ideated and plastered sticky notes all over the minuscule room until her brain fogged with exhaustion.

When she felt sleep creeping in, her mind wondered about her chances. She hadn't announced yet. *Was she late?* All the other candidates had millions of dollars. *Could she actually compete?*

It was always when she was about to walk out the door that her best ideas would come. Then she would just turn right back around and sit herself back at her desk all night.

Every night.

Until one night, she was accompanied by an intern, then surrounded by staffers. Soon she traded out that rickety storefront for a proper office space. Suddenly, one peculiar night, she wasn't such a long shot anymore.

Snapping back to the world around her, Emerald closes her eyes and takes a breath.

The rows of journalists before her appear only as silhouettes due to the blazing lights that stun her eyes. Their questions overlap one another on top of the incessant snaps of cameras and adjustments of microphones.

She unconsciously rubs the scar that wraps itself across her cheek and down her neck. Then she gets to it.

She finds a rhythm of answering questions. She gives the monologues she's perfected for hours in the mirror. She wields the words her team prepared. Finally fending off the endless sea of reporters, Emerald takes her leave. The press continues to throw questions at her back as she retreats, but it's done. The worst is over.

She heads backstage to celebrate her victory with her staff, anxious for a bite of that marble cake. She passed it on the way in, but Amelie wouldn't let her even take a quick taste. Apparently, having blue frosting on her lips wasn't appropriate for a press conference.

The adrenaline of the night begins to fade. The realization of her accomplishment begins to hit. An inescapable smile breaks through as she walks toward the elevators. Just as she is about to hit the button, one of her aides runs up, phone alight in his hand.

"Sorry Emerald, great job with the conference, but I have a caller on the line who says they're a sponsor and have urgent news for you. They were very insistent that you speak now."

Emerald sighs, she thought that she was finished with the public for the day. "Fine, fine. Thanks for bringing it to me."

The aide passes the phone to Emerald and walks away as she answers, "Hello?"

A gravelly male voice greets her. "Hello, Madam Mayor. Congratulations on your victory."

"Um, thank you. But may I ask who is calling?"

"My name isn't important," the man answers, "only that I'm speaking on behalf of our mutual friend in the golden tower."

Lowering her voice but simultaneously channeling her rage, Emerald answers, "You—how the hell did you get my number?"

The voice is unbothered, "Darling, when your name is on the tallest building in the city, you get what you want. Now don't hang up. I know you want to, but I know a little secret. A little rumor that might just make for excellent front-page news about the new mayor if it were to accidentally fall into the wrong hands."

"Go on," Emerald bites out through gritted teeth.

There is a smile in the man's voice as he answers, "Well, of course, everyone loves an underdog. And long shot political candidates almost never win. And usually, it so happens their issues stem from a lack of funds. Now, how did it so happen you miraculously found just the funds you needed? I doubt I need to go any further. I will assume the clandestine event I am referring to has been refreshed in your mind, has it not?"

Emerald holds fast, "I don't know what you're talking about."

The man lets out a deep, dry laugh. "Of course you don't, dear. And that's okay. All you need to know is we're going to meet. And when we do, we'll discuss how I can prevent any unfortunate slip of the lips."

Emerald can't believe it. She pushes back, "I don't need your help or your cover from whatever you think you know. I've got real constituents now, and we're gonna bring down your boss' energy monopoly."

"Ah, such bold words. Such brazen confidence," The man draws out the words, letting his ominous phrases hang in the air. "I think we can both recognize that's not how you felt when you thought you were alone in that shabby little shack of an office on the east side, hmm?"

Emerald's mind races, trying to determine how he knows all this.

The man closes as calmly as he began, "Anyway, I won't trouble you any longer. Just remember, next time we meet, bring a little more humility. You thought being mayor would give you power, but you're just like everyone else in this city. And we all work for the same man. Good day, Emerald."

4

OPPORTUNITY

Lucas Maamoun wakes to the vibrations of his watch and an overcast morning. Faded sunlight glows through his bedroom curtains, illuminating the room in a morning haze.

He opens his eyes and glances at his sleeping wife. Suzuka's straight black hair is a mess on her pillow. It makes Lucas smile.

Rising carefully, Lucas swings his legs onto the floor and begins his day. His first stop is always Sierra's room to check that she's still sleeping softly. She always is because when she wakes up, it's rarely subtle.

The main headline washes over him in a haze of blue-light as he heads to the kitchen down his worn stairs:

"PROTESTS ERUPT AS STERLING ENERGIES ANNOUNCES PLANS FOR NEW OIL PIPELINE!"

Lucas reads further:

Sterling Energies announced its planned construction of a new oil pipeline beneath the Aurietta Sea early Tuesday morning. The company defended its action by citing the 4 percent expected increase in output that will occur as a result of the network expansion.

While these statements have been verified by third-party reports, environmental activists immediately organized a protest in Sterling Square outside the company's headquarters. They are demanding Sterling reverse its plans and use the money to invest in green energy sources instead. They also point out the potential hazards of construction, leaning on lessons learned from the original pipeline network built fifty-five years ago.

Finishing his bowl of cereal, Lucas scans the picture. It features a silhouetted woman holding a sign stating, "*I demand a green future!*" as she shouts at the security guard outside the Sterling skyscraper. He shakes his head. His lips tugged in a thin line.

His heart warms slightly at the ragtag crowd of protesters taking to the streets. While he tosses his cardboard in the blue can outside each week, he knows his boss would kill him if he took off work to attend the demonstration.

At the same time, the images of the megaphones and the crowds and the shouting fill him with anxiety. Plus, *why would he risk injury?* The other day, images of a trampled protester filled the papers, their face disfigured and covered in blood. He can't risk that, and neither can Suzuka. He sees his wife's eyes spark whenever environmental news hits the TV, but they've got other things to worry about.

Returning the milk to the fridge, he pauses to look at his graduation photo. Standing in the middle of their football field, he, Nick, and Ezra are all sporting their dark green caps and gowns as they stare into the camera lens.

Nick smiles widely with his signature dimples. Lucas stands next to him with his long hair draping over his forehead, and Ezra stands in between them with his characteristically goofy pose. He wonders how they're doing. He knows

Ezra is in prison, but Nick remains in the city as far as he's aware. *We should meet up sometime,* he thinks. They never had a falling out. Life has just gotten in the way.

He remembers visiting Ezra once and bumping into Nick on the metro that one time, but recently they just haven't crossed his mind as often as they used to. Ezra is probably getting out soon. They should plan something for him. He marks the calendar, scribbling a quick note to reach out to his old friends.

Walking through the hall, Lucas passes the covered canvas of Suzuka's latest painting. It sits on an office desk, brushes soaking on the side in a soapy solution. He has the urge to peek, but he knows the rules. Suzuka doesn't like him to see until it's complete. She's pretty protective of her projects.

Finished art pieces line their hallway walls. The landscapes portray lush forests, oceanside sunrises, and harsh tundras. Lucas admires them all as he returns to their bedroom.

He finds Suzuka stirring, tangling the sheets in a pile at the foot of the bed. Lying on her back, she scrolls through her morning digital digest.

When Lucas approaches, Suzuka looks up. As per their routine, he walks up and kisses her as she sets her hand on the bold patterns that tattoo his forearm.

Suzuka wishes him a good day at work and reminds him of her overnight at her sister's on Saturday. Both joy and a spike of panic run through him at the prospect of caring for Sierra alone. He nods as if he hadn't completely forgotten before turning toward the doorway.

He raises his hand, signing, "*I love you.*" His thumb, index, and pinky hover in the air as Suzuka smiles warmly. He will never say those words with his lips, but signing that phrase to his wife each morning conveys more than the spoken words ever could.

She waves the sign back before he slips quietly out of their home, entering into an often hostile landscape of sounds.

Lucas' parents quickly realized his fever was a problem. How even after his forehead cooled and they rocked him in his cradle, he didn't seem to respond to their calls.

They brought him to an austere room with a man in a white coat who prodded him within dozens of weird-looking tools. In the end, the doctor provided his parents with his usual spiel as, after a while, even the most empathetic doctors become immune to the gravity of their words. He handed them a pamphlet and sent them on their way.

Those two hours spent in the doctor's office completely altered the life plan Lucas' parents imagined for him. As an oblivious two-year-old, Lucas didn't understand what was happening, but he certainly recognized the look of disappointment on his parents' faces.

Nonetheless, resolute to cope, his parents bought an ASL booklet on the way home from the doctor's office. They started from scratch. They reached out to the mixed Deaf and hearing school, and the community welcomed them graciously. Kind strangers sat with them in classrooms late in the night, gently critiquing their signs. It didn't take long before his parents were able to communicate proficiently. Lucas was raised with a community around him.

When he stumbled upon Suzuka at their shared first jobs, Lucas held on tightly to the soda can in his hand, his palms sweaty with nerves. He stood apart from his colleagues in the bland tan room, unsure how to engage with them. When

Suzuka walked up and introduced herself to him verbally, he simply shook his head furtively.

Most people would have been a bit surprised or confused, but Suzuka seamlessly transferred to ASL. Every time she tells the story of their acquaintance, she never fails to note the jaw-dropped expression on Lucas' face when she signed to him for the first time.

Suzuka was a CODA. Children of Deaf Adults always surprised Lucas every time. Suzuka was one of the few hearing people Lucas had ever met who actually knew how to *listen*.

At this point in his life, Lucas has learned to have mercy. The majority of people don't mean him harm. They are simply unaware of how inaccessible their hearing world can be to him. He laughs at their impatience when he doesn't understand their meaningless wild gestures. Being Deaf has made Lucas who he is. Many call it a disability, but Lucas has always thought of it as his superpower.

Walking down into the subway on his way to work, he sees a bassist playing. The audio cord snakes its way to an amp, the chords shouting into the air. As Lucas gets closer, he comes to recognize the beat. He immediately begins bopping his head to the vibrations as they blast their way down the street.

While he will never be able to enjoy the melodies of his favorite songs, Lucas appreciates the bass for providing the stability necessary for the other instruments to stun the crowd. Lucas will never be the lead singer or the fawned over electric guitarist, but he finds great pride in being the bass.

As a computer programmer, he provides base code for the world's digital interactions. There isn't much recognition in this job, but Lucas doesn't mind. He's never needed the roar of the crowd anyway.

Making his way into his office building, the security guard named Horace looks up. He waves and then finger-spells Lucas' name. Lucas waves back and signs his thanks. Lucas' name is the only bit of ASL Horace knows, and it took him a week to fully memorize and practice finger-spelling the letters in front of the mirror.

The first day he tried it, his hand was shaking, but Lucas understood. Every day from then on, he has finger spelled his greeting to Lucas. It isn't much, but it's more kindness than the world usually allows him.

The open-concept office of Lucas' digital software company is a Star Trek fan's dream.

Countless screens displaying different announcements and events embed the smooth, colored walls. The meeting rooms automatically identify him to adjust to his preferred temperature and lighting settings and checks him out wirelessly at the modern market-style cafeteria.

The only piece missing is beaming the employees up to their desks.

Lucas has always been a huge Star Trek fan, and he obviously loves technology. He finds the little tricks entertaining but has been careful not to fall too much in love with them. At the end of the day, they're just a few lines of code.

He's working on a similar piece of code at his adjustable desk when a notification slides into view at the top of his monitor. Usually, he can't stand the interruptive banners that invade his screen constantly, so he's carefully gone through his settings to ensure only those classified as important appear on his screen.

Unfortunately, this email from his supervisor qualifies for entry. At least her message seems exciting.

The subject of the message reads, "Amazing Opportunity!"

Interest officially piqued, Lucas clicks on the notification:

Hi Lucas,

I just received great news from our Engineering Fellow! I can't wait to share it with you and your new team. Have you worked with Tess and Jeff before? Meet me in my office at 14:00. I have an exciting new project for you.

Lucas wonders what could have her in such a good mood.

His manager is certainly well equipped for her job, a passionate extrovert among a sea full of introverts. But Lucas would never think of her as bubbly in the way this email indicates.

She is still a programmer, and numbers and results are what impress her. To make her almost giddy would require a huge business success.

A project assigned directly from the top must be an especially serious task. Lucas racks his brain for what could be going on but ultimately knows he'll have to wait until 14:00.

Turning back to the task at hand, he types away on his current project until the clock strikes 13:55.

Raising his desk upward with the press of a button, Lucas grabs his computer and heads to the elevator bay. He walks past his colleagues and through the smooth doorway to board an elevator to the sixth floor.

Arriving at his supervisor's enclosed office at the end of the countless rows of open concept desks, he finds the door shut. Extending his ID from the lanyard, he taps it against a slim black reader on the door. It blinks green twice, notifying her of his arrival.

For the next two minutes, he remains outside and looks out the window until the office door swings open.

An older man from graphic design—who he recognizes but doesn't know—leaves the office.

He has a slightly confused but simultaneously pleased expression on his face as if he can't quite believe what just happened. Without looking up, he makes his way down the hallway, and Lucas steps into the office.

His boss sits behind her sleekly designed desk, another office object that seems imported from the future. It has an embedded screen that mostly functions as a digital keyboard for his manager's two monitors but can also serve a host of other functions.

Two empty chairs sat in front of her desk, and she occupied the high-backed seat behind it. With her reading glasses on, the tall, middle-aged woman skims a report that Lucas assumes was part of the previous conversation with the man who just left.

Sitting down at his supervisor's desk, he looks up at this friendly superior and patiently waits for her to finish her reading. Within a few seconds, she looks up at Lucas and smiles. She waves. Lucas waves back.

Pushing aside the papers in front of her, Lucas sees she has already pretyped whatever she has to share with him.

She double taps an icon in the corner, and the screen embedded in the desk rotates to face Lucas. Folding her arms in a waiting posture, she looks away as Lucas begins reading:

Hi Lucas,

The Engineering Fellow has approached me with an incredible opportunity. As the result of a huge new deal, we are to write code identifying the top green energy companies in the city and predicting their growth! I am pulling together several people from different project areas for this assignment, and I would like you to join the team. Due to the agreement's price tag, I am happy to say a raise and promotion to Principal Programmer will accompany your appointment to this team. You have done great work, and I certainly think it's time for an advancement.

That said, your acceptance of this position comes with several conditions. Part of the agreement with this client is that we will keep the funding entity's identity confidential. You will be required to sign a nondisclosure agreement and will be unable to discuss this project with your other colleagues.

If you are ready to accept the conditions right now, use the pen tool to check here. []

If you require more time to think about this commitment, check here []

If you are deciding to decline this offer, I understand. I appreciate your continued hard work []

Lucas hesitates. This is huge. He can't wait to tell Suzuka of his promotion from Senior programmer.

He's been stuck in this position for the past four years, and he's been complaining to her at home that he's ready for the next step. He can provide even better for Sierra and maybe look into taking the trip to Italy he's been toying with for years.

But looking at the text in front of him, a red flag has been raised in his subconscious.

His manager had clearly laid out everything Lucas had wanted. So why does it feel wrong?

Ignoring this feeling and trusting his superior, he selects the pen tool on the left side of the screen and checks the first box.

Rotating the screen back to her, she grins and gives a thumbs up. It's a bit condescending as if he's a kindergartener who just turned in his stick figure drawing to his teacher, but he brushes it off. He's too busy being stunned that he's now a Principal Programmer.

His boss types a quick message and rotates the screen. It reads:

Congratulations, Lucas, and welcome to the team. We will have our first meeting a few hours from now, 17:00–18:00. I'm sorry to keep you late, but an outside guest is attending, and it's the only time that worked. The rest of the project should conform to mostly normal hours. Thank you once again, and I'll see you this evening in conference room 632.

With that, Lucas types out "thank you," rises from his chair, and leaves the office with the same disbelieving expression as the man before him.

Lucas arrives at the meeting at exactly 5 p.m. Having texted Suzuka that he'll be home late but has exciting news, Lucas spent the rest of the afternoon oscillating between the work in front of him and wondering what would be presented to him later that evening. *Did the company win a government contract? Is this a political campaign already getting ready for the next election in three years?*

As he walks into the room, he sees his manager at the head of the conference table with a very stuffy-looking young man next to her. He wears a black suit with a blue tie and a no-nonsense expression. He has slicked back his hair and wears an overly complex watch. Aside from his demeanor and dress, Lucas knows him to be the guest for his lack of an ID around his neck or on his hip.

Besides those two, there are three other employees already seated, leading Lucas to believe he's the last to arrive. One of them is the older man he saw leave his boss's office earlier. One is a glamorously dressed woman he guesses is Tess. The final team member is his cubicle neighbor, Anna. Thankful for a familiar face, he takes the seat next to her and waves.

She greets him with a wave back, immediately grabbing a piece of printer paper from her bag. Anna doesn't know any sign language at all, so they've developed a habit of writing in text-slang to communicate.

The room remains still as everyone continues gazing into their smartphones, and their supervisor fiddles with the projector. Anna's pencil is the only motion in the room as she writes, *"Do u kno wht this is?"*

Lucas picked up the pencil from where she placed it and wrote, *"No clu."*

Obviously unsatisfied, Anna contorts her face, evidently puzzled. She doesn't have to wait long, however, as their supervisor soon begins.

Lucas clearly doesn't hear her start but watches as everyone turns toward her and sees her lips moving rapidly. Trying to figure out what is going on, he tries to read everyone else's expressions to no avail.

Since Anna begins clapping politely next to him, he does the same. The serious-looking young guest stands, and a PowerPoint presentation appears on the main screen. Suddenly, Anna's claps freeze next to him. He soon realizes why, looking at the title of the PowerPoint, he reads:

Project RENEWED
High-Value Acquisitions Project
Presented by John Hadley
Sterling Energies

Lucas goes still as well. As John begins speaking, his manager passes around project briefing packets. Giving up his attempts to follow the PowerPoint, he opens up the packet Anna hands him and skeptically begins skimming through it.

The packet is thorough, but he still doesn't know what to make of it. This seems like an amazing opportunity. It is a chance to identify companies Sterling could use to move the city's energy grid into a new era. It seems absolutely phenomenal.

But Lucas can't shake the image he saw this morning of the protests at Sterling's gates. *Why isn't this initiative public? Why wouldn't Sterling want to showcase how they're modernizing their power grid?*

Lucas knows something isn't sitting right but doesn't know if he is just missing something in the words floating noiselessly around his head. Anna's face seems similarly suspicious, though, so maybe there is more beneath the words on the packet page.

Either way, Lucas feels the weight of this project. This morning Lucas watched from the sidelines of Twitter, but now he has been mercilessly thrown amidst the chaos.

Across the table, his two older colleagues seem shocked as well but eager to begin. John continues for another few minutes, although no one is listening quite as attentively as before. Lucas continues flipping through the dozens of pages of the "Company Confidential" briefing and hangs his head.

He knows he already agreed to work on this, but now he feels morally conflicted. *If this really is such a great assignment, why does this feel so wrong?*

Signing the final contract and NDA, he passes the contract back to his superior. Walking out of the room, Lucas can't help but glance back at the stately Sterling logo and wonder what he's just gotten himself into.

Suzuka is eating a salad at the kitchen table and scrolling through her phone when Lucas arrives. She smiles at him and signs, "*Welcome back. What's the news?*"

Lucas sets down his backpack and plasters a smile that he hopes hides the doubt in his mind. He signs excitedly, "*Guess who is a Principal Programmer?*"

Suzuka bounces out of her chair and rushes to throw her arms around him, signing, "*Fantastic! Congratulations!*" She hums with pride.

Lucas welcomes the embrace, but Suzuka's warmth doesn't quite feel the same.

5

SCARLET RAGE

Suzuka can barely breathe.

Her mind struggles to form a thought amidst the blaring noise.

She is thrown around by the people surrounding her.

But she's waited weeks for this moment.

She jostles her way through the crowded street as she chants along with hundreds of other voices. The speakers, on high, attempt to drown their calls for justice, but it's useless. Everyone here has a purpose. Their Saturdays are not lazy. Today they work for the planet.

All their passion is directed toward the infamous golden tower. As Suzuka moves closer to the tower, she sees the metal fencing. The gathering is large enough that Sterling has sent several henchmen to defend his precious gold-plated building. The police barricade themselves behind riot shields and armored vehicles. Ready to fight a war against peace.

Good. She's glad he's nervous.

Gradually the crowd settles on a chant, "Sterling! Darling! You're not Charming!" It steadily grows louder and louder until the roar reverberates through Suzuka's bones.

She feels absolutely triumphant. And when Sierra is old enough, she hopes she's proud of what her mother fought for.

Suzuka makes it to the front row, finally having a bit of breathing room. Other coalition members fan out beside her, and Suzuka finally spots their director.

The woman's gray hair doesn't dampen her fearlessness. She stares directly into the eyes of the expressionless riot guard as she screams about the climate. She hoists her sign above her head and turns back to the crowd, inspiring a wave of cheers.

Passersby stop to gawk, phones raised, and cameras ready. Some join in the chants. Others simply hang back. But all of them feel the electricity of the moment.

Suzuka is pressed forward as those behind her begin to close in. Lifting her off her feet and smashing her into the guard's shield. Dazed, she recovers, but the guard hasn't changed from his statuesque positioning. He didn't even blink.

Suzuka tries to stay with the other coalition members, but the tide moves them away. She begins to be thrown toward the coalition leader.

Her hands become clammy, and the sun suddenly feels very close as the friendly faces around her are replaced by strangers. Again, she's thrown up against a riot guard who doesn't budge. In the creases, she catches glimpses of the coalition director, boiling with the determination to be heard.

Suzuka struggles to move toward her. She is almost there.

The riot guards suddenly lift their shields and duck in unison.

From the corner of her eye, she sees a streak of orange. It curves like a violent shooting star, twirling as it splits the air. The arc falls toward the security guards—protectors of the guilty. As they scramble for protection, Suzuka has none.

Clink. Fwooom.

The glass makes such a small sound compared to the noise of the city, but it is all Suzuka hears as shards fly out mere feet away from her.

Flames bursts into the air as a shout rings out in waves through the crowd. The stoic guards are instantly agitated. They push into the throng of people, tossing many to the ground.

The world snaps back into focus for Suzuka. The guards draw their weapons and point them into the crowd as the masses run for their lives. More bottles and stones rain down as a cop shoots a canister above the disarray, leaving an arc of gas and disorientation in its wake.

Covering her eyes, Suzuka fights her way through the infinite disorder. Checking over her shoulder, she stops dead in her tracks. The coalition director lies on the ground, her face raised with angry purple marks. Crimson streams down her cheek as a guard brings his fist down, again and again, beating the older woman.

Before Suzuka knows what she's doing, she has a broken bottle in her hand and smashes it into the back of the guard's head. Blood splatters across her shirt, and the guard falls to his knees.

Leaning down, she traces red across his skin with the serrated bottle. In blinding rage, Suzuka kicks the officer with all her might. Even when he's down, clutching his head, she pummels him.

Only when Suzuka stands over his unconscious body, the bottle dripping with blood, does she regain awareness of the world.

Chaos still moves around her, and the director kneels in pain next to Suzuka, with fear in her eyes. When Suzuka moves to help her up, she flinches and draws back. But then Suzuka throws her arm around the woman, and they limp away.

The fires burning in the street reflect the orange glow of the Sterling gold. Guards continue shouting unintelligibly, and figures shift behinds the rising smoke.

Several people crash into the pair as they stumble toward an alleyway.

A stranger bolts past her, knocking her down, bringing the director with her into the ground. Suzuka's arm splits on the gravel. Her eyes see the dribble of blood running down her forearm, but she kicks the pain to the side.

She rolls to her feet, feeling the places where the bruises will form. But she grabs the coalition leader once again and trudges on.

Yelling and screaming continue to pierce the air behind her, and sirens blare. She does her best to pick up the pace, the director's breathing becoming ever fainter. Her walking grows weary until she finally collapses.

Suzuka sits on the asphalt and holds the director in the street. Both of them are bleeding with their spirits broken. Suzuka holds her until the blood has dried. Until the crowd is gone and the paramedics show up.

Suzuka holds her until her breathing stops.

In the small hallway indentation that acts as their foyer, Suzuka takes a moment to straighten her hair and smooth out her clothes.

Last night was supposed to be one of celebration. Instead, she spent it alongside others in the coalition, holding one another between fits of rage and waves of sadness.

She was allowed to take a quick shower at the hospital as the paramedics tried in vain to resuscitate the director, but there are several marks that will need much deeper cleansing.

She does her best to wipe the rest of the dirt from her palms, move her sleeve over her forearm, and stuff her bloodied sweater deep into her bag.

Taking a single breath to transition into mom-mode, she walks up to her door and into a surprisingly calm scene of Lucas watching basketball with Sierra in his arms.

Sensing movement, Lucas turns his head and smiles. He signs, "*Welcome home! How is Aina? Your sister doing well?*"

The question stuns Suzuka. She forgot the absurdity of her lie. But she doesn't know why it's always been easier to lie when she doesn't have to vocalize the untruth.

So, she just signs back, "*It was lovely. Got a bit heated at one point, but you know how we get. Thanks for watching Sierra.*"

Lucas signs back, "*Of course.*"

Suzuka responds, "*I'm gonna shower and then do some painting. I'm feeling some quiet time.*"

Lucas just nods and smiles again before turning his attention back to the game. Suzuka slips unchallenged into their bathroom.

Alone, Suzuka locks the door before sliding to a crouch on the floor.

Her chest rises and falls rapidly, still attempting to process the experiences of the day before. Her eyes sting as she rolls up her sleeves to look helplessly at her arms.

Feeling the phantom warmth where a life sputtered to an end. And the ghost of a bottle that held more rage than she knew.

6

SECOND FRIDAY

Aldrix Sterling slides open his dresser, pulling out a simple T-shirt and jeans from the dozens of suits and ties. He leaves his briefcase abandoned beside his nightstand. Instead, he picks up the everyday backpack that spends most of the month at the back of his walk-in closet. He still maintains his signature look. He slicks down his hair as he watches the financial news in his digital mirror. He picks out a wristwatch from the crystal case he keeps them in. He is trying to be relatable, but he still needs style.

Today is the second Friday of the month. Irrelevant to most people, this is the day that Aldrix spends his entire morning with the salt-of-the-earth of Sterling Energies: the mechanics, the engineers, the statisticians. They work in the smallest building in the Sterling Square complex and enter through the side entrance, but their work is monumental.

Today, he forgets about meetings and key performance indicators and does his best to remember the people making things happen. He realized the impact of these visits the first week as CEO. The people on the floor want to see their work appreciated.

His father passed on a growing company but left behind a workforce that barely knew him. He was always strictly business. He earned no loyalty despite the decades sitting above the laborers. Aldrix quickly realized the best way to grow was simply to get people to like him. If he could do that, then his workers could be proud of who they worked for. Thus, they would give more effort to the work at hand.

He acknowledges this was quite a shrewd way of looking at things, only socializing for the sake of his bottom line, but over time he has come to genuinely enjoy this little routine.

He now maintains strong friendships with many of his workers. Each month he receives updates of his favorites' lives. Bringing balloons to celebrate births and congratulate newlyweds. He has John pick out cards the week before. He always enjoys the smiles he gets in return.

He has the opportunity to use the company fortune to slide a little extra to those who need it. So he does. When his people lose a loved one, they often find a wad of cash in their lap. When a child is hospitalized, he rarely fails to leave a gift at the parent's desk. For all the criticism of Aldrix Sterling, he takes care of his own.

Aldrix finishes his breakfast and walks out of his house. His wife has already left for her law firm. Her Maserati is gone from the driveway. He continues on, passing his parked Cadillac. After walking four blocks through his neighborhood, he reaches the nearest metro stop. Paying his $2.20 in exact change, he enters the dim underground.

Truth be told, he loves riding the metro. He never took it as a boy, only being caravanned around in Rolls Royces. He always watched with curiosity as his parents drove him by the masses entering the tunnels, sitting among the dirt and grime for transportation.

Now, he tries to blend in and smirks as a mother scolds her child for trying to balance without sitting or holding onto a pole. The child stumbles, and the mother has to grab the kid, her aggravation bleeding through.

Aldrix wonders if he and his mother would have gone through a similar dance had he grown up among the lower class and his lineage were different.

Now he loves the lack of responsibility that the metro provides. His Cadillac is a constant reminder of his station and duties, regardless of how powerful he feels when the engine roars.

Aldrix much prefers the ease of paying $2.20 to sit and twiddle his thumbs if but for a little while. For these short moments, he can pretend to be just like everyone else.

On arrival, they welcome him like a king.

Matt, the security guard, jokingly asks for his ID while simultaneously opening the fencing of the facility grounds. Aldrix thanks him and asks whether his sister is settling in well to her new apartment. He's glad to hear that she is.

He strolls into the plant building itself and starts making his way around the floor. He sees Joseph first and waves before turning to greet Marissa as she leaves the locker room. He continues making his way along the long, narrow walkways, stopping briefly to make polite conversation and pass around his usual gifts.

Finally, he makes his way to the control room. His brilliant Engineering Lead, Nick, is there speaking seriously with a data analyst. *Hell of a brain on that kid,* he thinks to himself. *It's a shame he didn't finish MIT.*

Thank goodness Aldrix was able to snag him.

Seeing he's busy, Aldrix waves quickly and heads on over to see Mr. Rodrigo Martinez. With his back turned, Rodrigo doesn't see him coming, and startles slightly upon Aldrix's hand landing forcefully, yet amiably on his shoulder.

"Hey Rod, how's it going?"

The older man replies, "Hey Al, I'm doing well. Much better than you, it seems. I saw all of the posters on the way inside, and I am glad I am not you right now." Mr. Martinez says with a laugh.

Aldrix plays his part, "Yeah, well, the board's beside themselves about the PR, but people will calm down eventually. They know they need us. But forget about that, how's your wife? How're the kids?"

Rodrigo leans back in his chair, relaxed, "Wife's doing well, enjoying her retirement. She finds a new hobby every day, and I can't keep up. Last week she was obsessed with growing tulips, but that was too easy for her, so now she's into learning Arabic. She's so good at everything, and I can barely read these charts well enough to keep up with these newbies. Keeps life interesting though, can't complain."

Aldrix nods for Rodrigo to continue, "The kids are doing well too. Diego and Lucia are doing their own thing in their careers. Lucia's just got a reporting job with the *Chronicle*, though, so she's thrilled. Coming over for dinner this weekend, so I'm sure I'll get the lowdown then. How's your wife doing?"

Aldrix replies honestly, "Haven't seen much of her with how busy she's been at her firm. Sometimes it barely seems like we're living together between both our hours. We're working on it, though. Listen, I just wanted to check in. If you need anything, as always, let me know. I'm serious about that. You've been dedicated to this place forever. I appreciate that. Have a good weekend."

"Thanks, boss," Rodrigo answers. "Same to you."

As Aldrix moves toward the exit of the control room, Nick finishes up his chat with the data analyst.

Nodding at him, Nick makes his way over to Aldrix. Without any further communication, they exit the room together.

They walk beside each other down a few hallways. They barely make a sound before coming to a lesser-used corridor where Aldrix often has frank conversations with his managers.

Finally, Nick says, "Hey, Mr. Sterling. There's an issue with one of the instruments in the sea. It's giving us strange readings. The analyst and I determined we're going to send a team to look at it in the next few days."

Aldrix considers how Nick-like those few sentences were. Despite several invitations to call him Aldrix or Al, Nicholas Myelin continues to address him formally. He is also always all business. He happened upon this young prodigy nine years ago, but all Aldrix knows about him is he was a local, dropped out of MIT for some mysterious reason, has a brother and sick aunt.

It is clear Nick has some demons in his life, but it is also clear no one becomes privy to the details unless Nick wants them to.

He feels bad for the kid, but he is Sterling's best manager, so he never pushes too far.

So he just says, "I appreciate the update, Nick. Let me know what the mechanical team says once they check it out. How's the morale of your section been since the recent events?"

Frankly, Nick replies, "Not great, but they're pushing through. Most of them are just pretty conflicted. They like the company, and they like you, but lots of them share the protesters' sentiments. I definitely think you should consider at least partially satisfying the demands and moving in a greener direction."

Without even truly processing Nick's words, Aldrix gives his prepared answer, "You know that's impossible, Nick. Our competitors are doing just as well or better than us in other cities without all this green pressure. If we use up all our money investing in a fad, we're going to tank ourselves in the market."

Nick shot back, "That's what I thought you'd say, but you asked for my opinion, Mr. Sterling. The climate isn't a fad."

Aldrix replies while looking over Nick's shoulder, his attention elsewhere, "Fair enough, Nick. It may not be a fad, but people's energy to protest about it is. They'll give up in a few months and rotate back to other issues to concern themselves with. I want clean air as much as the next person, but there's time to become greener in the future. Presently we need to power this city and put food on everyone's tables."

Aldrix's eyes return to Nick's as he says, "You're brilliant with machines, Nick, but this is a people problem. I appreciate your input, but you can't solve this one by satisfying the quotient."

With that, Aldrix walks from the hallway to continue shaking hands, his charismatic smile plastered on his face once more.

7

AN INVITATION

The Monday morning after the protest, Suzuka wakes up, bruised. A combination of fear, shame, and guilt muddle her thoughts.

Despite knowing why she did it, the moment the bottle slammed into the cop's head plays on loop in her mind. She can't remember if he was breathing when she ran. All she remembers is her desperation to save her fallen friend.

What if someone caught it on video? What happened to the cop? Did she leave him to die, or did he wake up in a hospital bed somewhere? Did he get a good look at her face?

She scrolls through her social media, and it doesn't seem like she's trending or on any criminal watch lists, so that's a good sign. Still, the knot in her stomach is unshakeable. She puts her phone down on the empty space next to her. Now that Lucas has left, she has been left per usual to deal with Sierra and hop to work on time.

Her morning at the lab passes without much consequence. She lazily skims through the latest seismic reports from a Pacific island, entering the data into her growing earthquake dataset. Her fingers meander across the keyboard. She isn't even sure she inputted the information correctly.

Normally, Suzuka would be eager to have new data. More knowledge to improve her model. Something else she could add to her understanding of the world. Today, the knowledge doesn't seem worth it. She sits at her sleek yet bleak desk and wills the clock to move faster.

She plugs in her headphones and lets her mind wander away while her hands type digit after digit of numerical strings.

When she finds herself absentmindedly staring at the monitor, her stomach rolls with anxiety. The blankness in her brain is replaced by flashes of fists and glass and blood. The moments play on repeat in her mind. Her heart begins to furiously pump as she thinks about what she did.

She thinks of how the anger had burst out of her.

Her tears had stung on her lashes when she rubbed her hands raw in an attempt to remove the blood stains.

Suzuka snaps her head up when some of her colleagues walk by on their way to lunch. They look her way, but she knows she's long lost the right to an invitation.

All they know is she's turned them down every time their friendly faces have tried to convince her to hang out. So now they just stare as they walk by her.

Suzuka shakes it off. She has somewhere else to be.

Lucas has never worked on a project so fascinating.

He and Anna have been assigned to research and data collection for Project RENEW, feeding their developing algorithmic model as much information as possible. If they are to predict the most advantageous companies for Sterling to integrate into their operations, they need data. A ton of it.

However, the first day of Project RENEW was far less productive.

When Lucas first walked into his new office, his name was displayed digitally across the entry. He was stunned.

No longer did he sit in the crowded cubicles. His promotion had earned him a sleek space to call his own.

The first time he looked out the window, his mouth dropped. The lake shimmered below, and all he could make of the street were dots marching about their lives.

When he finally recovered, he ran over to Anna's new desk. He caught her staring out her window with the same expression he guessed his face showed just moments ago. Only, instead of the sea, the golden spire pierced the clouds before them.

Anna finally noticed Lucas and looked at the papers laid out on her desk. The sheets bearing the same insignia as the skyscraper in front of them. A small nod to the enormity and gravity of the task before them and the positive impact this could have.

Now Lucas barely glances out the window. He and Anna bounce between one another's offices, sharing meals while they pore over piles of profiles on clean energy companies: Alteryn, Electrusin, Hydromext.

These tech companies are revolutionizing the effectiveness of solar batteries. Green automated vehicle companies that could potentially replace Sterling's fleet. Everything from those studying marginal improvements in wind farming to businesses determined to capture carbon and pull it back down to the earth.

Lucas is amazed. *Who knew there were so many diverse, interesting enterprises? Why hadn't any of these taken off already?*

Anna taps him on the shoulder with her pencil, and he looks up. He looks at the digital notepad they always bring up on the desk to ease communication.

Anna had typed out: "*Just read through some financial reports for Alteryn. We'll see what the algorithm spits out, but it looks good. Have you noticed this logo?*"

Beneath her words is a squiggly attempt to draw a crest with the digital pen. Lucas looks at her with confusion.

She turns and projects her screen onto the wall. Pointing to the bottom edge, there is a small logo of three Cs.

Lucas types: "*What's so interesting about a sponsor logo?*"

Anna writes back, "*Not a sponsor, a coalition. These little Cs are on the pages of lots of these clean companies. Apparently, it means the Climate Cultural Coalition approves of their work. Like a little seal to say they're legit.*"

Lucas nods and types: "*Huh, that's cool. I've heard of them. They seem a little radical, though. But if their stamps of approval help the datasets, let's use 'em.*"

Anna responds: "*Yeah, from what I've seen, the CCCs approval is a great predictor of the success of lots of these orgs. It doesn't look like they provide much funding, but I guess they help share ideas and stuff? Not quite sure how it works, but it might be a cool variable to toss into the model. So, I'll look into it a bit more.*"

"*All right,*" Lucas writes, "*nice catch.*"

Suzuka walks into an absolute mess. Their small office occupies only a storefront, but papers litter the floor, along with the trash can that was clearly knocked over in rage.

The team of thirty-six Triple C staff stands divided, clumped in cliques in the community space of the office. Everyone looks up at her when she enters, and silence falls over the group.

Finally, someone dares to chime in, "Hi Suzuka."

All their eyes averted, her colleagues are careful, knowing she was the last to see the director alive. Someone else pipes in, "Are you... um, how are you doing?"

Suzuka ignores the question, responding, "I see we're all processing Saturday's events well."

That's all it takes to spark the match.

"They attacked us. How do you want us to respond, Suzuka? We need to do something back. Show we're still not scared."

"That's ridiculous. Are you kidding?" Another colleague pipes in, "The same thing will just happen again. Do you want another sprained knee? More bruises? A few more cuts? Or maybe you're just toying with death. But I'm not trying to end up like the director."

"How dare—"

"Everyone chill out!" Suzuka closes her eyes but only finds snippets of violence in her mind.

Images of the director's face flash behind her eyes. She opens them and continues, "Saturday did not go as planned. I know I'm not the only one who feared for their life, but we cannot afford to stop. Stopping just means they win. When I was in that crowd, my world shrank. All I could think about was getting back to my family. And that is exactly what Sterling is trying to do. Divide us into only thinking of ourselves. But we cannot afford to let them win. Sterling had a temporary victory.

"But we can't afford to let them treat us like that either. So no more mass protests. We'll find another way to make our voice heard. Let's just get more data. Let's get an estimate of how many people came on Saturday. If we can track down their demographics, we can use the data to reach more people. People want to speak out. We just need to show them we're here. They're not alone. Let's use the data, and we'll figure it out. Step by step. Okay?" Her voice falters at the end.

The room seems to take a moment to digest her words, but mostly everyone just gazes at the ground, trying to dodge the truth of the situation.

Then a ring sounds out, cutting through the tension.

The executive assistant looks to Suzuka first, and when she nods, he goes ahead and picks up.

"Hello, Climate Cultural Coalition office. Who do I have the pleasure of speaking with?"

Total silence hangs in the air as everyone collectively strains to hear if there is any more news regarding the aftermath—some with tears still running down their faces.

The executive assistant nods furtively.

The staff leans forward. Maybe a Sterling threat or a newspaper is looking to grill them for an out-of-hand event. Maybe more info from the authorities on the multiple investigations stemming from the events. But as Suzuka cranes to see the assistant's face, the awe it conveys eliminates all those possibilities.

"Yes. Of course. I… yes… of course. Um, give me one second." Holding the phone against his chest, the executive assistant says, "It's the Mayor. And she's… uh, she's asking for the *new* director."

The temperature in the room rises further, someone letting out a sob. Resolve fills the others.

Unanimously, all eyes turn to Suzuka. Without any pomp or circumstance, she grabs the device. She answers as confidently as she can.

"This is Suz... Director Maamoun of the Climate Cultural Coalition." The title feels traitorous coming from her mouth.

The mayor's voice sounds just like it does on TV, "Director Maamoun, I saw what happened last night, and I simply wanted to say I continue to support your cause. Your coalition's sponsorship meant a lot to me on the trail, and I intend to deliver on my promises to be a friend of the environment. Would you be available to speak with me regarding environmental policy? We would bring you into the office at an hour appropriate for you."

"I... Of course, it would be my honor Madam Mayor."

"Excellent. We will speak shortly then."

8

WHAT HE COULD HAVE BEEN

"Happy anniversary, boss!" Nick's reports shout as he walks through the energy plant.

"You renew your vows?" one asks Nick with a smirk.

"It get any better?" another calls.

Today is not his wedding anniversary. He's not even married. He hasn't been able to hold a steady relationship for years.

No, nine years ago today, Nick signed his name on the dotted line for a basic mechanic position at Sterling Energies.

Now the Engineering Lead, he looks back on the past decade with both pride and regret.

Graduating from high school, Nick wanted to be a mechanical engineer. He always brought home straight As to his Aunt Stacie. He never got below 96 percent in any science or mathematics class. So, when he sat in his high school's cinder block library, reading through college pamphlets, one place, in particular, drew his dreams: Massachusetts Institute of Technology.

Online, he read about the marvelous inventions, robotics championship titles, and epic pranks. When it came to visiting the school, he fell in love with the campus when his feet landed in front of the Great Dome. To him, the modern designs of the more recent buildings mixed seamlessly with the classical buildings. The engineering facilities were clearly unmatched, and the random posters labeled, "The Ethics of Hacking" made him smile mischievously every time.

When it came to applying, he spent triple the hours ensuring that his submission to MIT was impeccable. He reread his essays innumerable times. He ingested as much as possible about the history and values of the institution and ordered the presentation of his extracurriculars in the optimal sequence. He made sure he was the perfect candidate.

When the email came announcing his MIT decision was available, he was finishing up the day in his AP physics class. As soon as the bell rang, he bolted out of the building and bounded onto the bus. He usually waited to board the bus with his sophomore brother James, but today he ditched him.

He could've used one of the school's computer labs to view the decision, but he knew his aunt would kill him if he opened the announcement without her. She was almost as excited about his future as he was.

Nick's mind was racing as he sat on the uneven bus seat with foam ripping free of the fabric constraints. *Did he get in? What would he do if he didn't get in? The Stanford decisions came out today too, did his friend Ariel get in there? Was the announcement waiting for him in his portal going to make or break his life? If he did get in, what if he didn't like it?* All of the thoughts and doubts that had been haunting him for the past months suddenly came flooding back for the twenty-minute ride home.

Arriving at the house, he threw his backpack to the floor while simultaneously calling his aunt, "It's here!" There was no need for elaboration as she sprinted from her room and into the living room where their desktop was. Hands shaking, it took Nick three tries to get his fingers to cooperate and enter the correct portal password. Logging onto the website, a small box appeared in the middle of the screen, aptly labeled "Decision."

Slamming down on the enter key, a small graphic of confetti burst across the screen with the words, "Welcome to MIT!"

Without even bothering to scroll down to read the full letter, he jumped out of his chair, turning around in midair and throwing himself into his aunt's arms. Her embrace nearly crushed him, but he was too thrilled to care.

His future had arrived.

Now, as he enters his office, he looks at the personal items that line his desk and walls. A NASA poster depicting an ascending rocket with a team of engineers marveling at their own work hangs next to his office door. Beside that is a series of beautifully drawn design plans for various engines, cars, planes, and technological devices.

Several of the designs are Nick's own, not that he's told anyone that.

Second to last in his neatly arranged photographs is a picture of his high school friends at graduation. They lined up in their forest green cap and gowns. Lucas stood next to him proudly, and Ezra posed ridiculously in the middle. Nick wonders every day how they're doing but kicks himself every week for forgetting to reach out.

Maybe today will be the day he calls one of them to catch up. He sighs, knowing he'll do no such thing, and continues scanning over his wall.

Last in the line of decorations is an MIT banner. When asked about it, he always says his brother went there. That's a bold-faced lie. His brother went to Stanford, *the bastard.*

He was in an Advanced Mechanical Principles class his junior year when his phone buzzed. He didn't think much of the incoming text. But when he received five more vibrations to his pocket in the following minute, he quietly rose and slipped out into the hallway.

He quickly flipped the phone open and stared at the screen. There were several consecutive messages from his aunt, all variations of the same idea, *Urgent Nicky, call when you see this.*

He immediately pressed down on the little plastic home icon on the bottom center of his device and dialed his aunt's number from memory. After the first ring, she picked up.

"Hi Nicky…" she started.

"Hi, Aunt Stacie. What's happened?" His imagination running wild, he continued, "Did something happen to James at school? Is the house on fire?"

Tentatively, Stacie said, "Well Nicky, I'm actually in the… um… what's the word? Hospital! I'm at the hospital right now."

Nick's heart thudded, "Okay. Are you all right?"

"Well, yeah. I'm not hurt, I was just having a bad day at work, and some of my coworkers thought it would be best to come down to Lakeside Hospital for a quick visit."

Nick couldn't keep the panic from entering his voice, "What's happening? Can I talk to the doctor who's treating you?"

His aunt tried to keep the anxiety out of her words, but it didn't work, "No, no. That won't be necessary, Nicky. I'm just avoiding the issue. The thing is, well, you know I've been a bit forgetful recently. For the past few weeks, I've been really having trouble with my work. I just can't quite seem to get the numbers all lined up. Anyway, I was leaving to go to the subway as usual, but I stopped at the entrance because I couldn't quite remember where to go. One of my young colleagues asked me where I live, and I couldn't recall that either. He said it wasn't an issue and he'd drive me home himself, but instead of going home, he took me to the hospital. He checked me in, and now here I am. Don't quite know why, though."

A terrifying thought popped into Nick's head, but he pushed it away. "Okay, thanks for calling. Please let me know when you hear more. I'll be waiting for your doctor's call. Have you given the hospital my number?"

"Yeah, I think I did. I'm actually not supposed to be calling you. The doctor said he would reach out to my family, so you'll probably get another ring soon enough from the doc."

Nick tries to be calm, "Okay. Hold tight, Aunt Stacie. I'm sure it's nothing. I'll talk to you in a bit. If anything serious happens, make sure you or the doctor calls, all right?"

"Yeah, Nicky. Don't worry about it. I'll let you know when I can. Have a good rest of the day."

Nick hung up. His skin tingled as if he had spent too much time in the sun despite spending the past three hours in dark lectures. Refusing to let his thoughts overwhelm him, Nick decided to return to class.

If nothing else, the difficulty of following his crazy professor, who filled class time with esoteric information, would provide an escape from the fear rising up within him.

As he was about to open the lecture hall door, his phone rang once again. He paused, an unrecognized number, but he would bet anything it was the doctor calling. Stepping back out into the building's entry, he took the call.

"Hello?"

"Hi," a deep, baritone voice responded. "Is this Nicholas Myelin?"

"Yes."

The doctor continued in his practiced manner, "Hello Nicholas. I'm calling from Lakeside Hospital with some unfortunate news. I'm afraid we have your Aunt Stacie Jefferson in our care after a young coworker of hers dropped her off. My understanding is she lives alone, but you are her primary emergency contact."

"That is correct," Nick replied, growing more nervous by the second. "Is there any indication of what is wrong with her?"

"Yes, so... that's why I'm calling. I didn't want to raise any alarms until I had run our initial testing, but I am now fairly certain your aunt is suffering from early-onset Alzheimer's Disease."

"I..." Nick didn't know how to respond to such a statement. Stuttering, he denied the possibility, "But she's only fifty-eight. Isn't that a bit early? That can't be right."

A tad of sympathy tinged the doctor's words, "It is certainly unusual, but early-onset AD can affect those as young as mid-forties. With her forgetfulness and mannerisms, she is almost a textbook case of the disease. I'm incredibly sorry." The doctor paused to allow Nick time to process.

After a pause the length of a lifetime, Nick returned. "What do I have to do? I mean, how can I take care of her?"

"Well, we are going to hold her for a few more hours to run a few more scans and determine which medications may be best for her. While the disease isn't yet curable, we can take some measures to slow the progression of the illness. In addition to these remedies, I would recommend you either hire a caretaker or move her into a nursing home. There are several institutions established for this exact scenario equipped to deal with AD patients."

"My aunt isn't a problem to be 'dealt' with!" Nick shouted into the phone as his emotions finally crashed through the cool surface he had desperately tried to hold together.

Another short pause ensued before the doctor continued. "I'm sorry. I didn't mean to phrase it quite like that. All I meant to say is there are plenty of resources for those with this condition. I will give you a few days if you'd like, and then I will reach out once more with information on the next steps. Once again, I'm very sorry."

Stiffly, Nick replied, "Thank you. I'll look out for your next call. Please wish my aunt well."

Nick hung up. Standing in the lobby of a building that had become his home, he suddenly felt entirely foreign.

He thought about the caretaker his aunt now required. *Where would he get the money? Neither he nor his brother worked. They both attended their respective schools on the generosity of scholarships and financial aid. Now that their aunt would likely have to stop working, how would she sustain herself?*

He knew what had to happen and knew he had to do it before James found out. He couldn't afford to let his brother go all self-sacrificial.

He hesitated, knowing the past thirty minutes of his life had just altered his path forever. One rarely knows the gravity of a decision they are making. The entire world felt off-kilter. Nick couldn't grasp how others walked past him nonchalantly, joking with friends. Nick felt nauseous.

He peeked at the open lecture door which housed his brilliant classmates, many of whom were his friends. They took notes, just as bored as when he'd left them. Nothing about their day had changed.

He heard his professor's voice floating through the air. Despite his daily complaints, it was an honor to be taught by such an accomplished academic and knowledgeable teacher.

Feeling the sweat roll down his face at the dire circumstances in front of him, he closed his eyes and tried to forget about everything he was about to lose.

He knew he couldn't afford a caretaker, so he would become one. At the end of the day, giving up his life at MIT was a small price to pay for a few final years with a lucid Aunt Stacie.

She had cared for both him and Jamie for twelve years. There's no way he would abandon her now. By doing this, he knew he was disappointing three people—himself and two in heaven.

However, he also knew he was making those two extremely proud.

Walking much more confidently than he felt, he strode directly to the registrar and officially withdrew from all of his courses. He returned to his dormitory, bought a plane ticket home for the next day, and laid in bed thinking the same thought he would have sitting in his Sterling office nine years later: *What could he have been?*

9

SCARED OF THE DARK

The train rattles, jostling Ezra. He stands among plenty of strangers, his eyes looking around untrustingly.

Following his failed attempt at Sterling, Ezra's senses have begun to come back to him. His blinding rage wanes ever slightly, and he decides to clear his head at the downtown beach. The nicest parts are farther north, but he doesn't care about the quality of the sand right now. He just wants to set his eyes on the way the waves twinkle in the horizon.

When he arrives, it's even better than he remembers. He stops dead in his tracks at the first glimpse of water, mesmerized by the awe-inspiring sunrise and the bubbles that bounce over the surf.

Noticing a small boardwalk with a lantern, his legs finally decide to cooperate, and he makes his way to the water's edge.

He sits on the wooden planks of the boardwalk with his legs dangling over the water. He feels a perfect balance of cool and warmth as the water chills his legs and the heat emanating from the lantern at his back.

Looking up, the sun now peaks over the horizon, creating a watercolor masterpiece of the clouds above.

He closes his eyes and sits with the ball of anxiety, fear, guilt, and still-simmering anger toward Aldrix Sterling—both Sterlings, actually.

At least here, after ten years of turning his mind off to make it through, he can finally think.

After basking in his newfound liberty for a short while more, he gets around to thinking about how in the world he's going to survive in this strangely familiar city.

In his kindergarten class, each student had to present their future desired profession. Nick adorably described an engineer as an "invention maker." Lucas presented his drawing of his favorite Pokémon and wrote on the board that he wanted to be a "toy maker."

Ezra had surprised the room by announcing he wanted to be a "Newo surgon." He'll never forget how his teacher's head had tilted with a sliver of a smile that suggested she was already mourning the loss of his dreams.

Ezra remembers when he presented his stickman with an arrow pointing at the large pink mass of squiggles meant to be the stick figure's brain.

He knows his teacher's intuition was correct. He will never be a surgeon. He lacks the training, the grades, and the money. Not to mention he now has a criminal record. He wistfully feels sorry for himself. The will to help people, though, that was one thing he has in abundance."

As the sun continues to rise in the sky, an older man approaches the pier. He holds a long metal instrument with a bulbous end and a black bag.

The man is grumpily wearing a brown sweater with a neon-green vest over it. He glances quickly at Ezra and raises his brows as if in a shrug. As if he regularly finds thirty-year-old men pondering their lives alone at dawn. He continues past him to the lantern at the edge of the harbor.

Dropping the bag next to himself and raising the strange instrument to the flame, he places the round side around the base of the flame, smothering it. After holding the tool in place for a few more seconds to ensure the flame is out, the man bends down and rubs the tool on the ground.

The movement reveals an interesting tattoo, one with an inverted triangle and layered flame. Ezra guesses the man must really like his job.

He turns to saunter off, supposedly to put out the next beachside flame.

Ezra continues staring with shameless curiosity as the man passes him. Without warning, the grizzly-looking stranger pauses and says, “I’ve seen that look in many people’s eyes, son.”

Turning around, the man meets Ezra’s dark eyes with his own tired gray ones. Continuing, he states, “You have the eyes of someone who’s scared of the dark.”

Ezra quickly begins to retort, “I’m not scared of—”

The man cuts him off, “Yeah, you are, just not the darkness you’re thinking of. I don’t mean you need to go to the corner store for a night-light. I mean, you’re staring off into a future with no clue what to do. You’re fumbling through your life at night with no flashlight handy.”

Quietly, Ezra averts his eyes and mutters, “Yeah.”

The stranger responds, “There ain’t light in the night, so I get to make some. People say this isn’t a great job, maintaining fires all the time, but I disagree. I treat fires with the respect they demand. I’ve seen the scorched fields Earth leaves behind in a fury, and it ain’t exactly a heartwarming sight. But this view is, this beautiful sea is the only place in this wretched city untouched by us, the concrete and greed.

"I've walked this beach to light fires and take 'em out every day for forty years. Do it with no light at dawn and dusk, and it's got me thinking a lot about light. And you know what? I've often had a few thoughts."

Ezra, convinced this man is a bit crazy, sarcastically says, "Really? What kinds?"

Then, surprisingly eloquent for a man of his external appearance, he says, "As long as you rely on the sun, there will always be periods of darkness. But, if you make your own light, there will never be anywhere for the darkness to hide. Make a flame, buddy. You'll be all right."

Ezra looks at the man, stunned.

With that, the harbormaster simply smirks, walking down the boardwalks and disappearing into the golden rays and mist of the morning.

Turning back to himself, Ezra notices the man dropped a piece of paper. He grabs it and sees it's a flyer. Curious, Ezra reads the announcement.

A sly smile creeps across his face. He knows exactly how he'll burn Sterling.

10

A PLEASANT MEETING

Briefing, meeting, call, coffee—ever-fading thoughts of a power nap as Emerald runs with her executive assistant to the next event. Shuttled in an oversized black sedan, Emerald relies on the incredible organization of her chief of staff, Amelie. Emerald appreciates the help. Her head swims with agendas and schedules.

Amelie rushes through the flurry of meetings ahead.

"Ma'am, you have a meeting with the transportation secretary at 9:30."

"Thanks, Amelie."

"And that will be immediately followed by the panel with Alderman Liu at ten."

"Okay, Amelie."

"The new highway safety bill should be on your desk by eleven as well. They'll bring it over for signing then."

"Wonderful."

"I've also received your energy briefing from downstairs. You meet with Director Maamoun of the Climate Cultural Coalition over lunch."

"Which coalition?"

"The Triple C group, Ma'am."

"Ah. Well, no rest for the wicked, huh?"

"No, ma'am," Amelie says with a slight smile.

Emerald yawns her way through the morning. Her pen signs everything it must, her attention waning in and out while similar-looking men in slightly different colored ties try to lecture her on what she should be doing.

Until finally, the clock rolls to noon, and Amelie pops into her office with a salad.

"Good afternoon, ma'am. Here's your lunch. And your 'hand-written' note for TRU's COO is right here. It just needs signing, don't want them thinking their campaign donation was wasted."

"Thank you, Amelie. The climate director is next, correct?"

"Yes. I'll be sending her in shortly. I just received word that she's arrived."

"Perfect."

When Suzuka leaves for lunch today, she doesn't walk toward the coalition office. She walks to the main laboratory entrance where a black sedan sits waiting for her. She gets in on the right side but the driver quickly corrects her.

"Excuse me, ma'am. The mayor always sits on the right. Please use the seat on the left."

Suzuka was unaware there were protocols in place even when the mayor wasn't present, but she complies. If a little bureaucracy gets her in front of the mayor, so be it.

Without ceremony, the driver takes off and cruises confidently toward City Hall.

Unzipping the bag she packed after Lucas left, Suzuka adjusts the opaqueness of the glass separating her from the driver's row to provide some privacy.

She throws on her blazer and switches out her comfortable lab shoes for elegant flats, trying not to cause a fuss in the backseat.

Pulling up, Suzuka only lets herself marvel for a moment at the impressive building before the driver escorts her in. A lovely woman who looks fresh out of college and calls herself something French meets her. Then, she's whisked directly into an ornate room where the mayor sits before a stack of official-looking folders.

Emerald looks up at her within a second, a smile opening up on her face.

"Director Maamoun?"

Suzuka winces at the title. She addresses the mayor with respect but tries to move past the formalities. "Yes, Mayor Silva. But honestly, call me Suzuka. Still don't feel right about holding the title of someone who gave her life last week."

Emerald's face softens, "Yes, I heard. I'm sorry for your loss, Suzuka. Well, please take a seat. We have plenty to speak about."

Suzuka takes her place across from the mayor, and the conversation begins.

"Suzuka, firstly, I would like to thank you again for the support your coalition gave to me during the campaign. It was invaluable, and I look forward to working with you toward a more sustainable future."

Suzuka answers kindly, "You're very welcome. We're incredibly glad to have a politician who finally takes the crisis as seriously as it deserves."

Emerald smiles graciously at the compliment, "Thank you. I've invited you here today to have a look at the climate legislation my office is drafting. Of course, you knew my platform promises during the campaign, and this is our first stab at making those a reality. You are welcome to take the full draft home. It's quite chunky, but I wanted to chat about some of the key elements with you."

"Sounds great."

Sliding a single page toward Suzuka, Emerald says, "Here's a brief overview. I'll give you a second to read through it."

Skimming the pages, Suzuka feels like she's holding gold. The policies include a progressive carbon tax and the usage of the generated funds to provide upskilling for impacted communities. The document highlights the importance of providing subsidies for renewable energy companies and electric vehicle stations. It even dives into the importance of oceanic biodiversity and offers seaweed farming as a potential solution for oceanic acidification. It's more progressive than any legislation she's ever seen before. Real change.

Hope in her eyes, Suzuka asks, "This... Madam Mayor, this is incredible. Do you actually believe this will pass?"

Emerald leans forward, elbows on her desk, "That's why you're here. While my party won many seats in the City Commons, these policies need a few more votes to make it through. So, all I ask from your coalition is that you review the totality of the policies and publicly provide your approval for the legislation. Hopefully, that should change the minds of some of the aldermen on the fence. We only need two or three to flip for this to work."

Suzuka is stunned. "Wow." She pauses, then responds, her voice full of optimism, "This is fantastic. Thank you so much. We'd be happy to stand behind this."

Emerald rises from her chair, relief clear on her face, "Perfect. Well then, it was lovely to meet you, Suzuka. I understand you have to rush back to your full-time position, but it was a pleasure."

John hates bad news. A bad day at the stock market, an earthquake, or a serial killer on the loose. He doesn't care. The subject doesn't matter—just the fact he has to bring the news to Aldrix. Apollo opens the door to Mr. Sterling's office, and John walks in as confidently as possible.

Before he even says anything, Sterling asks, "What is it, John?"

Not exactly the welcome he was hoping for.

John shifts on his feet, aiming to find a comfortable stance. "Well, sir, I just received some reports from the team you asked to stay on top of the Climate Cultural Coalition."

"Mm-hmm," Sterling hadn't looked up once from the papers on his desk.

John continues, "As you know, there's that new director since the other one died in that mess at the front gates."

"Yes, John, I am aware."

"Okay, good. Um, well, that director just visited City Hall."

John thought Sterling's inattentiveness was bad, but his burning stare is so much worse. He now looks directly at John. "What was she doing there?"

John stammers his response, "Well, according to our… your friends in the mayor's office, she was invited for a policy conversation about incentivizing green energy."

"I see," Sterling says, drawing out the vowels. "And how long ago was this meeting?"

"It may still be happening, sir, or possibly just ended. I came right away when I heard."

"Good work, John." Somehow, he doesn't feel as though there is anything good about it. But as always, John responds in kind, "Thank you, sir."

John stands awkwardly for a moment before Sterling looks back at him, "Get out. And tell Apollo to come in. I need to speak to him."

That's all John needs to hear.

Emerald sits at her desk, glowing after the conversation with Suzuka.

The Director is lovely. Emerald is glad her policies ignited so much hope and validation in Suzuka's eyes. Forget about Sterling. His threats aren't going to stop her from preserving the world for the next generation—protecting the land and waters for those to come. The Triple C's support could really swing the tide.

Amelie pops in afterward, whisking her away to her next event. She drags herself through the endless pandering and politics. Still, she ends her day in the glow of the impact she might have on the climate.

On her way home in the back of the black sedan, Emerald scrolls through the news. The stock market has been shaky. A series of robberies are under investigation, a great opinion piece in the *Chronicle* about the ethics of AI.

Emerald swipes casually until an unknown message pops up on the top of her screen. Tapping, her heart drops to her stomach. She reads it over and over as her knee bounces ever more frantically against the seat in front of her. The message isn't long, but the menace in it is clear:

Disappointed to hear about your meeting today. I thought you knew to keep your nose out of my boss' business. Aritzen Park, 23:00 hrs. See you then :)

11

A WALK HOME

Suzuka's day in the lab closes like every other. She saves her data, sends a quick report to her lead researching fellow, and signs off her computer.

The lights seem brighter now that the sun is setting. Sterile blue illumination bathes the hallways as her shoes echo on the linoleum floor. The lobby is empty, her lab's metallic logo and the inattentive front desk manager the only occupants as she passes through and makes her way back out into the world.

The night air is refreshing after hours spent in the windowless confines of her desk, but there is still a grainy quality that makes her feel as though something trapped her in one of those first-generation TV sets. She saw the notices that today might have poor air quality, so she dons the mask she keeps in her purse and makes her way toward the bus.

The pollution weighs down her movements and obscures her vision of the downtown skyscrapers in the distance.

She turns her gaze to the quiet neighborhood around her. A few strangers pass by on the street: a group of college kids toting backpacks, a bald, muscular man in a brown T-shirt, a woman with a colorful paisley dress, and a couple dressed for an evening out.

Suzuka thinks of how their lives will change over the coming year. She wonders what they do, what the students study, whether automation or the changing climate will rock their professions. She hopes she can ensure they lead quality lives.

She is still stunned by the policies put forward by Mayor Silva. Her campaign was excellent, but Suzuka expected a certain amount of regression from her promises on the trail. The mayor is steadfast, and Suzuka will do whatever she can to help her bring change to the city.

She hits a busy intersection, waiting for the light to turn as she stands next to a Tex-Mex Cantina. She is joined by a few more commuters also making their way home.

She glances around at some of the faces, a man in an exquisite suit talking into his AirPods, a larger woman with a gorgeous pattern on her skirt, and a bald, muscular man in blue athletic gear.

The light changes, and they parade across the street. She keeps along her usual path and turns to cut through a neighborhood of beautiful townhouses only a few blocks away from the station.

The neighborhood is full of hills, but Suzuka likes watching the lanterns in front of the stunning homes light up as the sunsets, her bit of peace before returning to her frantic household.

She trips on one of the curbside gardens, her heel coming out of her flat and sending her stumbling into one of the trees along the street. She catches herself on the trunk. Her cheeks flush with self-consciousness.

She glances around from embarrassment, hoping that no one saw. Luckily there is only one other person on the block: a muscular man in a gray hoodie, a glint of something metallic on his hip.

Wait.

Suzuka's heart pounds, and she picks up her speed, mounting the hill as fast as she can.

The man behind her picks up his pace too.

Is he a cop? Is that thing on his waist a badge or a gun? Did they track her down? Did the guard she beat describe her face and send his partner to arrest her? Should she turn around and face him? Will she be charged with assaulting an officer? What would happen to Sierra? Lucas? What if he isn't a cop? What if he's just a creep following a woman home? Should she be sprinting toward the bus? If she ran up to one of the houses, would anyone answer? Would they save her, or would she just be trapped on the porch of a stranger? And if they even let her in, what's the guarantee they'd be good?

She is walking as fast as she can now, her shoes digging into her heel, forming what she knows will be blisters. She barely notices for the adrenaline rushing through her. She holds her head high. If she's going to be arrested, she won't snivel and apologize for trying to save the Director's life.

If he's just here for trouble, she's going to fight. She rips off her mask and stuffs it into her purse, trading it for pepper spray. She hits the pinnacle of the hill, and as soon as she begins to descend, she breaks into a sprint.

Suzuka runs as scenes from the protest flash in front of her, the memory of her desperation from that night triggered by the fear in the moment. She keeps glancing behind her, but it doesn't seem like the man has made it over the hill yet.

She turns the corner and keeps running despite her lungs begging for air.

She turns again, not knowing where she is, but becoming increasingly confident she's lost the man behind her. She slows to a walk, her muscles screaming at being pushed without warning.

She finally stops and rests on the stairs of one of the elegant townhouses surrounding her, the glow of the lanterns illuminating the block. She is alone on the street, but still feels haunted, hunted.

She takes out her phone and looks up how to get back to the station, only daring quick glances down before returning her gaze to the street. It maps a path for her, and she rises, walking swiftly along the prescribed route.

Her mind still buzzes with questions. *Should she even be going home? Will the police just be waiting for her at her door? Or is the threat gone, only the dangerous whims of a man up to no good?*

She turns the corner and is slammed to the ground.

Her skin tears along the concrete, scraping her legs and arms as she barely keeps her head from smashing into the sidewalk. Her purse and belongings scatter across the ground as the stranger comes closer.

The streetlights silhouette him. His hoodie hiding his face from view. He towers over her. His body dwarfs hers in stature. He says nothing, his silence more ominous than anything she'd imagined. He's no cop.

Suzuka scrambles to her knees, reaching for the pepper spray that flew out of her hand, but the man is faster. He kicks it away and pushes her back down.

Suzuka catches herself and surprises her attacker by screaming for help and launching herself at him. She grazes his cheek, leaving a small cut below his eye. But in return, she earns a kick in the stomach, and the wind knocked out from her. She tries to call out again, but no noise comes out.

The man stands above her, unmoving, features obscured.

Fear wells up in Suzuka, anxiety wracking her mind as she tries to think her way out of this corner. Her eyes dart around the abandoned street, looking for homes that may give her safe refuge, that might have someone who can help.

Then the man turns and walks away, her pain and fear seemingly having satisfied him.

She leans back against the unyielding concrete, tears streaming down her face.

She is bruised and scratched, but nothing else seems to be wrong. He was careful not to severely injure her. *But why?*

She gets up slowly, blood pumping furiously.

She goes to gather her pepper spray and all the belongings that fell from her purse. Among them, she finds one item that is not hers, a small white business card with a single symbol: A golden S.

Suzuka realizes the man wasn't a cop or a common creep. He's much, much worse.

That night in bed, Suzuka's mind races. Flashes of the hooded man loop through her mind, joining the scenes of chaos from the protest. She can't get the violence she's endured out of her head.

Lucas sleeps like a baby, but Sierra cries out from her room, sensing her mother's anxiety.

Suzuka gets up and places Sierra on the living room couch, her daughter playing with a ragged toy octopus while

Suzuka makes herself tea and watches from the other side of the kitchen island.

She admires her daughter, her uncoordinated fingers poking at the cotton tentacles of her toy, her mouth slobbering all over the head.

She wonders when her daughter will understand what humanity is doing to the home of that adorable octopus. That all the little fishies in her baby books are in danger.

She wonders when her daughter will realize the complexity of the world around her. The greed and the goodness. The hooded men and fearless mayors.

Suzuka finishes her tea and moves to hold her daughter. They rock together, Sierra's eyes shutting and the motion lulling her to sleep.

Suzuka's mind spirals, the anxiety attacking ruthlessly. Her brain scans through the darkness around her. *The hooded man. The bleeding cop. The broken glass. Her desperate attempts to wring the director's blood from her shirt. The horrid acidification report. The worsening air. The IPCC's dire warnings. The adorable octopus strangled by both her daughter's chubby arms and the plastic floating in the seas. The golden S. Aldrix Sterling's face.*

Sierra is fast asleep, but Suzuka continues to rock in the low living room light. She rocks to calm herself now to push away the fear.

It doesn't work. Because while the oppressive thoughts continue to swirl around her, she looks at her daughter and wonders what kind of world she will know.

12

DOCTOR'S VISIT

Nick thinks about his hallway conversation with Sterling as he prepares tea for Aunt Stacie. The quip hurt, but Nick knows it's true. Nick is a genius with machines. Math can't lie. Machines either work, or they don't.

People, on the other hand, are a mess. He knows his colleagues respect his brain, but they don't quite understand his heart. Neither does he. *What is he supposed to feel?*

No one can say he doesn't make the effort. He slaps some backs and encourages the junior engineers, but he knows his words fall flat.

He rips advice out of leadership books, and he knows it shows. He has let Lucas and Ezra slip away into the world, afraid to extend a hand for fear of losing it to the unknown dangers of the present.

In spite of the blessing of a brother, Nick feels as though he is dead weight every time they speak. It's true. Sterling is right. Nick is a complete failure with relationships. Except for one.

"Two sunny-side eggs, comin' up, auntie," he calls from the kitchen.

Stacie answers from her seat in the living room. "Right. Thanks, Nickie. Oh, jam? On the… the… um… what's the word? Please put some on."

"You're looking for some jam on your toast?"

"Right. Toast on the strawberry jam," her jumbled response.

Nick smiles as not to cry. "Already on it. Would you like some water?"

"He's going to the store," his aunt says.

Nick doesn't miss a beat. "Oh, not today. We're not going to the store today."

"Oh, yes. yes."

Throwing eggs on the griddle, he reflects on the impact Aunt Stacie has had on him. Since he was a kid, she has been his lighthouse, guiding him safely home.

Now, her light has begun flickering erratically, sometimes threatening to go out completely. Nick wishes he could just take out a replacement bulb and have his aunt back, but none of the treatments seem to be the right size.

When he returned from school to take care of her, she was mad at him. It wasn't a threatening sort of anger, just an expression of love that couldn't escape any other way.

She couldn't believe he gave up his future for hers. His brother was angry on the surface, but Nick knows he was relieved he didn't have to deal with it.

Once he arrived and got settled—moving back in with his aunt and beginning his new career track at Sterling—Nick got to thinking more seriously about his next steps.

He didn't quite know what caring for another person really meant.

He wanted to be able to watch over his aunt, but he didn't want to remove her from the familiarity of her home, especially considering the nature of her illness.

Since Aunt Stacie had paid off her house, it was also the best move financially, because now Nick doesn't have to worry about a senior home bill or mortgage. It's even convenient to his workplace since the metro is less than ten minutes away. So, he sleeps in his childhood bedroom and does his best to take care of her the way she cared for him and his brother their whole lives—until she couldn't.

The caretaking includes cooking for her, ensuring she takes her medicine, cleaning the house, doing the groceries, and all the other little things in between. Every three months, it also includes taking his aunt to her doctor's appointments on Saturdays. Today happens to be one of those days.

After waking up at 5 a.m., he pours her tea. The eggs are a bit burnt due to his wandering mind, but he doubts she'll say anything.

Aunt Stacie has never been critical. He makes sure to cook his best breakfast on Saturdays, eggs with cheese and ham, toast with strawberry jam, and sometimes even some partially burnt pancakes.

He nudges her back awake from her position snoozing on the couch and eats with her, mostly discussing events that have long since faded away into history.

In the past week, they've wavered between discussing how George HW. Bush was doing as president, the Gulf War in Kuwait, and going to the store to grab some cassette tapes of Madonna's new album.

As concerning as these conversations were when his aunt began losing track of the present in favor of the past, he's come to appreciate them. At their most basic level, his aunt is still herself, untainted by the latest scandal or complexity of the technological age.

Finishing up their meal, Nick says, "Remember we're going to the doctor's today. Once you finish, we can head on over. You remember how you like the plants at the doctor's office?"

Instantly, his aunt forms a quizzical expression. "Right. Yes. You're going to take me, Nicky? Don't you have school today? Your teacher will be very upset if you miss another day of attendance."

Nick pauses with his fork full of scrambled eggs hovering in front of his lips.

In the nine years he's been back with his aunt, she has always seen him as an adult. She may speak about the past, but he has always existed in the present.

Hesitantly he replies, "I think it'll be okay for the day. I talked to her about it yesterday. She just said that I need to bring a doctor's note tomorrow."

Consoled, she says, "Oh, okay. Sounds good, Nicky."

Walking into the kitchen with their plates, Nick replays what just happened in his mind. He dreads going to the doctor today and hearing what it may mean for his aunt's health.

The beginning of the appointment goes as it always does. The nurse measures his aunt's vitals and takes notes on their brief conversations.

His aunt is shepherded to her routine brain scan as Nick waits in the lobby. Afterward, they are put in a quaint room to await the doctor. Nick and his aunt each read in their own way, her from a magazine and he from his smartphone.

A doctor arrives shortly, reviewing the information provided by the nurse and asking his aunt whether she feels any different than normal. She never does.

Soon, a nurse comes in and briefly takes Stacie away so the doctor can speak alone with Nick.

The doctor begins as usual, "Okay, Nick. So, have you noticed any difference in your aunt's behavior recently?"

Nick tries to keep his hands and voice steady as he says, "Yes, sir. I was actually going to bring it up if you hadn't asked. She is struggling more with remembering words. And she mixes up grammar and stuff. Then sometimes, she's completely lucid, and we have hour-long conversations. But, um, this morning, she asked me why I wasn't going to school. It seemed for a few minutes that she thought I was a kid. Does that happen often? Does that mean anything?"

With a barely noticeable wince, the doctor responds, "I'm sorry to hear that, Nick. Yes, time-based incoherence is a common symptom of more advanced Alzheimer's patients. Unfortunately, it also seems to align with the MRI we performed today."

Pulling a copy of the scan from his manila folder, the doctor says, "If you look here, there is significantly more brain tissue shrinkage than your aunt's previous scan. What that effectively means is the illness is progressing into the next stage. It's tremendous she has maintained an exceptional level of awareness over the past decade since her diagnosis, but it seems like the disease is catching up to her. We're not going to speak about timelines right now. I don't have the full reports yet, and it's ultimately your choice if you'd like that bit of knowledge. But I'm afraid to say this isn't looking good."

13

ARITZEN PARK

Emerald clutches the keys in her pocket as she enters the park full of shadows.

Aritzen Park is one of her favorite places in the city during the day. She loves how the sun filters through the public conservatory and the manicured trees along the main walkway. The playground is full of memories of joyous swing rides and countless tears shed over scraped knees.

She glances at her phone, the time showing 22:58. A notification pops up from Amelie. Just a response to Emerald's lie that she's walking home late and wants her friend to know in case something goes south. All Amelie's response says is: *Kk, be safe.*

Amelie has no idea.

Pulling her thoughts back into the world, Emerald rests on one of the benches, sitting directly under the glow of a streetlamp. While the light reaches far, the night does not afford her the comfort she usually feels in the park. Emerald turns as a squirrel rustles through the bushes. The cutting breeze feels hostile as it steals across her skin.

Emerald just pulls her jacket close, thinking of warmer days. Her moment of sanctuary is cut short, however.

"Hello, Emerald."

Emerald flinches at the voice but recovers quickly. She stands to find a large but elegantly dressed man behind her. He is bald and wears a trench coat clearly styled for him, the quality evident even in the moonlight. His skin is tanned, but a fresh cut is below his eye, the skin red and angry. His face is surprisingly handsome despite the brutish voice.

Seeing her restlessness, he says, "There's nothing to be afraid of." She recognizes his voice as the same one from the call on the night of her election.

"Sure," she responds.

"Would you like to accompany me? I simply come as a friend for a midnight stroll."

Emerald shakes her head but moves to walk alongside Sterling's henchman down the maple-lined promenade. The leaves that provide such amazing shade are now casting shadows on the ground. As the trees sway, their shadows shift across the man's face, his expressions manipulated by the light.

"What is your name?" Emerald's question more of a demand.

The man replies, "That's of no concern to our business tonight."

"I thought you came as a friend? How can we be friends if I do not know your name."

He smirked, as if he found her fear adorable. "Then you may call me Apollo. But Miss Mayor, the more important question is how has *your* day been?"

Emerald shifts uncomfortably, "I'm not here to talk about me. Don't pretend you care."

"I certainly care."

For a few steps, the silence weighs heavy before the man gets to the point.

"My boss thought we had an arrangement. You do whatever you'd like, and he gets to run his business as he sees fit."

Emerald quips back, "I didn't interfere with Sterling. And I never agreed to anything that came out of your twisted mouth."

"Yet. You haven't interfered *yet*. But you are dangerously close." Apollo's face has darkened, his mask slipping.

Emerald stands her ground, "Aldrix Sterling's sponsorship of me was his choice. And you're right, I probably wouldn't be mayor without him, so gee, thanks. Do you want me to curtsy? Make sure he receives the treatment of a king? He's already enough of a spoiled man-brat."

"Your petty name-calling doesn't suit your office, Emerald."

"No? Well, ruling by underhanded threats isn't quite honorable either."

"I don't threaten," Apollo's voice softens.

"Really? You're going to say that when you have me here in the middle of a park in the dead of night?"

Apollo's words come more forcefully now, "No, really Emerald, my boss has only ever asked me to simply remind those who have forgotten their place. So here is your first warning. Don't ever conspire against Sterling again. Drop your carbon tax policies. And never meet with that lousy activist again."

"Why doesn't your boss schedule a meeting with me like everyone else, and we can sit in *my* office and look at all the ways in which he's destroying this city? Why doesn't he come himself instead of sending you on monstrous errands?"

"He has better things to do than speak with you," Apollo says, a hint of malice behind the words.

"Fine. But I'm not going to let you override the needs of this city. The people of this city."

"The needs of Sterling are the needs of the city. You don't think the city needs his power? His gas for their cars? Would you like to govern a powerless, impoverished citizenry?"

"We can get electricity other ways," Emerald shoots back.

"You think companies are the problem?"

"No, there are excellent companies. Teams of people who are embracing change."

Clarity shines on Apollo's face. "Ahh, I see. You favor that company Alter..."

"Alteryn."

"Whatever," he says, shaking his head.

They pace a few more steps in silence, the park still empty, the only sound the windblown leaves.

"Well, I have a recommendation for you, Emerald."

"And what is that?"

Apollo stops and looks directly into Emerald's eyes as he gives the message he was no doubt instructed to deliver. "I know you were not born in this city, and neither were your parents. They did not teach you how this place works, so let me educate you. There are forces here that most are not aware of. And those forces dictate the place and position of everyone else. The masses march along, ants unaware of the larger game. Then there are others who brush up against the true leaders, who benefit from them. That is me. My job is to protect the powerful, and their job is to rule. They are not always merciful, but they take care of their own. So join the club or make powerful enemies. Those are your only two options. Contrary to popular opinion, your role is not to govern. It is to enact the policies the people up top want.

You are a puppet to be used. And you are certainly, absolutely not at the top. Learn your place, Miss Mayor."

Emerald is only emboldened. "Or what?"

Apollo flashes a sliver of steel under his trench coat, his motion completely carefree despite the weapon it reveals. "We'll find someone else who will."

Emerald swears the air drops twenty degrees in temperature, her eyes widening in disbelief.

"I—"

"Now, let's not say anything we might regret."

Emerald feels off-balance, the ground swayed by the weight of the threat in front of her.

The man's voice never loses its nonchalant levity. "Do take care, Miss Mayor."

Apollo walks off, the darkness swallowing him into the night.

Heart thudding furiously and palms sweaty, Emerald makes her way back to the park bench and slumps in the seat. She whips out her phone and texts Amelie with shaking fingers:

All safe and sound, nothing to worry about, but thanks for looking out :)

As she presses send, she wishes she believed it herself.

14

NO ONE WILL NOTICE

Walking up to his mom's apartment building is surreal. It looks exactly the same. Ten years have passed. He has gone through torturous nights and dangerous days, but this building has just stood here as if nothing has happened. He shakes his head and swings open the door.

Ezra walks into the sloping entry and up the worn wooden stairs. At his door, he flips the welcome sign around and finds the spare key taped to the back. Nothing like old tricks.

Unable to sleep since his morning release, he collapses onto the couch. Within five minutes, he's out cold.

Mariah has seen her son every month since his incarceration. However, she has not touched him in ten years. Mariah relished every hug and kiss she received in Ezra's teenage years, and she has missed them every day since he left.

As she slows her car to a halt in her apartment building's lot, her skin is buzzing with the anticipation of holding her son. Getting out of the car, she can barely contain her excitement as she practically sprints through the lobby and up the stairs.

She opens the door and bursts inside. "Ez!"

Silence.

She calls again, "Ez?"

Walking further in, she finds him passed out on the couch. Walking up, she embraces him for the first time in 3658 days. She smiles as brightly as the sun.

The Monday after being reunited with his mother, Ezra arrives early to his first nightly emergency medicine class.

He's spent all day at the small convenience store owned by their neighbor, Maurice. Having done time himself, Maurice is willing to turn a blind eye to Ezra's record. He's a tad bitter, but he offered Ezra a temporary position while he studies, so he can't complain. Plus, the boring hours give him time to think. Think and plan, his near miss of Sterling still locked in his mind.

He passes the hours stocking shelves, only glancing at the door when the little bell sounds. The sky was overcast today, which was good for business, the light drizzling rain sending people running for cover inside the store. Still, he didn't say much to the customers. He just kept stocking the shelves, just like his repetitive, meaningless work in the pen.

After getting off work at the convenience store at five, he only had time to run home and make a sandwich for dinner, but he's made it here on time.

Entering a dingy-looking classroom in the back of Firehouse 97, he finds only one other person there. Awkwardly sitting at one of several desks in the fourth row, Ezra steals a glance at the mousy-haired guy sitting a few desks over.

The man seems to have barely registered Ezra entered since his face is in his phone. Trying to break the spell, Ezra tentatively says, "Hello."

When the other guy doesn't even flinch, Ezra sees his ears have those weird earbuds he's seen people walking around with. He decides just to give up and looks around the room instead.

At the front of the room, there is a whiteboard that bears the scars of past lessons.

A few feet in front of the board is a long wooden desk with a mess of equipment. There are layers of ropes and stethoscopes piled in the middle of the desk.

A few laminated charts detailing various medicines and medical techniques lie toward the side with a stack of pencils on top of them. Seeing plastic heads lying eerily on the other side, Ezra assumes they will be practicing with the CPR dummies today. Then Ezra's eyes land on the box of syringes and needles in the corner. Each has a label with the names of their contents. Just what he needs. He takes note.

As his eyes wander to the brick wall, he sees it lined with photos of previous classes of firefighters and EMTs. Each photo features a line of young people in matching blue shirts and signatures surrounding the picture. As he finishes observing the end of the line, his vision is broken by four figures entering the room.

Smartphone Guy is still absorbed in his own world, failing to acknowledge the arrival of new classmates. However, Ezra politely taps the shoulder of the woman closest to him, and she swings around. She wears perfectly round glasses in front of olive green eyes. Her hair is a dirty blond color, and freckles spot her face.

"Hi," she says in a friendly manner.

"Hi," Ezra responds. "Nice to meet you. What are all of your names?"

The young woman angles her body to include the rest of the women in the conversation. She says, "I'm Emma, but I actually missed everyone else's name. We just happened to run into each other since we all got lost trying to find the room. What's your name?"

"I'm Ezra."

As the group turns to face the next woman, she opens her mouth to speak but is interrupted by the sound of heavy footsteps.

A burly man walks into the room with a knowing air that marks him instantly as their instructor. He wears a clean white collared shirt with the fire department's logo sewn on.

Without any introduction, he drops a three-ring binder on the sole empty corner of the long wooden table. He says drily, "Welcome to day one of accelerated EMT night classes. I'm glad all of you have decided to take up emergency medicine. I'll be your instructor for these next four months."

Without even introducing himself or bothering to learn the names of his students, he says, "First, we're going to go over the basic materials. Can anyone tell me what this is for?" Ezra just stares at the bulky, red bag his instructor hefts from the table. It just looks like cargo pants in bag form to him.

Before the rest of the class has time to ponder the question, Smartphone Guy says, "That's a jump bag. It has everything you need. You can't leave your ambulance without it. It has all kinds of bandages, syringes, and drips, and stuff. It's a medical lifeline, dude."

The rest of them look at each other stunned, and even Burly Instructor seems shocked. The instructor quickly remembers himself and says, "Um, ahem, yes. That's correct, thank you. What about this?" holding up another alien-looking object.

The rest of the two hours follow a similar pattern. With his earbuds still embedded, Smartphone Dude jumps to answer any question the rest of the class hesitates to respond to.

The class quickly moves from being aggravated by the know-it-all to seeing him as their savior from the lengthy silences that follow any semi-difficult question asked. Finishing the basics, Burly Instructor quickly reviews all of the equipment and introduces the structure of the class.

Looking at the board and seeing the next few months written out in front of him, Ezra sees a road to a normal life again. The amount of material is completely daunting, but he will learn. Maybe he can get close to being that surgeon his younger self dreamed of.

He is determined to take hold of this new path forward. He doesn't care how many shelves he has to stock or medical terms he has to memorize.

Coming back into society is difficult, but that doesn't mean it's impossible. Plus, if he can pull it off, this will put him exactly where he wants to be. Two birds, one stone.

Emma walks out of the classroom, calling, "See you tomorrow!"

Ezra just smiles back and echoes her. But instead of following the rest of the class out, Ezra stares at his phone as though something very important has just come to his attention.

Once the room is empty, Ezra rises. Walking past the equipment, he makes a quick motion that not even a camera would have caught. A sly grab he learned during his time in the pen. As he makes his way out of the room, he figures that no one will miss a single needle.

15

TRESPASSING

When Emerald was twelve, the Sterling Energies Satellite Facility didn't exist.

The downtown square contained most of the Sterling empire with only a handful of external facilities. Nothing existed in the sprawling land on the outskirts of the city; nothing but trees.

The gentle giants spanned forever, blocking the distant skyline and providing a surround sound of birdsong. Living in this new place, surrounded by taxis and high-rises instead of endless fields and ranches, wasn't easy. When Emerald visited the seaside forest, she closed her eyes and envisioned the woods she grew up around.

Her memory projected the thin trunks and mangled brush. Without moving, her feet strode along the well-worn paths through the thicket, and when she finally opened her eyes, the reality wasn't too far off. The nature preserve settled along the coastline for miles, a light breeze swaying the branches gently.

Every fall, Emerald simply marveled at the majestic beauty of the season. The forest preserve was far from the battered row house where Emerald's family had landed, the only place they could afford. Despite the distance, her mom would take her every month.

Managed by the county, the park had paths and picnic tables weaved between the expanse of trees, allowing visitors a way to explore without losing their way.

Emerald and her mom would walk up to the pathway map at the entrance every month and select which color-coded track they would take that day.

They explored all the paths over the years. The green was Emerald's favorite, though. The two of them walked it frequently over the years. The orange trail with its sunflower-lined dirt path. The yellow with its magnificent skyline view through the trees. The blue which ended with an overlook of the Aurietta Sea, and the purple with its open meadows.

Besides being Emerald's favorite color, for obvious reasons, the green path was optimal for catching sight of families of adorable rabbits who could be found hopping through the bushes. They walked this path over and over again, never tiring of the natural splendor around them.

They spent countless Sunday afternoons chasing each other, simply exploring the natural splendor and talking. Emerald about school, her mom about work. About their home and their solemn moments of remembrance. The burn still marked Emerald's neck, along with several other scars that were deeper than her flesh. But what was said in the forest stayed in the forest, their own girl's club. She'll always remember her mom like that, in those moments of honesty in the midst of endless green.

Sophomore year of high school, Emerald got her driver's license. She was the first of her friends to get one, so naturally, that meant everyone now piled into her car to go to the forest preserve. Technically, she wasn't allowed to drive anyone under eighteen, but she figured it was okay. She was responsible. She was practically an adult anyway. Sixteen was close enough.

Every month for that entire school year, a few of her girlfriends would pile into Emerald's secondhand Prius, stop at the convenience store for popcorn and soda, and then drive up to the preserve. On arrival, they would find a wobbly wooden table and talk until sunset, stuffing their mouths with unhealthy treats and blasting music that no one could hear. When they were in the forest, time was infinite.

On the first Friday afternoon of junior fall, everyone hopped into Emerald's car. They grabbed their snacks and had a lively conversation while the radio played in the background. The stereo pumped, and when each song swelled to its chorus, they sang it out at the top of their lungs.

They collectively squealed when the first few notes of their favorite played, and they tried to do the artist proud with their off-key belting.

But no one cared. They felt free as the yellow lines sped by, the condensed city streets giving way to open air. As Emerald turned the corner, a fence blocked the entrance to the forest.

A collective, "No way!" echoed in the car as her friends rolled nearer to read the sign that repeated along the fencing. When they finally got close enough, they read:

According to agreement 296c, this land has been sold by the county to Sterling Energies

Private Property: Trespassing is Forbidden.

"No way," one of her friends said.

"This can't be happening," another echoed.

"And we already have the Cheez-Its and the ginger ale," another said, her priorities clearly set.

They'd known the county struggled to upkeep the several acres of property, but never in a million years did they think it would cave to business interests.

Selling the protected zone wasn't just a transaction of land. It wasn't just an exchange of cartons full of hundred-dollar bills. Selling the forest was auctioning off the memories of countless people. It was trading in a communal area of respite, a priceless habitat for the animals that dwelled here, and the life-giving trees that offered an unmatched air purity.

Yet her friends' disappointment was short-lived. The preserve was a special place to them, but soon one of them suggested they just go to the local mall. Emerald dutifully reversed, and before long, they were all singing at the tops of their lungs again.

They had a good time at the mall. Walking among the endless capitalism and trying on clothes they dreamed of owning. And when Emerald finally dropped her friends back at their homes, everyone had smiles on their faces.

Once the last occupant jumped out, Emerald drove only a few blocks before pulling over to grieve. She placed her head on the wheel, not caring about the wailing honk she felt reverberate from her car.

She still couldn't get over the concept that Sterling *owned* the land now. No one could own land. If anyone was trespassing, it was Sterling. The company already had the tallest building in the sky. They had other facilities around the city to collect their oil, and their logo was on billboards all across the metro area. *Why did they need any more*? In Emerald's mind, it wasn't just a frustration. It was a true loss.

Emerald finally lifted her head from the wheel and wiped the tears forming in her eyes. She shifted into drive and cruised forward, still battling the loss of a sanctuary. She left the radio off, sitting in silence, thinking about how a single signature and a stack of gold sealed the fate of nature.

16

CALM AMIDST THE STORM

Suzuka sits at her desk to paint, and the world falls away.

The threatening nights, continued grief, and twisted rage meld together as her brush moves across the canvas. For the first time, Suzuka has the peace she needs to mourn the life that passed through her hands.

She had sketched out a scene prior, pencil lines marking a peaceful mountainscape. The acrylic strokes tell a more harrowing tale. Her fingers rush the colors across the blank page. Dots of scarlet, cerulean, and amber hues splatter her smock. Her brows furrow as she brings a hostile landscape to life. She pours herself into the art, the brush flowing across the board, barely under her control.

The scene is the harshest she's ever made. It echoes the brutality that blew its way into her life. She presses down roughly, soaking the colors into the fabric until the canvas is dripping countless shades. Her phone alarm rings, and she pauses, stunned out of her haze—the trill pulling her out of her colorful trance.

She takes a moment to look over her work. Stealing the courage from the dreamy mountainside as she prepares to go face the world. Suzuka stands up, taking a few steps back to gaze upon the portal she created to another place.

The individual strokes form the beginnings of a snowy scene. The unfinished sky is midnight blue, absent of stars. The mountaintops gleam. Layers of icy sapphire mix with misty gray and brilliant white to form snowcapped peaks amidst a sea of clouds.

Although, Suzuka also sees where her emotions have bled through. The snow flies violently off the cliffs, the wind ripping the silvery crystals. Evergreen trees bend against the battering of the breeze.

Despite all the chaos, Suzuka lays her eyes on the centerpiece: a single torch. On a solitary ledge, the flame sits atop a triangular base, holding it fast despite the chaos surrounding it.

The cinders blow through the wind, glittering through the air. The fire flares. Suzuka hasn't yet decided whether it is the flame's last defiant moment or whether it will live on to see a calmer dawn. She'll have to determine that tomorrow.

Placing her tools down, she lets go of the warmth her passion provides. She slides the tarp over the piece, hiding it from prying eyes. She takes a moment in front of the hallway door, her mask sliding back into place.

Then she walks out the room, longing for the next moments she'll have to herself. She silently looks forward to placing the final strokes in the sky. She wants to see the awe on Lucas' face as she unveils the torch's fight against the relentless storm.

17

TWISTED WEB

Lucas takes another bite of his salad, but he barely tastes the greens. He sits in his office, mind completely spaced out.

He thinks Suzuka is acting strangely, but he wonders if it's his imagination. She came home the other night talking about a stomachache. Her eyes said something else.

Anna opens his door, and the movement brings him back to reality. She approaches his desk and types out her message on the digital surface.

"Hey, I've been following Alteryn's IPO, and they crushed it. They have raised $800 million. Plus, now they'll have to report out their earnings data, so we can model their potential better. The algorithm will love that."

Lucas types back, "*Wow, with what we have already, the algorithm is listing them on top, so then it looks like we have a winner. Have Jeff and the design team started on the recommendation deck? Probably gonna have the Alteryn logo all over it.*"

Anna responds, "*Idk, but I'll email him. I wanted to share the good news. Just think of a completely renewable-powered city. How cool would it be to know we helped make that happen?*" She is about to get up, but Lucas starts typing again.

He pauses for a second, and then he pulls out a slip of paper to write on instead, not wanting the system to know about this particular question. Anna looks at him quizzically, but she patiently waits as he scribbles.

"I know you had some concerns with this project too. The work is interesting, but why do you think Sterling contracted us to develop this software?"

Anna takes the pencil and writes back, "*Yeah, I was originally concerned that they have ulterior motives too, but I don't know. If Sterling buys Alteryn and they scale them up, that would be huge. Sterling Energies would keep their bazillion dollars, and Alteryn would now provide renewable energy across the city with a different logo. Seems like a smart move, wins all around.*"

Lucas writes back, "*But why keep it quiet? Wouldn't Sterling want people to know this? Might get the protesters off their backs.*"

Anna responds, "*Eh, who knows? Maybe Sterling's legal team doesn't want the target companies to rig the game. They wanna observe the clean energy corps in their 'natural habitat.'*"

Lucas replies, "*Yeah, guess you're right. Lawyers are annoying. Those protestors have been screaming for weeks but haven't gotten anything done. So if we can change Sterling from the inside out, then we can hold our noses and deal with that stuck-up John guy a few more weeks, huh?*

Anna chuckles at that. Lucas smiles.

Anna gets up and moves toward the door. But upon getting there, she doubles back. She sits back down and writes out, "*Lucas, are we friends?*"

Surprised by the question, he writes, "*Yeah, of course. What do you mean?*"

"I know we're colleagues, but I care about you. And I found something as part of my research you may want to know."

Lucas nods his okay, urging her to continue.

"You'd only vaguely heard of the Climate Cultural Coalition before I mentioned it, correct?" Anna bites her lips nervously as her fingers fly over the paper.

"*Yes.*"

"And your wife's name is Suzuka, correct?"

"Um, yeah. What does she have to do with this?" Lucas leans forward, a frown tugging at the edges of his mouth.

Anna furrows her brow as she writes out, "Well, this environmentalist outlet listed her as the current director of the CCC. Instated after the last one died in the protests a few weeks back."

"*Wait, what?*" Lucas is confused. That can't be right. *Suzuka is so calm and measured nowadays. Plus, she works at a research lab. When does she have time to lead a climate organization?*

Anna taps her digital pad and slides a website link over to this desk's surface. A small box in the corner of the page lists rising climate figures to watch. It is a sizable list, but Lucas only cares about a single line:

A lesser-known figure in the CCC takes control, Director Suzuka Maamoun

Lucas' heart hurts. *Why has she been lying to him? Why wouldn't she share something so pivotal? And it's not like she's a criminal overlord or something. Has she been trying to say something, and he's just been distracted? Or has she really been obscuring this from his knowledge? Also, how could she be so irresponsible? If the last one died, is she in harm's way? How could she put herself in a situation that could end with him as a widower, Sierra motherless?*

Lucas keeps his composure in front of Anna, just writing back a barely concealed lie, "*Oh yeah, she did say something about this the other day. Just didn't make the connection.*" He smiles tightly. Anna's clearly not convinced but nice enough to take the hint.

All she writes out is, "*Cool. Well, I'll go email Jeff.*"

She gets up, leaving Lucas to question what other lies might be waiting for him at home.

18

GRADUATION

The weeks of class pass without much of a fuss. Ezra puts in the work, doing his shifts with Maurice and studying in the evening where he can. He's been surprised to find all this medical stuff has actually been interesting.

Studying has become less of a chore and more of a hobby as he sits by the lamp light every night reviewing anatomy and memorizing crazy Latin words doctors use to make them feel like they're not just passing out street drugs.

He feels like he can help people with this knowledge. He knows he can care for all the neighbors he sees walking funny but refusing to see anyone cause the docs don't treat them right. Ezra's still focused on other things, though.

He's now slipped everything he needs from his class—vials, pills, and syringes kept in a stash beneath his bed. He's learned how to mix them too.

So far, no one at the firehouse has seemed to notice. In the moments before bed, Ezra always double checks the safety of his pile and pulls out the stored maps he has alongside them.

He knows there's novel technology and advanced mappers, but he's on a mission. He doesn't have time to learn all that fancy stuff.

Plus, he's heard about several people in the pen who got caught before they ever really did the crime. So Ezra sticks to paper maps of the city. Maps that now have highlighted paths all along the streets. Color-coded lines that follow the elegant avenues and fanciest boulevards, plotting the daily habits of one Mr. Aldrix Sterling.

Pencil marks note times next to each pit stop. The places where Ezra has seen Sterling frequent whenever Ezra takes his weekend escapades to the city center.

Only after Ezra has reviewed both his EMT homework and his 'passion project' does he roll everything back into its hiding place and turn off the lights.

Ezra has pictured this graduation since the day he started training. He never completed college, and his high school graduation seemed forced, simply a box that society dictated he must check off. Now he's actually proud. He has exactly what he wanted sitting under his bed, and he's also happy to take the certification and a shot at a postprison life.

He reminds himself this isn't just a celebratory ceremony. The firehouse's graduation event doubles as a reveal party as well. Their instructor has been contacted by each of their potential employers, and he will disclose their matches tonight.

Ezra waits impatiently in the classroom. Despite the nervous energy, no one speaks a word. The only movement is expressed through bouncing knees and trembling hands.

Ezra's mind works at a breakneck speed, worrying about the outcome of the ceremony. *Will his record hold him back? Could he have been rejected by every site he applied to? What would he tell his mom if his exhaustion and late nights these past four months resulted in nothing? What other options does he have? Would he actually spend the rest of his life working at Maurice's?*

An unfamiliar firefighter knocks on the doorway. She doesn't mince words, ordering, "Follow me."

The EMTs to-be rise as a unit and follow her down the familiar hallway and out into the concrete training deck behind the building. Usually filled with practice tools, exercise equipment, and secondhand footballs, the small outdoor area is empty except for a single long table with a blue cloth draped over it. Six folders with each trainee's name lay on top, and Instructor Burly stands rim-rod straight behind it.

Some of the on-duty firefighters kindly hung string lights along the back wooden fence and now watch from a neat line on the side. The firefighter who led them out onto the patio now moves to join her comrades and leaves the soon-to-be graduates standing in a line in front of the table.

Ezra stands with Emma on his left and Smartphone Dude on the right.

After a few moments of silence and a cough from one of the firefighters on the side, Burly Instructor finally says, "I'd like to welcome our EMT trainees to their graduation and employment ceremony. I'm excited to award each trainee their National Registry of Emergency Medical Technicians certificate and letters of decision." His voice doesn't quite ring with excitement, but Ezra doesn't care. He just wants to open his envelope.

"I will begin alphabetically by last name. Once you receive your folder, you may return to the line, but do not view the inside contents until I permit you to. First up, Jason Altman."

For a moment, the entire class is confused until Smartphone Guy walks forward to accept his folder. Ezra knows that everyone is thinking the same thing, *Who knew he had a name? Much less Jason.* Well, that's one mystery solved tonight.

"Emma Caldwell." With practiced steps, Emma approaches the table and returns to the group.

"Ezra Coleman." Heart pounding out of his chest, Ezra steps forward, the room swaying as he puts his entire focus into not tripping or embarrassing himself on his arduous ten-foot journey to collect his folder.

Instructor Burly holds Ezra's packet straight out in front of him, and with a single word of thanks, Ezra snatches it and pivots back to his companions.

They call the final three names, but Ezra doesn't notice. He is just staring at the folder in front of him with the District 97 crest on it as if it will give him the X-ray vision he desires at this moment. After what feels like an eternity, their instructor says, "You may now open the folders."

Ezra rips the spine as he looks inside, his certificate on the right and his decision letter inserted on the left. His eyes focus on the words, and he reads:

Stratford Hospital is pleased to extend an offer of employment to Mr. Ezra Coleman for the position of Emergency Medical Technician (Basic).

Thank goodness.

All of the newly employed EMTs look up from their individual papers and see the smiles plastered on each one of their faces, making them grow even larger. From out of nowhere, the firefighters waiting on the side cry out in celebration and champagne appears from thin air. Those on-duty aren't able to partake, but they happily serve up bubbling glasses to the graduates.

For the next few minutes, Ezra enjoys this feeling. *Step one, check.*

19

FIGHT

Lucas senses Suzuka's excellent mood the moment she walks through the door.

He greets her with, "*Happy Friday! It's the weekend! What happened at work? You seem happy!*"

Smiling, Suzuka signs, "*Happy Friday! Yeah, I had a good day at work.*"

Lucas pauses, waiting for more, but when nothing comes, he prods further, "*That's it? You practically danced through the door. Something special happened, let's celebrate it.*"

Her smile fading a little bit, Suzuka signs, "*Well, we just got some really exciting data from the Oceanic Research Society about this underground volcano. It is going to really help some of my team's research.*"

Becoming frustrated, Lucas signs on, "*Okay, that's great. But… not to push, but is there something else? That sounds fascinating, but you're way too happy to just be excited about some new data.*"

Suzuka throws off her bag and tosses it hastily to the side before signing, "*Why don't you share about how your work has been going with your promotion? You were all excited about that new fancy office, but now I've barely heard a peep about what you've been up to."*

Lucas knits his brows as he responds, *"I told you, they had us sign a nondisclosure, so it's not that I don't want to talk about it. I'm just complying with the policies."*

That clearly didn't satisfy Suzuka. She wildly signs as she shoots back, *"You can't talk about it? Really? There have been many other projects where you've signed NDAs, and that definitely didn't hold you back from grumbling about them before bed. You love to talk about work. You love complaining about work, and now you've been silent for weeks."*

Lucas›s signs are equally aggressive as he replies, *"At least you know the reasons why I can't talk about work. It's not like what you're doing is so classified and important at a research lab. Why can't you just share something personal and fun about your day? That's all I wanted. Why is this such a big deal?"*

Suzuka fires back, *"Don't come at me like I'm the only one with secrets around here. And while we're at it, you've been talking so much about how your promotion is providing for us so much more with a slight pay bump when I'm still the one stuck every morning caring for our daughter cause you can't be bothered to do more than kiss her before you hop over to your 'Mr. Big shot' job."*

Lucas pulls the trigger. *"When were you going to tell me you're leading a climate justice organization? Why wouldn't you share that with me?"*

Shock hits Suzuka only briefly before her face turns red with rage. *"Why wouldn't I share that with you? Why wouldn't I share my activism with the man that shakes his head when he scrolls through the protest articles on Twitter? The man who is so passionate about providing for our daughter but then is content to just shrug at her future? Why do you think?"*

Lucas reacts with, "*I don't shake my head cause I disapprove of the movement. I shake my head because it's messy. It's dangerous, and I can't believe you are in a position that killed the last person who held it. How good will Sierra's future be without a mom? Believe it or not, my new project is a job to help Sterling acquire Alteryn. If this goes through, it could revolutionize the city's power grid and make Sterling and Alteryn a ton of money. So why are you putting yourself in danger by fighting the system when I'm making a bigger difference from the inside? We're all on the same team. Just use your head instead of throwing your emotions all over the place!*"

Lucas throws down his hands after his tirade, steeling himself for Suzuka's response, but she doesn't explode as he'd thought. Instead, she just simmers in cold fury, a sight that makes him even more terrified.

Suzuka's attention breaks away, and she looks down at her phone. Lucas presumes it made some sort of sound and takes the moment to get a handle on his shaking hands and rising blood pressure. Suzuka lets him sit in anxiety, fearing her response.

Slowly, she turns her attention back to him and raises her hands to respond, "*Sterling doesn't play for any team other than himself. You have no clue what you're dealing with. You're a complete fool for thinking he'd actually let things change.*"

She takes a brief pause, then continues signing, her hands trembling, "I *can't do this right now. If you want to know why I was in a good mood, fine. I just got an email about speaking with the mayor for a second time in two weeks.*"

Lucas signs, "*The mayor? What? Suzuka, congrats.*"

"*Go to hell, Lucas. And when you come back, then we can talk. I need some sleep.*"

Lucas brings his hands up to shoot back, but he doesn't have anything to say. His palms just hang in the air as his thoughts lay in a shattered mess.

Then she walks away, leaving Lucas to regret having ever mentioned anything.

Lucas dreams of a memory—a memory that happens to be one of his favorites.

The entire audience holds their breath in the darkness. A single laser pierces the sky, faintly illuminating a stage encircled by a pool of perfectly still water.

Dum-ba-dum, ba-dum, ba-dum, ba-dum, dum, dum, dum

Slowly, the water begins to tremble, the speakers beginning to rumble with sound.

Dum-ba-dum, ba-dum, ba-dum, ba-dum, dum, dum, dum

The laser splits into multiple, illustrious sound waves of green, shooting into the arena's dome.

The music shakes Lucas' feet, the beat resounding through his body. The waves crashing through his bones as the beat rises.

Dum-ba, dum-ba, dum, dum, dum, dum, d-d-d-d-boom

The first bass drumbeat sends a ripple of cheers through the crowd.

Boom-pa, boom-pa

The water surges up with each drum strike, shooting up to create a circular wall of ever-moving glass and obscuring the stage from view.

The bass drums fade as the water reaches full-height, ten-foot-tall sheets of moving glass.

Dum-dum-dooo

The arena is still dimly lit, the laser beams the only source of light.

The drum fades entirely.

Lucas feels the anticipation, Suzuka nearly shaking from the suspense next to him.

Raaahhhh

The guitar hits a single note, holding it as the crowd goes insane.

The arena explodes with light, the wall of water splitting like curtains to reveal the band.

The chords feel smooth under Lucas' feet, combining with the quick successive drumbeats, the two musical elements harmonizing within him.

People launch out of their seats and into the air as the band gives everyone the show they came for. The lead singer belts out notes, face contorted with passion.

Lucas can't hear anything coming from the mic, but he's not looking at the artist anyway.

He's looking at the interpreter, spotlighted on the side, hands flying to the beat, completely jamming out.

Her signs are truncated to fit the music but convey so much more than just simple words. Her body is in constant motion, telling a story with her movements.

The bassist goes on a rift, her fingers flying over the strings and sending waves raging through the audience.

Lucas dances along, jumping to the beat as Suzuka bounces next to him.

As the show goes on, the moat around the stage rises and falls, creating clouds of light mist that shimmer under the lights.

Suzuka's silhouette radiates green, purple, and red as the lights strobe, her figure surrounded by a pulsing halo.

Somewhere a confetti cannon rockets beautiful strips of metallic paper through the air, sparkling as the light refracts off them.

Taaa-taaa-taaa-pah-pah-pah-bum-bum

Ba-da-da, pah-pah-pah-bum-bum

They are among thousands of others, screaming at the top of their lungs, but Lucas only sees the angel dancing before him.

Lucas takes in the electricity running through the people around him. The fists thrown into the air, the heads nodding to the rhythm. All moving to a language they all understand, collectively forming a shared experience.

The music swells, the bass reverberating through him as the final song comes to a close. Fire shoots from the stage, playing off the water and causing the whole stadium to glow. The world turned golden.

He looks to Suzuka, who is clearly belting out the final note, completely enthralled by the show. Her eyes are closed, but she leans into his arms.

He feels radiant.

The lights cut out, the final beat hitting like a thunderclap, leaving whispers of sound in the air. Only a single green laser strand remains in the air, pointing directly toward the sky. Then it slowly fades, and the audience is left in complete darkness once more.

When the arena floodlights turn on, Lucas is on his knee, his trembling hands trying not to drop a precious box. Still bursting with the energy of the night, Suzuka's expression turns to one of disbelief. Lucas barely opens the box before Suzuka throws her arms around him.

When the memory slips from his grasp and the morning welcomes him, Lucas can still feel the drumbeats reverberating around him. He can still feel the warmth of Suzuka's embrace and her kiss on his lips.

Though, when he reaches for his partner across the sheets, his arm finds only an abandoned pillow and empty space.

20

SEEING COLORS

Ezra enters Stratford Hospital for the 8 a.m. orientation.

In the small lecture hall, he finds two others already seated and one other taking her seat. Glancing around, he sees "*Welcome to SH!*" scribbled on the dry-erase board in front of room in red with surprisingly artistic balloons drawn around the letters.

About five more new hires join them in the room over the next few minutes. Three of them engage in some brief exchange, but the majority remain quiet, preferring to stick to the comfort of the phone screens.

The sudden scraping of the doorstop being removed and the portal being shut causes everyone to cease their polite chitchat and look toward the front. A paramedic has entered and is now walking toward the main desk.

His back turned, the paramedic drops his bag onto the front desk and withdraws his laptop. With shaggy blond hair, an oval face, and long limbs, the paramedic looks less like an emergency services professional and more like an awkward basketball player. He sinks in his chair like he just ended a night shift. However, the moment he looks up with his piercing blue-gray eyes, Ezra is transported to a different time.

The first thing Ezra noticed about Nick Myelin on the first day of kindergarten were his eyes. An intense icy blue, they were difficult not to note. Whenever Nick was upset or tired, they turned a bit red, but this simply added to their brilliance. In the sunlight, his eyes shone.

This often resulted in Ezra forgetting to catch the ball as Nick sped around the kickball bases, but Ezra was completely fascinated by their coloring. Looking in the mirror as a child, he often wished his eyes were as cool as Nick's and continued to envy them well into high school.

In seventh grade, Nick sat with Ezra one day at lunch. He looked a bit green, and when Ezra asked, Nick replied, "I think I have a secret."

"What?" Ezra said back.

"I think I like Amanda."

"The girl from your robotics club?" Ezra asked.

Nick just nodded, green turning to a bright red blush. "Ez, you can't tell anyone. I don't know what I'm going to do. I want to ask her to the dance, but I don't think she'd say yes. Do you think I have a shot?"

Head hung low for the entire beginning of their conversation, Nick now looked up.

Ezra smiled, but it died as soon as Nick's eyes met his. He noticed a fleck of gold he'd never noticed before. Not a lot, just a tiny sliver in the sea of blue. It struck Ezra he had never quite felt like that about a girl before. He'd never looked at any of his female classmates the way Nick stared across the room toward Amanda now.

But there was a boy that made him feel all the colors at once. Feel as though he was a shooting star. Nick's perfectly blue eyes captivated his attention. The way he wore his red and brown glasses made Ezra dizzy. Even Nick's pink blush made Ezra's stomach tumble.

After a brief moment of realization, Ezra felt instantly ashamed. *He didn't want to be weak.*

Trying to hide his spiraling thoughts, Ezra decided to pump his friend up as much as possible. So, he finally responded, "You should ask her, Nick. You never know. She might say yes." But even though he gave the advice, he secretly wished that Nick would ask him instead.

In ninth grade, Ezra met someone who brought questions bubbling to the surface of his mind. His classmate was gay, and everyone knew it. He was flamboyant and loud and basically walked around the school halls with a rainbow flag wrapped around his shoulders. Ezra didn't like him very much and didn't think he was very handsome, but he was the only other gay person he knew existed in the world.

One day in class, Ezra slipped him a note asking him to hang out. The boy accepted, and the next day they met in a neighborhood park. They had a painfully one-sided conversation in which Ezra heard all about the other boy's life. How old his siblings were, that he wanted to study finance in college, how he already knew he was going to be a banker, everything. It was a horrible ninety minutes, but at the end, Ezra made sure they were sitting on a park bench with no one else around. Ezra made his move and leaned in. The other boy was surprised, but once he recovered, he leaned in as well. With that, Ezra had his first kiss.

It was enjoyable. He didn't know what that meant for him.

The two of them left the park after an awkward goodbye, unaware one of their classmates watched the entire scene out the window of his apartment across the street. Their classmate was all too eager to snap a few photos, and soon the word spread like wildfire.

The next day, photos of Ezra kissing his extremely extroverted classmate were on every phone that walked the halls. Ezra was knocked around during passing periods and received anonymous messages all day calling him malignant words he hadn't even known existed.

Nick and Lucas were great. Nick told him, "You're still you, Ez. Don't let them make you feel different. We still love you."

Lucas wrote him an incredible letter that ended with, *"I'll be expecting an invite to your wedding."*

They showed nothing but acceptance, and Ezra loved them for it, but his friends weren't with him every second. Any time they weren't around, he felt the target weighing heavily on his back.

Things started to calm down after a few weeks, but for the rest of his four years, Ezra was seen as different by the whole school. He became incredibly aware of his actions and avoided anything someone might interpret the wrong way.

At graduation, Ezra was careful to lean away from Nick in their friend group's photo. He posed in a silly manner but never unmanly.

In prison, he hid his identity completely. He worried anyone finding out about his sexuality would spell death or serious injury. He spent extra time at the gym, buffing up his physique and practicing his tough exterior. If anything happened, he needed to be able to take the guy challenging him.

His fourth year in, a new guard joined the ranks. He had sandy blond, wavy hair, and a perfectly kept beard. He stood tall and had kind brown eyes.

Every time Ezra passed the guard, his eyes lingered on the man's lips.

In the end, though, Ezra pushed his feeling down. Each morning as the guard brought him food, he thought about saying something. In the end, he figured it was too dangerous. It wasn't worth it. So he continued to hide himself. To be ashamed of who he was.

He buried that part of him so deep he almost forgot he had the capacity to fall in love. The only thing that saved him was the memory of his friend's eyes. Despite everything he'd endured over the course of those years of confinement, he still held onto his feelings for Nick.

They say to fall in love with eyes as they remain long after the beauty of youth burns away. Ezra sees no reason to doubt this saying. After all, it must be true. His love for Nick hasn't dimmed one bit.

Snapping back into the reality of orientation, Ezra averts his eyes to the ground. The paramedic's eyes are the closest thing to Nick's he's seen in a decade. Despite all of his experiences in lockup, he will never forget the exact blue of Nick's irises.

For the rest of the orientation, Ezra concentrates as much as possible on the board. Flicking his eyes as sparingly as possible at the paramedic. At the end of fifty minutes spent discussing the tedium of how to log hours, find their equipment, and activate their IDs, the paramedic announces it's time to meet their partners.

Gesturing to the back of the room, the class notices seven emergency technicians have snuck in. They are of varying heights, ages, and experience levels, but they all appear untouchable at that moment. An intimidating unit that has come to choose its victims from the still disoriented rookies. Without a hitch, the left-most technician calls out the name of their new partner, the man next to Ezra rises, the two disappearing out of the room.

This happens twice more before Ezra hears his name called. The fourth technician is a middle-aged, short, blond woman whose hair is cut perfectly evenly, as if with a laser. She is unsmiling as she calls Ezra's name in a much deeper voice than Ezra would expect out of her petite body.

Rising, Ezra walks toward her with increasing intimidation. Before he even reaches her, she turns and strides out of the room, clearly expecting him to follow.

He enters the hallway, where she waits.

"Hi, nice to meet you," Ezra says as unconfidently as he feels.

"Nice to meet you too, Ezra," she says deadpan. Not bothering to introduce herself, she says, "Let's go to the cafeteria."

They walk in silence as they make their way through a series of identical-looking hallways.

Upon arrival, his partner takes Ezra over to a table evidently laid out for the new hires. It has a few salads, small sandwiches, and small cans of soda. Ezra grabs a little of everything before joining his new partner at a small circular table for two.

As soon as Ezra seats himself, his partner begins, "So, hi Ezra. My name is Meghan, but I go by Meg. I've been in emergency services since I got out of school twenty-two years ago. In those years, I've had great partners and lousy partners. I've been thrown up on, bled on, burnt, and had several guns pointed at me. I will not slow down my pace when someone's life is on the line just so you can learn what you missed in NREMT class when you zoned out."

Barely pausing for breath, Meg continues, "I will not treat you like a rookie, so I expect you not to act like one. If I tell you to do something, do it. Arguing just wastes time when seconds could mean life or death. If you stick with me and do what I say, I will help you become the best EMT of your class, and you will be a full paramedic in no time."

Ezra doesn't quite know how to react to her brief speech. The woman had just scared him completely with her searing remarks, but he knows without a doubt that he will be learning fast. Additionally, where there was once complete terror, respect now peeks through the surface.

"And finally, despite what you may think now, I do like to have fun. I also believe a partner is not just an on-the-clock relationship. For better or worse, you are now my partner. Sure, that means we save lives and ride in the ambulance together. But that also means we watch out for each other, eat together, and joke around during downtime. We can play cards together, grab a beer together, or go bowling together for all I care. What I mean is when you're my partner, I will pick up the phone regardless of what time it is, and if I call you at 1 a.m., you better pick up too. Is that understood?"

Stunned more than he thought possible by the woman in front of him, Ezra merely nods. The horror he had felt just moments ago is gone. In its place is absolute awe.

In response to his bobbing head, Meg says, "Good. Now eat. We only have thirty minutes for lunch."

Ezra still remains frozen.

"What did I just say about listening to me? Eat!"

Ezra instantly remembers himself and shoves food in his mouth, knowing he is in for the ride of his life.

21

AN ACCIDENT

Suzuka walks toward the seaside, last night's fight replaying over in her mind.

She ran out this morning before Lucas was awake. She needs time. At this moment, she needs to stay focused.

Suzuka had seriously weighed going to the seaside today, her stomach still bruised from that encounter with Sterling's thug. She sat in her kitchen for a while, leaning against the faux-marble island, stirring a cup of apple cinnamon tea.

She doesn't want to admit it, but that beating got to her. Yet, it also activated her deep-seated anger. That rage she felt at the injustice of the protest, at the director's life slipping away. So when she went to kiss Sierra, dropping her off at the nursery for the day, her love for her daughter only added to the determination that she had to stick it to Sterling.

Plus, now she knows to look out, walking the streets with her guard up. If he tries again, she'll be ready. She refuses to succumb to the fear. Not when her daughter's future is at stake.

The mayor is waiting on a park bench overlooking the water. Her aide and a security guard are beside her. "Hi Suzuka, I invited you here today to discuss more specific policy measures. I apologize for taking up some of your Saturday."

"It is not a problem, Mayor Silva," Suzuka still basks in the glow of being consulted by the mayor.

Uncharacteristically, Emerald stumbles over her words. "Well, you see, the specific thing I wanted to discuss with you is the possibility of extending the timeline for our green energy policy."

Suzuka tilts her head, "Wait, what? You want to postpone what is arguably the most consequential race against the clock in history?"

Emerald responds warily, aware of the impact her words will have. "Well, it might be the only path we have forward."

Suzuka's voice rises sharply, "I can't believe this. With all due respect, what you're saying doesn't line up. You can't have it both ways." All of the deference Suzuka had given the mayor goes out the window. She has betrayed Suzuka's trust.

Emerald tries desperately to explain. "I don't like it either, but we simply don't have the renewable capacity to cut off the oil pipelines tomorrow. This transition will take time."

Suzuka rails against her in frustration. "I'm not saying tomorrow, but we don't have a lot of wiggle room. Anything other than what you proposed isn't aggressive enough." Suzuka seethes as she asks, "What happened to shift your policy so much?"

"Suzuka—"

"Director. Director Maamoun," Suzuka corrects.

"Director Maamoun, I will admit I had a conversation with key oil players in the city."

Suzuka throws her arms out in disbelief. "Why are you listening to those people? And why are you saying, 'key oil players?' I know it's just Sterling. Of course, he's going to try to convince you of anything that'll make him more money. He's a greedy bastard."

Emerald refuses to cower. "I didn't particularly enjoy the encounter, but I cannot ignore the fact they provide almost the entirety of the power to this city. And they're right in one regard. If they switched off the lights tomorrow, there would be madness. So none of my policies have changed. I'm just elongating the timeline."

Suzuka screams, "That is a policy change! That's a huge policy change!"

All Emerald wants to do is tell Suzuka the impossible position she is in. To make her feel the threats of Sterling and the vulnerability of midnight encounters with armed men. But she doubts she would understand, Suzuka's fearless. As they walk along the seaside, Emerald just continues to pitch a perspective she knows is faulty.

Emerald isn't surrounded by the safety of her office's privileges. She can't just lean back and hide behind a mahogany desk. Only Amelie and a solitary guard trail them now, being cautious to keep a respectful distance.

Not that it matters for all of Suzuka's shouting.

Emerald had arranged the informal meeting in hopes of relating on a personal level with Suzuka and clearing this hurdle keeping the government and climate coalition from making real progress.

Suzuka is making it incredibly difficult. Emerald does her best to give a measured response. "I don't see any issue with supplementing renewables with fossil fuels while we transition. We can't go cold turkey on this and—"

"But we have to," Suzuka cuts in. "Our coalition represents a diverse set of voices. And honestly, we don't agree on much. We all come at this issue from different directions. But, we all agree *drastic* action is needed. We can't afford to take our time switching to clean energy. To be frank, it should have already happened. And you yourself criticized your predecessor for his slow pace on climate action. We endorsed you because you promised to take decisive action. I'm coming to this table in good faith, hoping to actually be heard by a politician."

"I'm not a politician," says Emerald.

"You're not a politician? You're the mayor. Of the government. Of one of the largest cities in this country. What do you mean you're not a politician?" Suzuka's face scrunches in anger.

Clearly aggravated, Emerald responds, "I'm just a person. I'm doing my best!"

Suzuka retorts, "But you're just a person who holds the future of our city! I—"

"Um... I'm sorry to interrupt, ma'am," Amelie says as she quickly closes the few yards that had separated them.

"Not now, Amelie," Emerald says briskly.

Amelie persists, "I... well, ma'am, I've just been told you're needed urgently at your office."

"You're kidding." Emerald can't believe this timing.

Timidly, Amelie continues, "Unfortunately not, I was directed to bring you back right away, ma'am."

"Who told you this? It's almost 5 p.m. on a Saturday. Who is even at City Hall right now?"

Amelie runs her hand through her hair nervously, "Um, not sure ma'am, I just know it was actually a secure communication. I don't quite have access yet."

"I won't keep you from your work, Mayor Silva," Suzuka says. "But we will certainly need another meeting."

"No," Emerald replies. "I'm not leaving our discussion like this. We're on the same side."

"Are we?" Suzuka asks, arms crossed.

"Yes, believe it or not," Emerald says. "So please, ride with me to City Hall. I can have the drivers take you wherever you'd like afterward."

"No, that's not necessary," Suzuka replies stiffly.

"I insist. Again, our conversation isn't over."

"Fine," Suzuka says, following Emerald toward the car.

"So," Ezra says, "Any first call tips? I'd appreciate some—"

Cut off by their radios crackling to life, "Ambulance 28, requested response on Corso street between Temple Ave and Madalena."

Without hesitation, Meg responds. "Thank you, dispatch. We're on our way." Then she turns and begins jogging toward the ambulance bay.

Ezra rushes to follow her, adrenaline pumping as they run to the vehicle.

Once in the ambulance, Meg says into the radio, "All right, dispatch, we're on the road, ETA ten mins."

The sound coming out of the radio box is grainy as the dispatcher says, "Copy, fire, and police also en route."

Ezra plugs the directions into the GPS, and Meg takes off.

Emerald squirms under the weight of the silence in the car. Five minutes have passed, and the conversation never quite found a rhythm.

Amelie sits in the passenger's seat, scrolling through emails as per usual, her face entirely blank. An expression Emerald has come to recognize as the "trying hard not to listen" face.

The guard drives, his expression bearing the same stoicism as all the others that security assigned to her.

And, of course, Emerald sits diagonally from the driver, her designated seat for all eternity.

Beside her, Suzuka tries to pick up the conversation again. Emerald desperately wants to salvage the discussion, but her mind is much more preoccupied with figuring out whatever crisis is about to greet her at the doors of city hall. She hasn't received any unexpected secure communications in these first few months in office, so she has no clue what to expect.

Her stomach rolls as her mind considers anything from a PR nightmare to a notice from the President about an impending war could be on her desk. And then, in the back of her mind, she fights back against the intuitive whisper that Sterling has gone public with her secret.

"Madam Mayor, you're not even listening, hmm?" Suzuka asks.

"I'm sorry," Emerald says, returning her focus to the woman next to her.

"No, you're not. You were confident and electric on the trail. Your support for renewable energy was unshakeable."

"It still is!"

"It clearly isn't. You're already under their thumbs."

Emerald shoots back vehemently. "I'm not. It's just a bit more complicated than it looks on the outside."

Suzuka begins, "I can appreciate that, but—"

"Do you? Really?" Emerald asks, the weight of her position evident on her face.

"Look," Suzuka says, bringing the tension down slightly, "have you heard of the Future World Analysis Tool our coalition created?"

Emerald reluctantly replies, "The one that illustrates the various climate dystopias? Yes, Amelie showed me. It wasn't the most hopeful thing I'd ever seen, but it was impressive. Your team's work doesn't go unappreciated. You know we referenced it in some of our policy research for the trail. And we will work to make sure the predictions don't become a reality."

"But it is reality, ma'am. And it is a future defended by force." Suzuka pauses in exasperation.

Only the hum of the engine is audible for a moment before she continues. "I… I was at the protest at Sterling the other week when the guards shot blanks into the crowd. And before everything started, I felt so… so triumphant. The passion in the crowd was unexplainable. I'm sure you know the feeling from your rallies. The complete electricity. That feeling of peace in a swarm of complete madness. It is such a magical experience to be in a crowd like that.

"But then… when it turned violent. I hate to admit it, but my passion went out the window. I was almost crushed by everyone running. I was thrown to the ground and kicked around. And, I mean, I was scared. I could've died. And when I was running for my life, I wasn't concerned about the earth. I just wanted to get home to my family. To my husband. To my daughter. And when a guard hit one of my friends… I… fought back. But not for the planet. Just out of sheer panic and anger and hatred. And I'm still ashamed I abandoned my cause. All it took were some guards and smoke. So, Madam Mayor, yes. I know it is complicated. You don't have a family yet, but I know you're getting pressure from all sides. But we can do this. We *have to* make this happen."

Emerald looks Suzuka dead in the eyes and takes in the determination staring back at her.

"The next day, I got up and started organizing the next protest because if I stayed silent, Sterling would have won. And he has tried to beat me down, but I'm not letting him win. So please, I'm just asking you to push the boundaries of what people tell you is possible. Together we can—"

The car comes out of nowhere.

And for a moment, they are weightless. Suspended in a second of terror as the glass turns to spiderwebs.

Then the force of the impact throws Emerald to the side, and blood immediately covers her. It takes a moment for her to process the sound, but once she does, it is the loudest thing she's ever heard.

Glass showers her, and she keeps her eyes firmly shut as the car skids to a halt.

She keeps her eyes closed as she fumbles to unbuckle. She throws the door open and stumbles from the car. She carries an avalanche of glass shards along with her as she crawls along the asphalt, away from the heat she feels at her back.

For an unknown number of minutes, she simply lays there on her side, furious and confused. The shock is insurmountable, and her head feels as though she had a run in with a brick wall.

She registers some movement around her, and through her mind fog, she remembers others had been in the car too. Wiping glass from her face, Emerald finally dares to peek at the remnants of her ride. The street dangerously tilts as she attempts to take stock of the chaotic sight that greets her. Metal and glass litter the ground, shining in the evening light, flames smoldering under the hood.

Where the driver's door had been is simply a concave mass. There is no sign of the guard.

Emerald's fear finally kicks in, and she rises. Something that had felt impossible mere moments ago. She peers behind her to the back row and finds an unmoving, bloodied Suzuka. She pulls the Director to the ground, gritting her teeth and hoping the crackling of the flames doesn't climb any farther.

Turning to the front seat, Emerald immediately becomes nauseous. The guard's eyes are open, his skull crushed against the dashboard. Amelie's chest is barely rising and falling, but blood streams from her neck, scarlet soaking into the leather cushions. Emerald tries to drag her assistant, her friend, to safety, but she won't budge. The distorted metal traps Amelie in a cage as the car begins emitting a menacing clicking sound from the burning hood.

Emerald slides the SOS icon on her phone and a voice that sounds far too collected for Emerald's liking answers.

Still barely processing the situation, Emerald cries out, "Please. Car accident. I'm the May... ayor... We're on Corso street. We were going to City Hall. Please. We need help."

Climbing back into the fresh air, Emerald vomits. When she is completely empty, she slowly notices no one has come out of the other car. It, too, is burning, but she doesn't care. Fury now sweeping through her, she makes herself hobble over to the vehicle against the pounding heat and rips the door open.

But no one is there. The front of the car is completely crumpled, but there are no signs of blood. Almost as if no human had been in this car. Emerald reels and wracks her brain to understand how an automated vehicle had rammed their car so fiercely; until she sees the note taped to the steering wheel.

I couldn't have you forgetting who your real friends are.

Emerald finally succumbs to the nausea and collapses to the asphalt.

Finally, John has some good news. Even though he isn't quite sure what the news is. All the voice on the phone said was to tell Sterling "it worked." That was enough for John. Mr. Sterling loves hearing his ideas were right.

He enters the office and finds Mr. Sterling at his desk per usual.

"Yes, John?"

"I was instructed by Apollo to tell you that 'it worked,' sir. He said you'd know what I meant."

Sterling's shoulder slump as if a weight has been removed. "Yes, that's excellent news John. Thank you very much."

Stunned at the nicest response he'd ever gotten, John turns to leave.

"Oh, one more thing, John, could you please take this note downstairs to Nicholas Myelin?"

"Of course, sir."

Ezra has no idea what he is walking into, but he knows something is deeply wrong.

Meg speeds through the streets, taking hairpin turns and moving the ambulance like it is a sports car. Under the steering wheel, her knee is bouncing like crazy.

Meg finally turns onto Corso, and the first thing Ezra notices is the smell. The burnt rubber and smoke and… oil. Then both he and Meg take a deep breath as the scene unfolds before them.

Ezra has never seen a car crash this bad. It is almost like the offending vehicle was trying to do as much damage as possible. And he can't believe who he sees lying on the ground in front of them.

The mayor is sprawled out a few yards away from two burning cars. Ezra stands in disbelief before Meg punches his shoulder and begins shouting orders. The mayor is a safe distance away along with another severely bruised female, so they rush to the front of the car.

Ezra takes a look at the driver and knows he's a goner, but the passenger is still breathing. The heat pulses on his skin as he tries to pull the woman out, but she is trapped. Meg called the fire team, but since they hadn't arrived, Ezra pulled desperately. He isn't sure if the flames will stay at bay long enough.

In the meantime, Ezra and Meg load the mayor into the ambulance. It wasn't until they were lifting the second woman that Ezra realized she looked familiar.

"Ezra. Ezra! Quit staring deeply into her eyes and get your head in the game. Fire just rolled up." Meg pulls him toward the reinforcements.

The firefighters are blasting the flames that had engulfed the front of the car. A pair of them ripped the car apart with shears, heaving out the passenger, her body severely burned.

Ezra and Meg rush to meet the fire team carrying the woman and find she is still breathing. Ezra looks to the fire captain and thanks him. In response, the fireman just grimaces. "You better get outta here. That one needs all the help she can get."

The two of them haul the third woman into the ambulance before Ezra jumps in to care for the patients as Meg hops in the driver's seat. And while wrapping the wounds of the burnt woman, Ezra searches the face of the familiar-looking lady. Meg's aggressive driving becomes even more frantic as the sirens blare.

Ezra tries to keep himself from being thrown around and thinks about the brutal scene they are speeding away from. He might be new, but if the mayor was involved, he has a sneaking suspicion this is much deeper than it appears.

The ambulance slams to a halt, and the doors are thrown open. Ezra hauls the first woman out on a gurney, and he and Meg roll into the ER… where everyone is frozen, distracted by the TV.

22

DISASTER

Sterling calls a man he despises.

The man picks up immediately. "Did it work?"

Sterling cuts to the chase as well, "Yes."

The voice on the other end asks, "And was the cop beater taken care of?"

Aldrix replies in the affirmative, "You can tell the police chief she's paid her dues."

The voice only gives a one-worded response. "Excellent."

John steps off the elevator, a horrendous scent immediately hitting him. He frowns as he makes his way past the mechanics and machinery, the most wretched place in this building. He finds Nicholas in the control room as John restrains himself from placing his handkerchief over his nose.

"Nicholas Myelin."

Nicholas doesn't even have the decency to rip his eyes from the panel of blinking lights and number-filled monitors. He replies, "Uh, huh."

John holds back his commentary. *This is why he's down here in the pigsty instead of upstairs with the real leaders.*

"Nicholas Myelin, I have a note for you from Mr. Sterling."

He pivots to John, "Really? Okay, thanks for dropping it off."

The moment Nicholas reaches for the note, an alarm begins screaming. John startles, eyes widening under the red lights that now wash over the floor.

Nicholas turns back to the control board, frantically scanning for the issue.

"Rodrigo, what's happening?"

The older man replies, "It looks like a leak sir, the old pipeline just burst."

"What do you mean it burst?"

"I don't know!"

John doesn't need to hear the rest of the exchange. At least this gives him an excuse to go back upstairs. Bolting toward the elevator, note still in his hand, he jams his finger into the seventy-fifth button and watches the doors close on the blinding red lights.

Nick cannot believe the pressure readouts scrolling across the main screen.

"How could we have missed this?" he mutters.

Rodrigo shouts back, trying to make his voice heard over the toll of the alarm. The data shows how the pressure rose day after day. The pipe was slowly overpowered, and small bits of oil likely seeped through the cracks. Months of someone not caring that the indicators had risen by 0.5 until this happens.

Someone throws the news onto the monitors. Everyone in the room drops what they're doing and stares in distress.

The wind blasts Lucia Martinez's face, her wavy brown hair flying in front of her. The air is freezing despite the jacket she threw on hurriedly as the team ran out to report on the tip they received. Some random call about an oil leak.

Mark sits next to her, his camera dangling out the side, taking in the view of the ground. They're not live yet, so he just swivels in his chair, looking toward the sea.

She never wanted anything to do with the news growing up. It was so boring to watch stuffy people in bland suits and dresses drone on about the weather. Now a bachelor's in biology and PhD in oceanography later, and here she is in a helicopter with the *Chronicle.*

Five minutes out from the sea and Lucia scrolls through the comments on social media:

@Lora_the_unexplorer40

There's something in the sea. Why does it look like that?

@depressed_jock58

Heard something happened in the sea today. Kinda hope it is the loch ness monster. At least an apocalypse would get me out of this job.

@Xu_like_shoe1

My dad is a fisherman, and he just came back home talking about a messed up catch. Anyone else hear anything?

@beach_bae365

Oh my goodness, I was just at the beach relaxing, and my hair got completely covered in this black stuff. It's so gross!

Lucia smirks, sounds like this will be a good story. At least there'll be some local drama tonight about a few dropped barrels of oil.

Mark jolts up and swings the camera around. Lucia reacts as well, and for a moment, she's confused. *Where's the water?* Looking down, all she sees is black. As if the beach just turned into asphalt.

Just then, a realization hits her. The darkness moving through the waves, the dirtied sand and the usual blue now only shimmering in the distance.

Then there are the fish, rows upon rows speckled upon the beach. Unmoving.

Mark swings the camera around to face her, counting down to live. Five... Four...

She's not ready, smoothing her hair back hastily and trying to put on a façade of calm.

Three... Two...

Lucia takes a deep breath, her eyes stinging, thinking about the effects this will have.

One...

Mark signals to her, and the live light blinks on.

Lucia tells the truth, "This is the greatest environmental disaster I've ever seen."

PART II

INTERLUDE I

THE GREAT HORNED FALCON

The Storyteller gathered all of the children in a circle, some rolling restlessly in the grass, others sitting perfectly and straight-backed. Some were unable to find comfort among the leaves and twigs. Their discomfort only ever lasted as long as it took the Storyteller to begin. Once his words began to flow, all of them followed him into the legend. And every tale began the same way:

"A long time ago…

… the Creator was watching over all of nature. All was in harmony: all the creatures, including humans, took and gave in equal parts. Our ancestors gathered berries and fashioned houses while the spiders weaved their wonderful webs and the lions feasted on prey. High in the sky, the Great Horned Falcons watched over the Creator's skies.

The Greatest of the Great Horned Falcons had spires atop its head which denoted the wisdom it held. The length and strength of its horns were said to be superior to any of our ancestor's tools and spears. It made its home in the trees of the forest, never settling once on the ground, even when swooping down for a meal.

One day, a group of young Horned Falcons, for they had not yet achieved the title of 'Great,' were practicing their flight amidst the treetops when they noticed a plume of smoke rising above the canopy.

They saw a man wrestling with a fire spirit, trying to subdue the spirit into submission on behalf of his people. The man's pride had convinced him that if only he could command the fire, the whims of its mood would never be a threat. So he had snuck deep into the forest where the sprites and elements dwell, looking for the fire spirit's resting place.

He leaped upon the spirit, strangling it and attempting to force it into service of man. But fire spirits are not inferior. They are not mortal either. They dwell among us at the behest of the Creator, and the Creator alone has command over them, just as the Creator alone knows our fates.

The man was foolish to think humans could ever rise above nature, separating themselves from the intricate system in which we live. So as he tumbled in the grass, struggling with the fire spirit, the spirit burned the trees and the grass and the leaves, spreading its fury across the land.

The young Horned Falcons laughed at the man but then yelped when the first cinders touched their feathers. Crying out in fear and watching their ground-bound friends scurry amidst the bushes pushed fear into their hearts, and they flew as fast as they could to the Greatest Horned Falcon in his perch on the strongest branch of the tallest tree.

Now the Greatest Horned Falcon had already seen the flames but was unafraid. He knew the Creator used the fire spirits to maintain the balance of the forest. He had seen plenty of blazes in his time and was amused to see the young Horned Falcons flying clumsily toward him.

His entertainment was short-lived. The young Horned Falcons explained it was not by the Creator's command that the fire spirits had set the ground to ashes. They told him of the man who fought the fire and thought he could make it his servant.

Alarmed, the Greatest Horned Falcon leaped from his perch, flying higher than any other. Then he dove toward the flames, rushing into the heart of the battle between the foolish man and furious fire spirit.

Finding the two combatants, the Greatest Horned Falcon used his majestic horns to pluck the fire spirit off the ground and into the air. The fire engulfed his horns, melting them as the fire spirit continued to rage, and the fire grew toward the community of man.

With no heed for itself, the Greatest Horned Falcon flew to the humans' meadow where the flames surrounded their young. The fire spirit still atop its head, the Greatest Horned Falcon used its tremendous wings to calm the fire and protect the meadow of humans.

When the smoke cleared, the Greatest Horned Falcon landed for the first time ever upon the ground, letting the placated fire spirit down from its head. Disgraced, the Greatest Horned Falcon had lost its horns to the fury of the spirit and the cinders of the forest.

From that day forth, the humans gave great respect to the Horned Falcons and recognized the bravery of their kind. The foolish man learned only the Creator could command the elements. He became content in the knowledge humans would never extricate themselves from the natural world they lived amongst.

So that is how the Great Horned Falcons lost their horns and how our guardian Flamekeepers came to be. Those whose skin has the mark of the torch. The inverted triangle for our earth with the fire spirit atop as a reminder of its power.

The Flamekeepers are those among us who are most in tune with the commands of the Creator and are most respectful of our place in nature. They maintain the fires that heat our homes and cook our foods, always recognizing the power of the flames.

They never try to subdue the fire spirits but rather work in tandem, respectfully requesting their aid to further the survival of our community.

One day when your hair turns to moonlight, your children will call this land home. And the respect you show to our land and neighbors will have consequences on the lives of those to come. So take care. For it's a powerful thing to sacrifice for the generation yet unborn.

So never forget children, there is no separation between humans and nature. We are nature. Just as the Creator has blessed us with fire and surrounded us with both wild friend and foe.

When we take more than the Creator gives, the fire will grow angry and unkind. The Flamekeepers know this, and that is why they are charged with praising the Creator and fostering friendship with the fire.

We must never think ourselves superior, or next time we may not have a Great Horned Falcon to save us from ourselves."

23

SHATTERED

Emerald sits in an empty room, yet she is not alone. Nightmares fill the space around her.

Her face is tearstained.

She sits in pitch darkness though brilliant flames blaze in her memory.

Her guard gone. Suzuka's status unknown. Amelie seriously injured. Their blood was not spilled by her hands, but the guilt is heavy on her shoulders.

The walls of the hospital meditation room are embedded with screens. The display showed a forest when she arrived. It looked like Emerald's home, the breeze flying through the swaying branches. She turned it off instantly, staring instead into nothingness.

She can't hear the frantic hospital halls in here. There are no harsh lights or wails of pain. There are no demands. For a few moments, she is no longer Mayor Silva. She is just Em.

A salty sting returns to Emerald's eyes, streaming down her cheeks. She's glad no one can see how her mascara runs, how her chin gathers a pool of liquid sorrow.

The attention is the worst. The media, the authorities.

The police chief just left.

He asked about threats. He asked about power. He asked her endless questions. None of them were the right ones.

They all missed the mark, and she lied to the ones that most neared the truth.

His face was stern as he interrogated her, but his eyes betrayed his detachment. He does not care about her.

The chief promised a full investigation.

She doesn't expect anything from it.

When the paramedics woke her up, everything felt hazy. Her head swam, but her mind was lost in the abyss. She barely heard the words being thrown at her.

"Madam Mayor. Oh my goodness. Can you move your feet? Your fingers?"

Some part of her knew to comply though she barely knew where she was.

They told her it was a miracle. That she only required a few bandages and a couple of stitches. They told her sheer luck saved her life.

She knows it was by insidious design.

Emerald runs her hand along her neck, feeling the raised skin of her scar.

She remembers the flickering orange—the childhood lost in the ashes. The feeling in the moment she knew her life would be eternally altered.

That same mysterious emotion greeted her when the collision threw her car into the air. The sudden realization the future she envisioned was no longer viable.

Pieces of her shattered.

Emerald once read about the art of kintsugi—the Japanese style of weaving gold between the shards of broken pottery pieces.

Embracing the imperfections. Creating something even more spectacular.

She tries to sow her inner cuts with golden memories. For a brief moment, she imagines the crispness in the air as she played in the winter fields. She pictures her mother, walking the colored trails, the breeze creating a collage of falling leaves around them. She tries to substitute pain with laughter, tears with joy.

Then the demons creep back into her thoughts, tearing through her childhood fantasies and replacing them with the horrors of her reality.

Emerald guesses kintsugi isn't meant to work when gold is your enemy. Instead, she faces the darkness head-on. She sends an invitation to her devil. It lands across town, seventy-five floors up.

She will meet the silver-cloaked man.

24

SPEEDING

Lucas thought his day would be predictable.

He sits on his couch, watching the oven timer anxiously. The smell of dinner wafts through the air. He glances at the TV while cooking shepherd's pie—Suzuka's favorite. He's hoping it'll be a suitable peace offering but knows it won't be enough. He doesn't know where she went in her fury.

All he wants is for her to walk through the door and look him in the eyes, to acknowledge his existence instead of slipping away, eyes averted. His thoughts swing between the fight and the news. The oil spill coverage is everywhere, and it makes Lucas sick.

As a child, like most children, Lucas loved Disney. His parents would put on the subtitles, and he'd spend the afternoon in Neverland. He cheered when the heroes triumphed over the villains. Disney isn't real life, though. The villains in this city aren't evil. They don't wear black cloaks or carry magical serpentine canes.

Sometimes they look like polished men in front of elegant buildings. And sometimes, they look like nerdy thirty-year-old programmers.

The oven timer hits zero and flashes green. Lucas pulls out the steaming pot.

Every day, someone reminds him of the good work he's doing. His boss sends article upon article about green energy and how Sterling could revolutionize the industry if they buy the right company.

Although, nothing about Sterling's actions or recent comments denote any inkling of a thought toward a green mindset. Lucas places the shepherd's pie on the counter, removing the cover. The sweet, tangy scent that rises with the steam is terrific. He hopes it tastes as good as it smells. Deep inside, he knows how much the raise pushed him toward a decision. How much the allure of the spacious office tugged his hand down this path.

Is he truly turning the villain good? Or is Suzuka right, and he's just another fool being played?

His phone suddenly lights up from an unknown number. He swipes it away. Can't believe robocalls are still a problem in this day and age. Then the voicemail drops. Intrigued, he presses play as he turns off the TV. Lucas looks at the phone as the AI transcribes the message for him:

"Hello, I am trying to reach Lucas Maamoun, Suzuka Maamoun's husband. My name is Thora Burke, and I'm a nurse at Stratford Hospital. I'm afraid to say your wife is here in our care after a car crash. Please call back whenever you get the opportunity. Thank you, bye-bye."

Lucas leaves the food on the table. The steam rises behind him as he rushes out the door to face a terrifying reality.

Lucas can't breathe.

The space around him seems as though the air has been removed, vacuumed out of his lungs.

He speeds faster than he's ever gone, zooming along the highway. He picks up Sierra early from her play group, frantic and scaring her caregivers. His only explanation is a crumpled piece of paper with a single word: *emergency!* His usual clean handwriting slants with the fear of shaking hands and sweating palms.

He just grabs his daughter and gets back in the car.

Together, they race toward her mother.

He cruises through the historic district, the cobblestone streets jostling him.

He turns, weaving through the immaculate streets of the elite, ritzy townhomes melding together as he breezes by.

He merges onto the highway, speeding along. The yellow dashes below blur into a solid line as his vehicle rockets toward his partner.

Then the car in front of him slams on its brakes, and Lucas finds himself locked in traffic. Tears of frustration, fear, and helplessness well before his eyes.

He slams his fist into the horn. He does not hear the noise, but he hopes it sounds awful to everyone around. He hopes their ears register a fraction of the pain he feels.

His seatbelt is restrictive, his breathing uneven. Despite the slight rain, he opens the windows. Still, he feels as though he is hyperventilating.

Finally, he sees the reason for the slowdown, everyone staring at the sea as the highway barrier opens up to a view.

It looks horrendous. It looked pretty bad on TV but viewing it in person is a whole different experience. The aerial views didn't capture the death.

Lucas scans the sand, oil-covered fish lying motionless on the ground. A few seagulls peck at some of the fish, themselves covered in filth but alive enough to attempt a feast.

That's only a momentary distraction, though. Lucas is not here to gawk.

Each moment is an eternity as they inch their way past the fire trucks and emergency vehicles. Lights flaring as teams of people begin the months-long cleanup.

Lucas sits in absolute agony.

He glances back at Sierra, her eyes mesmerized by the stuffed octopus in her hands.

He's going to make sure she sees her mother.

He turns back to the road and moves ahead—inch by inch.

Lucas bursts into the hospital lobby, Sierra bouncing fast asleep in her holster at his back.

The nurse at the desk flinches when he approaches, no doubt because he looks like a mess.

The nurse's mouth begins moving, but a frown begins to form when Lucas doesn't make any sort of reaction.

He whips out his phone and types, the phone speaking on his behalf.

"I'm looking for Suzuka Maamoun. In for a car crash, I'm her husband. I'm Deaf. Where is she?"

The nurse's face finally shifts into understanding. Kindly, she hands him a visitor's badge, writes down directions, and circles the number forty-six, pointing Lucas down the hall.

He does his best to give her a grateful look before he's gone again, barreling through the halls.

His wife is on a gurney, the monitor lines bouncing to a steady rhythm, the only source of hope in the room.

Lucas' heart stops. For a few moments, he is breathless. His eyes take in the scene around him, but his brain refuses the images.

His knees fail, Lucas catching himself on the hospital bed and closing his eyes in hopes that the world will fade. His mind is unable to reconcile the scene with his dreams for the future.

Lucas feels Sierra stir and reach for her mother.

He is glad Sierra is too young to understand her mother isn't sleeping. Her young eyes simply gaze widely at the scene in front of them.

Placing Sierra on the gurney, he watches her wriggle in close. She hugs her mother's limp arm.

The lights are off, and Lucas doesn't bother to turn them on. The darkness shows enough of her suffering.

A nurse comes in to check on Suzuka and waves.

Lucas types through bleary eyes, Siri once again announcing:

"Hi, I'm Lucas. Suzuka's partner."

The nurse responds and gestures to use his phone. She types a quick message back:

"I'm sorry you're here. Your wife sustained multiple severe injuries, including traumatic cranial damage. Her status is currently critical, but our team is doing everything we can. I'm just here to do a couple of checks before a doctor comes to meet with you. I've also received a few requests to visit by members of a group called the CCC. As her husband, you have the right to grant or reject those requests. I'll get you a list shortly."

When the nurse leaves the room, Lucas thinks back to his proposal, to the way she radiated in the lights.

He thinks of his awkwardness when they met, a huge contrast to her confidence and energy.

He thinks of all the ways in which his wife is beautiful. The woman in his memories looks nothing like the shell of a person in front of him, barely clinging to life.

He thinks of the future they were supposed to share.

Walking Sierra into her first classroom.

Dates dressed in finery under starlit skies.

Dropping Sierra off at college, driving away in peace.

Traveling to cities of limestone archways and dazzling mountaintops.

Listening to the adventures of their grandchildren.

Looking out over the sea, admiring the gray in each other's hair.

Loving one another.

Smiling.

Lucas holds Sierra tight and spends the night remembering all the reasons he hopes his wife will open her eyes.

25

VILLAINS

"The world watches, son. As do I." Alfred Sterling's voice is one that commands obedience. Confidence drips from every syllable.

Even though his father cannot see him, Aldrix bows his head, shrinking into himself, "I understand, Father, but I can manage well enough." Aldrix sits in his office's plush leather chair, weathering through the criticism of the last owner of the desk.

His father replies, "Can you now? I should have never entrusted you with our legacy. Our family's history. All I hope now is you don't manage to destroy decades of work before you get to pass it on to your own son."

Sterling's stomach sinks. It is not a feeling he is accustomed to.

His father continues, voice rising, "Aster has the steel you never had. Thank goodness he gets to build himself up now, in his residence hall, studying hard, making connections, away from your sniveling cowardice. Your son already has more grit than you've ever known."

Aldrix is alone as he listens to his father's scorn. Both Apollo and John sent away when the call came buzzing in. He plays with a pen on his desk to maintain his composure. This is the only relationship in which Aldrix wields no power. Though gray is beginning to tint his beard, he will never stop being a boy before his father.

The tirade isn't over, "I knew you were weak from the beginning. How your mother coddled you. Shielded you from strength. You always did grovel before true leaders." Revulsion hangs on his father's every word.

Aldrix attempts his defense. "I may not lead like you. I may not rule with an iron fist. I do not command obedience, but people adore me. You may have built wealth, but your people cursed your name. I will not let that be *my* legacy. I will navigate this storm *with* those who comprise this organization. I will not leave them out to dry simply because I do not want to burden the costs of an oil cleanup."

His father is unswayed. "You think they adore you because they show up to work? That you're all some sort of family because they have the privilege of wearing Sterling shirts while they slog through the muck and mire? Never forget Aldrix, they hate us. Those at the bottom scorn our success because they are incapable of doing it themselves. They are too feeble, too daft, to command the assets of our family. We have earned the right to ignore their weakness. They merit nothing."

Although Aldrix knows it is a losing battle, he holds his ground, "I think you're wrong, Father. Times have changed, and if I am to survive the media storm brought upon our company, I need every employee on my side. A collective front."

His father laughs hollowly, "You never learn, do you? Only the Wellsworths and their associates are on our side. You cannot make a team of lesser men. That is why you will fail."

Aldrix rests his head against the smooth wood of the desk, replaying his father's wrath over in his mind. His attention oscillates between his family duties and his horrendous situation.

He can't believe his luck. He glances at the authorization papers for the new pipelines. The stack of dozens of pages of ridiculous bureaucracy. He thinks of all the work he's done over the years, and now his reputation is on the line because of a single accident.

Red-faced, he throws himself out of his high-backed office chair. He throws his fist at the wall, creating a completely unsatisfying *thud*.

Why can't people just do their jobs right?

His eyes can barely focus as he skims across the lines of John's report.

"Lack of proper upkeep..."

"... five miles of piping"

"... millions in lost revenue"

"... lawsuits filed for damages."

Aldrix rips the paper to shreds. *A living nightmare. Those moronic mechanics made his life a living nightmare.*

From his office perch, the oil is just a small stain on the water, as if it is a drop of soy sauce that fell on someone's shirt and just needs a good run in the washer to fix it. He knows barrels and barrels of oil are lying there wasted, staining the water in a way only a multimillion-dollar cleanup operation is going to fix. He pivots back to his desk and sits down. He can't bear to look at all of those squandered profits.

Why does everything have to be pinned on him?

Aldrix wasn't the one to make the mistake. He wasn't the one who checked the 'a-okay' box without really making sure the pipeline was truly secure.

Everything he's done for this company has only moved it forward. His employees respect him for that. Why can't the world? Why can't the papers understand this is just business? If the protestors really want change, why don't they switch the financial incentives instead of harassing his employees?

Aldrix turns on his office TV. A talking head is tearing Sterling Energies to pieces. He changes the channel. His own face immediately greets him with a red X over it, the reporter practically screaming. They make it seem like he went out on a boat and hacked the oil pipeline himself. Like he laughed while the sea creatures suffocated. A notification slides across the top of Sterling's phone. Results from the internal pulse survey. He taps it immediately. *Thank goodness,* he thinks. *Some silver lining.* Eighty-eight percent CEO approval.

He beams with contentment. His people love him.

Why doesn't the media report that? Why can't they see that Aldrix isn't a monster?

His pride is defeated moments later.

Aldrix checks the market. STRLG stock has plummeted. His grip on the phone intensifies.

He refreshes.

The stock price drops another few cents. The temperature in the room rises.

He refreshes again.

The little red line lowers itself further into the negative.

It's okay, he desperately thinks. *Maybe it has been a rough day for the markets. A crashing wave ripping all boats under.* A bead of sweat rolls down Aldrix's face as he types.

He checks Alteryn. A line of towering green fills his screen below the ticker ALTYN. He slams the device into his desk.

A hairline fracture appears.

At the end of the day, he just wants to provide for his family just like everybody else. The allure of public opinion draws him back to his device, to Twitter. This time his anger drives him to join the conversation.

He clicks the feather pen and types out his message to the world:

"Power is power. Not words, or pathetic protests, or public outcry. Why can't you all get that into your ungrateful brains?" His finger hovers over the publish button. His better judgment saves him. He deletes the draft.

He knows he'll be expected to make a real public statement soon. He knows that he will be made out to be a villain. It's already happening. In the meantime, he just scrolls through his feed. His anger festering. His resolve hardening.

What no one tells you about being successful is how much people will hate you for it.

Like everyone else, Emerald's eyes are glued to her office's TV. This disaster is a mess, but Emerald's fury is much deeper.

Her body is sore, but she does her best to stand tall. Her staff has been babying her. She has to project confidence.

She watches the screen, hair pulled back so her team can see the strength she hopes she is exuding.

Her shoulders still slump, though, the weight of Amelie and Suzuka's fate still heavy in her heart. Regardless, the man on the screen is a murderer.

Her entire team is in the office atrium, coffees in hand, tension evident. Emerald glances at Amelie's empty desk outside her office.

Her phone constantly buzzes in her pocket.

Emerald has been blasted with messages since the news dropped. People blaming the government for not stepping in fast enough on the oil spill even though she was literally unconscious. A few concerned citizens are saying how glad they are she's safe after the "freak accident."

In the hours after the crash, she scoured the internet for photos, a story meant for the front page, limited to a couple of hidden articles.

They are so clinical. It shreds her to the core. No one cares about her. They scream her name in press briefings and rallies, but she is not human to them. In their eyes, she is only the sum of her policies and position.

The oil spill affected them all. Plus, she's not a native, the label of Droughtie still hanging over her. So, of course, she earns no sympathy. She's the villain.

She watches with hatred as Sterling takes the podium in front of a background bearing the company's proud seal. He places a speech down in front of him.

His pitch-black suit is perfectly fitting for the situation. No doubt bought with the profits of his greed.

"My fellow citizens," he begins. Even at these words, Emerald's blood pressure surges.

"Yesterday evening, an unfortunate incident occurred in which a pipeline ferrying natural gas to our Sterling Energies Enrichment Facility leaked its contents into the Aurietta Sea. This regrettable occurrence is currently under investigation, and reports are expected shortly regarding the cause of this accident."

Emerald draws her mouth into a line. She feels the gazes of her colleagues turning toward her. She keeps her gaze pointed toward the screen.

"However, regardless of what the reports say, I want to recognize the damage this will undoubtedly cause to many across the city. Sterling Energies recognizes the spill will impact fisheries, boating companies, and countless other businesses. We have already reached out to many in the area and are working to rectify the situation through direct payments for the inconvenience. And—"

Heat burns into her as she senses her entire team taking in her reaction. In barely tempered anger, Emerald scoops up her bag and walks out of the room.

She's heard enough.

26

ALL HE CAN ASK FOR

Rodrigo Martinez Ramos leaves the house before the sun has even dared to cross the horizon. He walks briskly for two blocks before stopping to wait for the M12 bus. As always, it arrives at 6:32.

Greeting the driver, he sits in his usual spot by the window of the fifth row. As the bus continues along its route, he notes all the usual scenes. Mr. Cortez rolls up the grate of his bakery on the corner of Taylor St, the sweet smells wafting down the block. Eighty-year-old Mrs. Hernandez waters her hopelessly shriveled hydrangeas on the small balcony of her apartment. Young Luis holds his even younger brother Ricardo's hand as they make their way to before-school care. He remembers when his daughter was that age, and she marched to school, not with her siblings but rather her four best friends. Now she rides helicopters on TV. Blaming his boss for an accident no one caused.

He's watched these neighborly scenes for over forty years. While some people have moved away and new faces have appeared, Rodrigo has always loved seeing the block wake up each morning.

He drags himself out of bed for another shift, but he appreciates the little things that make this his home. More than the new buildings and the modern amenities, his daily interactions are what have turned this city into his home.

Books, newspapers, or now, phones, fill the hands of many others on the ride. Instead, Rodrigo has always been captivated by the tiny miracles occurring each day outside of the bus's grimy window.

This neighborhood mirrors the scenes of his island. When he closes his eyes, the language, culture, and music that embrace him almost make him forget palm trees do not fill these streets.

As the bus turns, not a single fancy townhouse is visible. Some here wish they had cash like that, but they'll settle for one another.

They'll settle for neighbors who leave the warmth of their houses to shovel piles of snow from people's driveways; for the smiles on their kids' faces when they pick them up from a neighbor's care; for the spray of the fire hydrant and blasted music that fills the air to celebrate successes.

Rodrigo will settle for opening his weathered door to find warm meals and kind gifts during the worst days of his life. As he sat next to his wife as she faded, lying on the couch as only a whisper of herself.

In his book, that isn't settling. That's why he never considered moving in all his years.

The bus jolts him as it slams to a halt outside of Sterling Square. He steps off, and it is immediately clear the bond he shares with his neighbors does not extend to the rest of the city. He walks by countless posters that line the chain-link fencing:

Home of evil in this city!
Sterling's morally bankrupt!
Terrorists work at Sterling!
The Leak is YOUR FAULT

He lowers his head as he walks by. He understands many young people are concerned. He has avoided this particular conversation with his own daughter since it is practically her life's work. He's not quite sure what he thinks. He's glad the next generation is so engaged, though he sees hubris in their youth.

They're probably being a bit overdramatic. Hasn't the earth gone through changes before? And he's not a scientist anyway, so what does he know? The leak is unfortunate, but it will be cleaned up.

All he knows is that this job has been solid, honest work for decades. It has allowed him to provide for his family in the winters and even steadily grow their savings. Rodrigo may not be working for a nonprofit, but he has never gone a day without being able to put a hot meal and a bowlful of fruit on the dinner table.

Rodrigo stores his backpack away before donning his neon green vest. Now 7:48, he has twelve minutes before signing in and starting the day. His coworkers also begin to flood in. They all strap on their respective outfits and get to work. Just good, solid people.

Looking across the aisle, he sees a young man lacing his black boots in preparation for a day of heavy lifting. In his youth, Rodrigo was also assigned physical duties. He transported and installed mechanical equipment. Today, just looking at all that equipment gives him back pain. Now he is just responsible for sitting in the control room and recording meter outputs. It's not glamorous work, but it's straightforward. That's all he can ask for.

He takes a deep breath, grabs the door handle, and begins his day.

27

TAINTED

Meg and Ezra arrive in the midst of the firefight.

Bang. Bang. Bang.

In quick succession, the sounds ring through the night sky. Ezra watches the bullet spark off the side of a police cruiser that sits midway down the residential block. Two pairs of cops lean against the side of their cars and fire into the dark, several figures fleeing from the broken windows of a home.

Bang. Bang. Bang.

One cop is down. Ezra, a distance away, can't see where the bullet struck, but a second officer tries to simultaneously fire at the thieves while tending to his partner.

Meg parks the ambulance at the corner, a safe distance from the fight. Meg calls into the dispatch, "Dispatch, we're onsite, active shooting situation in progress."

The response is immediate, "Copy, Ambulance 28, standby until law enforcement clears the area."

Meg clenches her jaw, "Copy. Understood, standing by."

B-B-B-B-B-Bang.

Ezra ducks on instinct as an automatic weapon fires toward the cops. His adrenaline surges. His world sharpens as he and Meg grab their gear. Ezra hefts his jump bag, his body buzzing as shots continue to sound off down the block. Meg is standing behind the ambulance, foot tapping anxiously, her mouth drawn into a thin line.

"Let's just go," Ezra says, energy rushing through him.

Meg shakes her head, "We can't. It's a hot zone. Dispatch told us to wait. That's protocol."

Even as she says the words, Ezra sees she is trying to convince herself. Ezra shifts on the balls of his feet. His body feels powerful in this heightened state. It wants to jump into the action.

"Ahhhh!"

Meg and Ezra hear the scream as a second cop is shot. Meg says, "Screw it," and bolts toward the shooting. Ezra races after her, his mind barely processing the danger he's in. His feet fly over the asphalt. The scene comes into focus as the two near the cruisers.

Two officers now lay on the ground, one shot in the shoulder, the other has multiple wounds to his abdomen. Ezra crouches behind the left cruiser, sidling up to the one with the injured shoulder. Meg takes the abdomen patient on the right.

Before Ezra can open his mouth, the cop lashes out at him. "What took you so long? Why'd you stand around instead of coming in and helping us? What type of medic watches cops get shot?" Ezra doesn't respond, holding his tongue. He just opens his kit, riffling through the bandages.

B-B-B-B-Bang.

Ezra flinches, throwing himself to the ground. The cop tries to shift but grunts in pain. For the first time, Ezra peeks at the gunmen. He sees three figures dash out of the cover of the house and toward a vehicle parked across the street. The two engaged cops fire.

Bang. Bang. Bang. Bang. They miss.

Ezra turns his attention back to his disgruntled patient, blood seeping through his uniform. "Stay still," he commands. His hands shake as he applies pressure to the wound and binds the bandage with his specialized gauze. He looks briefly at Meg. Her focus is centered intently on the wounded officer, with blood oozing from multiple holes.

B-B-B-Bang.

Glass rains down on Ezra as bullets fly through the cruiser's windows and over his head. His heart skips a beat. His hand feels desperately around his head for blood. Nothing, he's fine.

The cop in front of Ezra yells at him, "Get me out of here!"

Ezra flicks his eyes back toward the fleeing perpetrators. He watches as a cop's bullet hits one in the shoulder as he hops into the car. The perpetrator's gun glints under the streetlamp as it falls to the dark ground below. It doesn't seem like anyone else saw the weapon. Even in the midst of horror, Ezra sees the opportunity. He just needs to survive the next few minutes. He calls out, "We're moving!" He throws his arm around the cop and stands. They're exposed, but the other cops fire several rounds to cover them. The injured thief has been given a replacement and sends bullets flying as their vehicle speeds away.

B-B-B-B-Bang.

Then the wheels carry the thieves away, the cops calling into their radios for backup to follow them. They need to take stock of their injuries. Ezra hobbles with the weight of the injured cop at his side, but they make it down the block to the ambulance. He grimaces as his muscles strain to load the man into the vehicle. Meg isn't far behind, one of the unscathed cops sharing the weight of his partner as they walk. They load the other wounded cop into the ambulance, and Meg gets ready to take off. The two uninjured cops return to their battered cruisers.

Ezra calls to her, "Ah! I left some equipment down the street."

Meg frowns. "Run," she shouts. "We need to get outta here."

Ezra bounds down the street, further than where the cruisers were. He walks into the grass lining the street and searches for the reflection of metal on the ground. He sees it, blood rushing to his head as he swoops down to pick it up.

He places it into his bag and walks briskly back to the ambulance.

Ezra is exhausted when he gets home late in the night. His mind still bounces frenetically through the scenes he just witnessed. He passes his mom in the kitchen without saying a word. She looks at him, seeing his posture, and leaves him be. He goes straight to hiding his treasure beneath his bed. He sits on his comfortable tan couch, video games flashing across the TV as he tries to destress. On the screen, his character shoots for a goal, but the goalie picks the ball out of the air. Ezra smacks the cushion, letting out the stress that still wells in him.

His thoughts are interrupted.

"Ezra Coleman!"

His mom never uses his full name.

He rises from the living room, throwing his controller aside. He runs toward the kitchen, swinging around the doorway to stand before his mom. Where water should be, black liquid streams out of the faucet. Dark splotches stain his mom's shirt.

She looks at him in shock as the oil clogs the sink and rises up along the edges. Her eyes are wide in disbelief, "Ez, I... what in the world is happening?" Ezra throws himself past her and turns the tap off, the blackness left swirling in the sink. His mom wipes her hands on a paper towel, but they are still covered in gray grease. Voice shaking, she tells him, "Grab my phone."

Ezra complies, but he questions, *who can they even call? Will the city help them?* She calls one neighbor, and then another, and then another. And one by one, the neighborhood discovers that suddenly they have nothing to drink.

Where's all that money the mayor promised to invest in his community on the trail? Mayor Silva talked a good game, but she hasn't done a thing for them in these past few months. His mother sends him off to grab packaged water, and he imagines Maurice's corner store is about to make more money than ever. Not for the right reasons, though.

Just cause the mayor is like all the other politicians cycling through that fancy city hall. Pretending they are different. Everyone always stupidly believes them. While they shovel millions to Sterling for cleanup efforts. As he walks, his anger grows. Aldrix Sterling is worse than his father. While he gave that pretty speech earlier today, Ezra knows deep down not a single penny will be given to his community. Ezra turns onto the block of Maurice's store. It is almost midnight, but a line has already formed halfway down the street.

Ezra can barely stand still in the line, pacing in short strides back and forth, his mind still not free of the events earlier in the night. His system slowly begins calming down, and he takes stock of the others in the queue. People have bags and baskets of all shapes in hand, just hoping to get in before the shelves run out. He sees some are still in pajamas, and others are in various professional uniforms. Some wear the newest high-tops with chains, and others are in tank tops.

It doesn't matter, though. Everyone's equal when the clean water is gone.

28

HEROES

Emerald clasps her hands to keep them from shaking. Footsteps resound off the hallway floor. Footsteps that carry pride in every stride. Emerald bites her lip. The footsteps draw closer. Emerald smooths her hair and steels herself.

Then Aldrix Sterling is standing in her office entry. His face pulled in a smug expression.

"I was surprised by your invitation," Sterling says as he enters her office and closes the door.

"I'm surprised you came," Emerald replies curtly. Despite him coming to her turf with security outside her door, Sterling's presence still makes her feel like prey. Just having this visit on the books doesn't change his menace one bit. He is close to how she imagined him, his oily hair and arrogant gaze just as apparent in real life as on TV.

What she was not prepared for is the fear he instills in her. How her skin prickles as he strides confidently toward her desk.

At least he's here in the flesh. He can't hide behind his shadowy henchmen or make vile threats here. She wields power in these halls. They are supposed to be discussing the cleanup efforts, but they have much more to discuss than the public knows. She doesn't waste any time. "You're a murderer."

Sterling doesn't sit. He simply stares nonchalantly down at her. "I don't have the slightest clue what you mean."

Emerald fumes. "We'll get to the leak, but first of all, my chief of staff is in critical condition, a member of my security team is dead, and a key environmental figure is in a coma."

Sterling feigns empathy. "I saw the terrible news. I'm so glad you got away with such minimal injuries. I heard it was quite the miracle occurrence."

Emerald explodes, "You're in *my* office, Aldrix. Don't you dare play your games with me. We come here every day and work as public servants. Everyone in this building comes to work so people can put food on their tables, so their voices are heard in this government, so the next generation still has a planet and will be able to have it better than we do right now. All you do is make money. And then what? You sit on it? Hoard it and watch your net worth climb? You think I wanted to invite you here today? The only reason you're in front of me is because I have to pretend for everyone out there that you're not the manipulative psychopath you are."

Sterling doesn't miss a beat. "You think you deserve power because you 'fight for justice?' You think you're the little heroine, don't you?" Sterling scoffs at her.

Pure contempt replaces his confident demeanor.

There are no signs of remorse for his actions. "Well, Emerald, let's do some math, shall we? In the past few months of being mayor, your social service programs have helped a few hundreds of thousands of people, if I'm being generous. There are a couple of hundred people in your employ here in this quaint little castle. You parade around and give speeches and write policies, most of which get denied as soon as they hit the Commons. Then you turn around and complain everyone is against you. As if you're even important enough to warrant opposition."

Emerald begins a retort, but Sterling cuts her off with a simple wave of the hand and an ominous look. He continues, "Now it's my turn. In the past few months, I have enabled every single drop of electricity and gas power in this city. I have employed thousands of people for years, people that are no doubt fueling this economy. Oh, and that's no thanks to your sky-high taxes. And ah yes, I have donated *millions* of dollars to charities. So I'll let you in on a secret: everyone thinks they're the hero."

Sterling now rounds her desk, leaning down to whisper.

Emerald's pulse beats in her ears as he says, "And you think you run this place? I know everything that goes on in this building. *I* decide everything that lands on your desk. You have no idea what real power is, Emerald. You're in that chair because it is advantageous to me to have someone who will stay out of my business. Your predecessor got a little too nosey, and so I arranged to remove him from that chair you sit on. His curiosity was annoying, but it was no threat. You, on the other hand, are becoming an active pain. Your little miracle was my final warning. Next time my people won't program the car to miss."

Emerald simply stays frozen in her chair, her muscles completely tense as Sterling makes his way back to the door. "And by the way," his cool, confident edge back, "if anyone asks, we had a great conversation about the leak. I was a gracious guest, and we look forward to moving forward on this cleanup together. Isn't that right?"

Emerald doesn't respond, but Sterling nods regardless.

His footsteps echo once again on the way out, the sound dripping with arrogance.

29

FAMILY FIRST

"Checkmate." Seven-year-old Aldrix watched as his father knocked his king off the board and sent it tumbling onto the ground below.

It laid on the pristinely clean maroon carpeting of his father's study, the cross tilted down into the floor. Surrounded by the refined environment of mahogany desks and oakwood tabletops, Aldrix had been invited by his father, Alfred Sterling Jr., to play a game of chess.

His father's face was stern but encouraging. "You have to think ahead of me. You left your king completely undefended to attack my queen. You have to be *patient*. Reset the board. We'll play again tomorrow."

"But it's hard, Pa," Aldrix complained. "And you definitely cheated."

His father let out a brief laugh at his son's melodramatic despair. Then he said, "There are harder things still. And yet, we succeed. You will get better over time because you have to. You have to succeed. If you don't win, then you lose. And if you fail, there will be many who take pleasure in our family's fall. Do you understand?"

"Yes, sir." Aldrix rasped.

"What do we say?" his father asked.

"Family first," Aldrix replied.

"Good. You will inherit the world, and I will prepare you for it." His father picked up a piece of paper from his desk, sliding the board aside. "But for now, return to your room. I must speak with Mr. Wellsworth."

Obediently, Aldrix rose and crossed the room toward the door. It opened for him as he neared it, a dark-haired man appearing in the frame accompanied by three unsmiling men in trench coats, a *W* imprinted on their breasts. Mr. Branson Wellsworth gave a twisted smile as Aldrix left the room, "Glad to see you once again, boy."

Aldrix only response was to quicken his pace, retreating to his room.

At his gothic-styled prep school, twelve-year-old Aldrix walked nervously into an opulent room filled only with dark-wood tables and twelve candled chandeliers. At the front, a mean-looking man with rectangular glasses and a round belly sat at the lecturer's desk. He looked Aldrix over with something like disgust as the boy entered, as if children inherently repulsed him. Walking up tentatively, Aldrix asked, "Is this chess club, sir?"

While the man answered, he didn't seem too pleased. "Yes, lad. It seems you've come to the correct place."

Speaking up once again, Aldrix said, "Great. Where should I go now? How are partners selected? Are we matched by skill level? How long does the club convene for?" The chaperone ignored the burst of Aldrix's questions and simply pointed to a corner table where a solitary student about Aldrix's age sat.

His classmate occupied one of the corner desks, face obscured by the shadows as he looked down at the board in front of him. As Aldrix approached the table, his soon-to-be-opponent raised his eyes, and they lit up with recognition. Aldrix's heart sank at his horrendous fortune. *Of course, it would be Liam Wellsworth.*

The Wellsworth family. Owners of the titanic financial entity Onyx Bank. The bank of the elite. Even among the privileged students at Aldrix's school, including himself, Liam was in a league of his own.

Although, money was not the only reason his family was untouchable. And, unfortunately for everyone else, Liam knew it.

As soon as Aldrix sat down and Liam uttered a stiff, "Welcome Sterling," the two boys knew this would be more than a friendly chess match. Sterling returned the acknowledgment, "Wellsworth."

Without another word, Liam slid his white pawn forward two spaces, and the game began.

In his twelfth year, Aldrix sat alone in their dining hall, engraved pillars of bronze and mural painted walls around him. He preferred to eat alone. It was better that way. Friends only complicated things, distracted him. He needed to focus.

He was eating a freshly made panini and reading over a pamphlet comparing the Laurel League. The six most exclusive schools in the country. Tomorrow was decision day, and the dining hall was full of anxious chatter.

Aldrix had applied to all six, but he fixated on one in particular: Rhenhurst University. A photo of campus showed students lazing collegially in the gardens, a culture of collaboration emphasized. Then he peered at Osgrave, the stone archways menacing and lanterns looming above the pathways. Aldrix tapped his foot nervously under the table.

Liam walked by Aldrix, then paused, turning to approach. "Sterling," he muttered.

Aldrix played into their practiced dance. "Wellsworth."

Sarcastically Liam stated, "Looking forward to sharing Osgrave's campus with you next year."

Aldrix shot back, "That confident you'll be accepted?"

Liam smoothed his hair as he replied, "Is that truly a question?"

Aldrix could barely stand Liam's presence. He didn't respond.

"Worst of luck tomorrow, Sterling," Liam said under his breath. He crossed the hall, sitting down to be surrounded by friends and admirers. Transitioning to complete ease. He gave one more brief glance toward Aldrix. When their eyes met, Aldrix saw only malice locked in Liam's eyes. A look reserved for those beneath him.

A moment later, Liam turned to a friend, expression shifting entirely to a comfortable smile. But Aldrix still felt the weight of Liam's disrespect.

Looking once more at Rhenhurst's prideful colonial buildings and classic marble walkways, Aldrix decided to be patient.

Sterling received a stack of acceptance letters the next day. Four of the letters were Laurels: Palladius, Osgrave, Iriden, and Rhenhurst. He ran up to the door of his father's study, peeking in just as he'd done countless times throughout his childhood. As per usual, his father sat at his polished desk, rifling through papers and jotting down scribbles in his leather-bound notebook.

Upon hearing Aldrix swing open the door, his father simply raised a hand, signaling Aldrix to stay put. Aldrix's flaming excitement instantly froze, neutralized by his father's indifference. A man stood to the side of his father's study. He looked Aldrix up and down as if assessing whether he was a threat to his own father.

Only once Alfred Sterling had finished writing did he turn toward his son. Aldrix flicked his eyes toward the stranger in the corner, and his dad simply waved him away. "Don't mind Harold, he's just some extra protection, some of Mr. Wellsworth's clients have been running into trouble recently."

Aldrix didn't dare challenge the explanation. Instead, he placed the acceptance letters on the desktop. After a few moments of tense silence as his father scanned the document, he looked up. A smug smile filled his face. "Excellent, Aldrix. Congrats on all, but I will be proud to walk you through the Fordven Gates of Osgrave."

Aldrix clasped his hands tightly in his lap and corrected his father. "That may have been Father, but I'd rather enter the Quintus Gates of Rhenhurst."

A look of confusion filled his father's face. Son, you've known you've been destined for Osgrave your entire life. That is where Sterlings go. That is where Sterling Hall stands, our namesake plastered above the archway. That is also where Wellsworths go, and your relationship with the Wellsworth boy is the most important partnership you will have in your life. Rhenhurst is a fine school, but it is not your path."

Aldrix steeled himself as he said, "I disagree."

His father stood from his chair slowly, his anger rising. "Pardon me?"

The blood drained from Aldrix face, but he forced himself to be bold. He stood as well, face to face with his father, "I am not a child anymore, Father."

His father's face showed his infuriation, his son's insolence unimaginable. Alfred Sterling tried a final time to override his son, "This is a matter of family first, Aldrix. This is not about you. This is about the institution that will permit you to engage with the necessary individuals to continue this family's legacy of distinction in this city. That institution is Osgrave."

Aldrix only shifted on his feet, glancing toward the stoic man in the corner. Harold's face was calm as if he was not even aware of the vicious fight unfolding in front of him, but Aldrix knew this would get back to Branson. Wellsworth associates were loyal only to one family.

Alfred Sterling rounded his desk, grabbed his son, and thrust him against the wall. He spit his words at Aldrix, "I have spent your entire life preparing you for success. I have loved you and groomed you as an heir, and now you risk it all because you are unappreciative of your choices? Would you like to be a Droughtie: no home, tattered clothing on the street?"

Although his father railed against him, Aldrix still remained firm. "On this, Father, you will not sway me." Then he pushed back at his father, freeing himself from his rough grip.

Alfred Sterling was stunned by his son's insubordination. Aldrix watched as the proud man he had always known turned bitter toward him. The transformation evident in his mannerisms and the words that haunted Aldrix for the rest of his life, "You are making a mistake. And if you fail, I will not be there to soften your downfall. Ever again. From today, your actions and the fate of our family are on *your* head."

With that, Alfred turned back to his work, the obvious clue Aldrix was to vacate the study. Aldrix straightened his clothes and walked out, Harold's eyes following him until the door shut.

Aldrix made his way to his room and enrolled in Rhenhurst.

30

DONE

Aldrix steps off the elevator—basement level, his first time here since the leak. In all his second Friday visits, he's never known the morale to be this low. His workers drag their feet, shuffling along. The security guard greets him, but there is no hint of laughter, only a brief acknowledgment. He'll deal with that later. He has to see Nick.

His seat is empty in the control room. Rodrigo and the others sit dutifully at their stations, but the manager's chair lays vacant. "Rodrigo." The older man turns around and smiles. Aldrix gives a sigh of relief. At least some people are still on his side.

Rodrigo says, "How are you doing today, sir? I'm sorry about the incident. You don't deserve all that bad press, man."

Sterling only smiles. Rodrigo doesn't know the half of it. He responds nonetheless, "Yes, it is quite unfortunate. But I'm grateful I still have people like you around. Speaking of which, have you seen Nicholas at all?"

"Um, no, sir. He came in briefly this morning, but I haven't seen him since. I think he left something on the desk, though."

Aldrix grimaces.

"Thanks, Rodrigo, always great to see you." Aldrix turns and picks up the note that lies in front of Nick's monitor.

When he opens it, his suspicions are confirmed. Nick's trademark, precise handwriting does not mince words:

I'm sorry, Mr. Sterling. I'm done.

Respectfully disrespectful to the bitter end, Aldrix thinks. No clear rationale, no lengthy soliloquy. Nick just made up his mind and resigned. It tracks with his personality, but still. Sterling wishes he could have spoken with his star manager for a moment. Had the chance to convince him not to believe the slander in the papers. Nine years of developing the kid, and now he decides he's done because of the gossip in the press. Aldrix doesn't let himself feel the frustration. There is too much to do. He just solves the problem and moves on. He'll deal with Nick later.

"Rodrigo."

"Yes, sir?" he responds.

"Congratulations on your promotion."

31

LITTLE PACKAGES

The first time Ezra's dad sent him to get a package, he was eleven years old. Most kids love receiving mysterious gifts, so for the first few months, he skipped merrily out the door each time his dad requested. It was the same spot every time. Ezra came to know the way by heart over time. Only the first time, he had to repeat his father's instructions again and again in his head. *Down the block, take a right, one more block, take a left and enter the park. Meet the man near the big oak tree.*

As he reached the end of the block, he turned right and repeated the instructions to himself. *Down the block, take a right, one more block, take a left and enter the park. Meet the man near the big oak tree.* He continued reciting these quick phrases to himself under his breath as he took large strides. He was still small and hadn't hit a growth spurt, but he understood the importance of his task. He wanted to walk as confidently as an adult, proving he was a grown-up to whomever he was to meet.

He entered the park and saw a man in the fanciest clothes he'd ever seen. His dad always told him not to stare, but he couldn't help it. The man had smooth chestnut skin and was leaning against a branch of the oak tree. Ezra thought it odd the man's brown suit had a super-duper complicated pattern and that it just sat on top of a white T-shirt that mirrored his own. Ezra was pretty sure he'd never seen anyone else who looked quite like this guy.

His beard was neatly trimmed, just like the beard Ezra imagined he had when 'shaving' alongside his dad. Unafraid to meet one of his dad's friends and encouraged by the man's interesting but friendly appearance, Ezra walked toward him.

Upon his approach, the man in the suit asked, "You Ray's kid?"

"Um, yeah! Nice to meet you. What's your name? My dad told me to come get a gift from you. He told me it's like a Christmas present." Ezra innocently asked.

The man smiled darkly, "Yeah, something like that."

From the inside of his extravagant suit, he pulled a small Ziplock bag filled with a white dust that looked like fluffy snow. He passed the packet to Ezra, who looked at it with curiosity and wonder. "Thank you," Ezra said brightly.

He then ruffled around in his pocket for the cash his father had entrusted to him. Handing the man the bills absentmindedly, he looked back to the stark white substance that he held in his hand.

"Put it in your pocket, kid. Don't take it out until you get home and give it to your dad. This is a special gift that other people might try to take from you if they see it, okay?" Ezra nodded and slid the package into his pocket.

"Have a good day, kid. Enjoy the present," he said with a fox's smirk.

"You too!" Ezra said with a wave.

Ezra liked the man, and he liked the activity of walking to the park. To him, it was a great excuse to get outside and use his legs. With boundless energy, he was always itching to move throughout the school day. He came home with a display of exuberance that his mother would often refer to as explosive.

He wanted to use this energy to join the soccer team, especially since he saw Nick and Lucas heading to the field each day, but his dad forbade it. Every couple of months, Ezra would try to persuade his father again, but he always received the same response:

"We don't got money for no games, Ez!"

The answer always confused Ezra; fun-filled memories of them playing basketball together in his head. His dad loved some games, smiling wide as he tickled a squealing Ezra.

One day, Ezra finally pushed further. He approached his father while he was sitting in front of the TV in their kitchen. Acting as confidently as he could, he declared, "I want to join the soccer team, dad." When his father provided his usual response, Ezra tried a new tactic.

He said, "We have money for your packages. Why not sports?" His father paused, shocked his child had the guts to speak back. In the silence, Ezra looked around and realized one of his dad's little packages was lying half-empty on the table. Looking back at his father, he didn't seem to be himself. Ezra blanched, unsure of what his father may do in this altered state of being.

His father suddenly erupted, slamming his palm flat on the kitchen table, and yelled red-faced, "You ain't understand what's in those packages! They are a necessity to keepin' this house in order! Your little dreams of playing sports with yo' rich white friend and yo' mute Arab friend don't matter! Buy yo' own uniform to play dress up in if you wanna, but I ain't gonna give you none of my hard-earned pennies!"

His father immediately left the room, found his mother relaxing in bed after a long day of working at the supermarket, and slammed the door shut. Within seconds, Ezra heard the low swoosh that precedes only one other sound. *Crack.*

As the belt fell a second time, Ezra's eyes filled with tears, themselves filled with the raging emotions of hurt, guilt, and sorrow.

Connecting the little packages with his father's anger, he vowed to never get another package for him again. However, as his mind continued to process his thought and emotions in this critical moment, one sentiment rose above the others, determination. He suddenly had an epiphany.

So, at age thirteen, Ezra learned how to extort. The next time his father demanded he collect the little packages he now knew to be cocaine, he didn't fuss. He went to meet the man in the suit who he had once admired and exchanged his dad's money for the drugs.

When Ezra returned to his father, he said, "Here, dad," tossing the packet onto the table. "The price went up twenty bucks, so here's the rest of your change. Your guy said there were some troubles with the guy he gets the stuff from." He set down his father's leftover cash on the table next to the package.

His father blinked, saying, "What? Twenty bucks? That's a rip-off! Next time I see him, I'll let him kno' I ain't gonna put up $20 bucks just because he don't know how to handle his biz'ness."

Just as Ezra hoped, his father was much too hooked to risk speaking to the man in the brown suit. When Ezra returned to his room, he removed the $20 he kept for himself and slid it into a small envelope under his mattress.

At age fourteen, Ezra spoke with his mother. When his dad was out getting a haircut, he entered his parent's room. His mom was just getting in from an all-day shift at the grocery store, but she smiled when he entered anyway. As she untied her shoes, her long-sleeves rose up and revealed light black-and-blue marks from his father's most recent episode.

"What's up, baby?" she asked.

"Mom, I… I just wanted to know… why haven't you left dad?"

She froze, unprepared to answer such a question. "I love your dad, baby."

"But why?"

"Your dad is a good man, Ez. Don't you dare disrespect your father, baby. He has some… issues sometimes, but he ain't never stopped putting food in front of us. And anyway, I ain't never done life alone. My whole life, he has been there wit' me, and I know I can't survive on my own."

Defeated, Ezra hung his head. Turning to leave, he paused. "I love you, mom."

"I know, baby."

Silently, Ezra left without another word.

At age sixteen, Ezra finally stood up. The night before, he had spent running through his plan in his mind and steeling himself for the day ahead. His friends all asked him what had his head in the clouds, and they teased him about crushing on the classmate who sat across from him in algebra. They had no idea.

When Ezra returned from school that evening, his father was already home, watching TV, a few beers next to him on the side table. When his mom came in at eight, Ezra made his move. He went briefly into his room before calmly asking his mother to meet him outside. She was confused but promised to be there in a few moments. Ezra walked through the living room on the way to the front door, his prepacked bag lying next to the exit.

His dad noticed the movement, turning to see Ezra making his way outside. "Where you headed, Ez? You done finished your homework?" Ezra made an earth-shattering mistake. He told the truth, "No. Mom and I are leaving tonight."

As the words fell out of him, it seemed as though someone else was speaking. He became completely disembodied as his mind rushed through the infinite ways this could go wrong. Not understanding what he meant, Ray Coleman replied, "What? Where you going? There a trip you been planning?"

Ezra mustered all his courage and said, "No, dad. I mean, we're moving out. I can't stand you treating mom like garbage every day anymore. So we're leaving."

His dad's eyes immediately shone fury. At this point, his dad hadn't been the same in years. When his father rose from the couch, there was nothing left of the man who had read Ezra's bedtime stories or sung the Lion King soundtrack with him as a kid. It pained Ezra to see the man so sick, torn down by forces out of his control. Coping by any means necessary.

But that didn't change Ezra's terror as his father stalked menacingly toward him. Ezra immediately went to turn and run. One instant, he saw his father barreling toward him, and the next, his head was thrown to the side by a fierce strike. He found himself on the floor as his father's leg rose to kick him. On pure instinct, Ezra rolled out of the way as his father's foot sliced the air next to him. Ezra scrambled to his feet and punched his father in the gut, the larger man barely stumbling backward.

Faster than ever, his father undid his belt and whipped the metal end toward Ezra. The end caught him in the cheek, blood gushing from the wound and knocking out a tooth. Ezra grabbed at his face as another attack came. This time the metal missed, but the leather stung as it wrapped violently around his forearm. With his other arm, he grabbed hold of the belt and pulled sharply, throwing his dad off balance. Ezra wrested the belt completely away and tossed it to the side.

Ezra threw a punch, but his father batted it away. His dad's firm hands grasped onto Ezra like a vice, picking his body up and throwing him back. His head smacked into the wall, his vision filling with gaps.

Shoop

Ezra's stomach dropped.

Gathering himself from the ground, he rose to find his father holding a knife, his face purple with rage, veins bursting from his neck. In all these years, in spite of the sloppy nights, beatings of his mother, and verbal abuse, he never thought his dad would kill him. Not once. Until then. Ezra launched himself at his father, his entire energy focused on freeing the knife from the man's hand. His father reacted immediately, swinging the knife toward his chest.

For a moment, time slowed as Ezra brought his hand up to block the blow.

In the next blink, he would either be dead or free.

Ezra made contact with his father's arm before the knife was able to plunge into him, but for several seconds the two stood in an awkward embrace. Ezra trying to rip the blade from his dad's hand, and his father attempting to advance the knife into him.

With a guttural growl, Ezra pushed with all his might.

His father fell back into the kitchen table, the knife landing on the carpeting below.

Ezra grabbed the weapon and moved toward his dad. Ezra stood over his father, knife in hand, weighing his options.

In milliseconds, his brain rushed through the good and the bad—memories of laughter and love mixed with the sounds of whipping and the pain of new scars. Ezra shifted, time running out as his dad pushed himself back up.

Ultimately, Ezra made his choice.

He drove the knife into his dad's thigh.

Mariah rushed up from the basement at the sound of shouting and destruction. She found Ray on the floor, blood welling around him, a knife embedded in his thigh.

Before she could even properly react, she was being flung toward the door by Ezra's strong hands. Her eyes widened as she took in her injured son.

In all of their years of marriage, Ray had never touched Ezra. Mariah could suffer herself, but she had always believed they shared absolute love for their son. Seeing this was no longer true, she summoned her own valor and let her teenage son usher her out the front door.

Ezra had made sure his blow would not end Ray's life, so the knife did not keep him from hurling threats behind them.

The pair ran down the stairs and across the street toward the park. Still fearing for their lives, Mariah and Ezra raced into the park until they finally relented among the trees.

Wide-eyed, she looked at Ezra and cried. "What are we supposed to do now, Ez?"

Too bloodied to say a word, Ezra pulled a crumpled folder from the bag he snagged on the way out. The front was labeled in his scribbled handwriting: *Mom Fund.*

32

LAUREL LEAGUE

Emerald entered the gates of Palladius University, the sun gleaming off the bronze roofs of the ivy-covered stone buildings. She had made it to a Laurel. The state capitol's meager skyline sat in the distance, but Emerald didn't care. She was glad to have left the concrete cage of the other city behind.

In her favorite summer dress, she walked across the quad toward Lupis Hall. She watched as upperclassmen milled around in the grass, laughing and hugging after a summer apart.

The air buzzed with the particular combination of excitement and nerves that comes only from the beginning of a new adventure. Emerald walked briskly toward the welcome celebration but with uneven steps. She saw first-year students around as well, but their gaits were smooth, heads held high. Emerald did her best to copy as the gothic building loomed large before her.

She primped her hair. She checked her mirror, too, her full face of makeup obscuring the fire's stain along her neck and lower cheek. She took a deep breath, eyes closing, envisioning all the moments that had led her here.

She entered.

The ballroom was gorgeous. The experience was sickening.

Emerald immediately had a sensation of drowning. Hundreds of people filled the room, all of them immaculate. She looked down at her clothing; it didn't compare. Symbols of status marked their attire. Icons of brands she only dreamt of owning. The words that swirled around her were too loud. The space twinkled with glittering gowns and spectacular lights, but Emerald was not charmed.

Seeking refuge, Emerald made for the table of hors d'oeuvres. She was not as graceful as the other women gliding through the crowd, smiling lightly, and drawing envious glances. People looked at her, but not with anything resembling adoration.

As she walked, the comments followed her, always just out of sight.

"Droughtie."

People whispered under their breath as she gathered her food.

"Is she lost?"

She pretended not to notice.

"At least she's pretty. Except for that horrendous scar."

She tried to turn herself into a ghost.

"What do you give her? A year before she drops? Two?"

Emerald fled to the wall, observing the scene, but not daring to enter the conversations floating around her.

She'd heard it all before, the same comments as her grammar school teachers.

"It was a miracle a rural kid had learned so much from those outskirts schools."

"Emerald is lucky, must have some innately high IQ."

"She was so much better than all the other rural-borns."

"Such a shame her old teachers weren't able to provide the environment for her to blossom."

Emerald thought this place would be more tolerant, more equal, but instead, she felt more excluded than ever.

Emerald watched as those around her spoke in a language she'd never heard. It was a language told in cutting glances, high-class pronunciation, and thread counts. Family connections, boarding schools, and gated communities ruled the grammar. It bore no resemblance to the caring speech of her parents. To the subtle syntax of the neighbors who accepted her family to the city with kindness. Who looked to a family who had lost everything in a drought and gave despite their own hardships.

Emerald did not belong in stiff environments with even stiffer people. She kept to herself—eating food that looked delicious but tasted bland on her tongue. She was just finishing her plate when a couple dressed in finery approached her. The man's digital watch alone likely cost more than her parents made in a month.

Emerald stood up straight. She plastered a light smile on her face, trying to mimic the ease of those around her. Her mind raced. *What would this couple want from her? Would they offer to bring her into the fold? Were they just here to spit further insults at her for wearing the best dress she owned?*

When they neared, neither happened. They simply dropped their dirtied plates off in her arms and moved on without another glance.

Emerald held back tears.

She placed the plates on the nearest table and made her way out of the opulent room as elegantly as she could. The moment she passed through the doors, she broke into a sprint. She ran out of the building and along the various pathways, not knowing where she was going as the evening light faded. Then she crossed into Amethyst Court, and her nerves began to finally slow.

The courtyard was a bonified garden filled with violets. Greenery and a calming pond surrounded her, the water dripping in a sweet song. It was like home. Like the fields before they turned brown. Like the trails before Sterling robbed her. She sat on the stone bench in the center, smelling the freshness that only nature could provide. That's when the emotions kicked in.

Rage and sadness and disappointment and melancholy melded together in her heart. *How could she survive four years? Were they right? Should she give up on day one? Could she compete? Did she want to? Were there any nice people? Would she be alone?* She looked up to the stars, searching for a reason for her suffering.

She didn't find an answer, but she found resolve.

Emerald received a call early on her first day at the state housing bureau. Her nerves rattled. The internship had begun. She picked up. "Hello, office of the assistant secretary of housing."

A melodic-sounding female voice picked up. "Hi, ma'am. Sorry to bother ya. Just calling again about the processing of my state disaster relief. House went in a mudslide after the crazy rain a few weeks ago."

The hair stood on Emerald's arms, thinking about the horrific scene this lady had experienced. Emerald could smell the smoke of her home as it burnt to ashes, sharing this woman's plight. This was exactly the population she wanted to help. She picked up the nice pen on her desk, preparing to write down the details of this woman's case.

Emerald responded, "Ma'am, I'm incredibly sorry to hear that. Truly. I apologize we haven't gotten back to you more quickly. What's your name? And how many times have you called previously?"

The woman answered without hesitation, "Name's Marlene. And seven."

Emerald stopped her writing. "I'm sorry, you said you've called this office seven times already?"

"Yes, ma'am. Spoken wit' most of your colleagues. Heard there were some switch-ups in the office, though, so I figured I'd try again."

Emerald received nonstop calls the entire day. Not a single one of her cases were processed with any immediacy. As she walked out of the colonial building, heels clicking on the stone steps, Emerald threw on her coat. The wind's howl echoed her frustration. Her hopes dashed in a single day.

So she took it into her own hands. She graduated and went straight back to the housing bureau. This time, she was in charge—manager of a division. She blew through the ranks to become secretary of housing at age thirty. But still, it wasn't enough. She quit and moved back to the bustling city, full of people who had rejected her, but also faces who welcomed her back with a smile. She spent years working for the conservation center. The work was good, but that wasn't her focus. She spent her energy during late nights and early mornings in a small hole-in-the-wall office. The east side storefront where she dreamed until she dreamed so big her ambitions broke into the heavens.

Ambitions that an angel answered. An anonymous donor. A generous stranger. A backer whose funds revolutionized her life overnight. A person Emerald conjured in her mind as a progressive billionaire, atoning for a ruthlessly lived life. Her guess was close, but he wasn't atoning.

If only she'd known the angel's name was Lucifer.

33

SUCCESSION

Aldrix admired the angelic figure atop the Quintus gates as he walked into Rhenhurst's quad. From the moment his feet hit the ground, every interaction he undertook served a single purpose: win.

He walked the marble walkways and entered every immaculate courtyard with determination. His classmates were interesting, but they were also ruthless. So that's what he became.

Aldrix also joined a student-run business club that provided various services across campus, including a café, bank, grocery store, and smoothie bar. It became his life. While everyone else was off at frivolous parties, Sterling worked. While the clock ticked away and the library cleared out, Sterling sat by the window on his laptop.

Others passed by, inviting him out. Telling him how much fun it was to get completely wasted. Sterling politely declined most offers. He maintained elite company. Other children of titans. Those who he would need in the future. He built his own network, not the slimy circle his father and the Wellsworths predestined for him.

Over the summers, Aldrix returned to his father's company, holding a high-level analyst 'internship' created for him alone. His father continued to groom him to take over the company, but his eyes were no longer kind. His father saw him as an heir but no longer as a person.

Nonetheless, Aldrix learned as much as he could from his father's leadership and the actions of his executives. Especially Dean Carlson, the Chief Operating Officer. Aldrix truly admired Mr. Carlson. He was a diligent worker, an inspiring leader, and, most of all, he was fiercely honest.

Mr. Carlson unabashedly told Aldrix's father when he disagreed with an action. Sometimes this led to shouting matches between the two men, but Mr. Carlson was almost always correct. He was a measured voice among the chaos and one of his father's real friends. Aldrix had the opportunity to witness Mr. Carlson's wisdom at work and then enjoyed his generosity when he and his wife invited the Sterlings over for cocktails.

Of course, Aldrix was a shoo-in for his club's CEO position senior year. He applied everything he learned from his father and Mr. Carlson over the summer and directed the club as best he could, using the same principles as Sterling Energies. The club grew and even opened an off-campus branch of the business serving the residents of the college town.

Each time he made a decision, he heard his father's voice. The messages that were drilled into him over his young life and now reverberated through his skull:

Win. Every day. Whatever happens. Make sure you're still standing at the end. If you have to sacrifice others, that's the price you must pay.

Not everyone liked this, though. When Aldrix announced his plan to change the organizational structure of the club, he received many retaliatory remarks.

A sophomore in the club posted on socials that he had a much more efficient way to progress the organization, that wouldn't include a messy reorganization. Seeing this challenge, Aldrix knew what he had to do.

As his father taught him, this subordinate was impeding the progress of the club. He spoke to the sophomore's supervisor, and they asked the student to leave the club that same day.

But a few days later, a small seedling of doubt grew.

Around Thanksgiving of his senior year, Aldrix scrolled through his feed while sitting by the fireplace. After passing through several of his friends' bad jokes and celebrity nonsense, a *Chronicle* announcement fell into view.

Breaking News: Sterling Fires Dean Carlson Over Operations Disagreement. Matthew Sessetti Set to Fill the Position.

Aldrix couldn't believe his eyes. *This must be wrong. Surely even the Chronicle made mistakes, right? Mr. Carlson was one of his father's most loyal colleagues and stalwart friends. Why would he be let go?*

He reached into his bag and retrieved his thick cellular phone. He called his father. He endured several rings before his father's voicemail delivered its monotone request to leave a message. He didn't bother, instead hanging up and sending his father a text message on the clunky keyboard: *"What Happened?"*

After five minutes passed without a response, Aldrix resigned himself to waiting. He went about the rest of his day distracted. The lectures went into one ear and out the other, his left-hand scribbling notes subconsciously. His eyes scanned the page, but none of the information entered his brain. His mind repeatedly sought the reasoning behind this development. He picked apart his summers, looking back in an attempt to find any trace, a single clue that pointed toward his father's unhappiness with Carlson's work. He drew a blank.

His answer finally came later that night as he laid in bed. His phone gave a small ping, and a message from his father flashed across the top of the screen. The answer was brief, devoid of emotion or any semblance of real depth: *"He was holding us back. He didn't want us to expand into new territory."*

Aldrix found this response entirely inadequate. He responded immediately:

"He just wanted you to be careful. That's not a crime."

The reply came seconds later: *"It's one thing to be careful, it's another to be contrary. Carlson was a great partner for many years, but he just became too complacent. We have to continue pushing forward to compete. Mr. Wellsworth and I decided he needed to go. It's not your place to question my decisions, boy. You may be in charge one day, but not yet. I did this for us. Family first."*

With that, it was clear the conversation was over. But Aldrix still wondered why Mr. Wellsworth had any hand in a decision that had nothing to do with banking.

Aldrix immediately called the sophomore who had publicly questioned his organizational decision.

After a single ring, a baritone voice picked up. "Hello."

Awkwardly, Aldrix said, "Hey, uh Michael? This is Aldrix."

His classmate was unimpressed. "It's Matt and, um, what do you want? You already fired me from a college club. I don't really think I need anything else—"

Aldrix cut him off, "I want you for a new position I just decided to create: Growth Officer. You will oversee the rest of the board's decisions and play devil's advocate when necessary. I'm sorry I was frustrated with you before, but I realize your voice is important. I can learn from you. You don't have to respond now, but please email me within the next two days if you'd like the spot. I apologize once again."

The sophomore hesitated for a few seconds, drawing out a long silence. In that time, Aldrix feared he'd made things even worse than they already were.

Then came the deep response. "I'll do it. But any more disrespect, and I'm out. I'm not going to let you play any more games with me."

"Agreed. Welcome to the team, Matt."

Three months before Aldrix was to succeed his father as CEO of Sterling, he received an invitation to the Wrightman Executive Conference for Young Business Leaders. He was excited by the prospect of hearing cutting-edge practices, but Aldrix always dreaded the parade of elegant people with less elegant motives.

Nonetheless, Aldrix was here to become the best. Not what his father considered the best, but what would move Sterling Energies into the future. What would secure his family's legacy. Despite his father's scathing remarks, Aldrix still put family first.

The conference's venue was inside the Mountain Point Hotel. Upon securing his name badge from the black-velvet clothed registration table outside, Aldrix entered the room.

A large stage was at the far end of the space with five colossal screens suspended above. Chairs lined the navy blue carpeted floor, suit coats, and the purses littered about. With fifteen minutes until the official event commencement, the attendees milled about the room, enjoying the two gratuitous refreshment bars.

Finding an available seat, Aldrix dropped his own suit jacket before making his way over to the rest. He took note of the high fashion surrounding him. His contemporaries dressed in their finery, each diamond-encrusted necklace and elegantly crafted ring meant to impress.

Arriving at the bar, Aldrix was about to order when a hand landed on his shoulder, and a voice said, "Excuse me."

Aldrix spun around to find himself face to face with Liam Wellsworth, a dazzling woman dressed in a simple maroon dress standing next to him.

Liam began menacingly casual, "Aldrix Sterling. It's been a while. How've you been?"

Unsure of how to treat the situation, Aldrix decided to give Liam the benefit of the doubt. "I'm doing well, Liam. How are you? Is Onyx treating you all right?"

Shrugging the question off, Liam said, "Yeah, it's been fine. Let me introduce you to my fiancée, Almendra Wrightman. You have her family to thank for putting this leadership event together."

Warmly, if not a bit condescendingly, Almendra said, "Nice to meet you, Aldrix. Liam has told me all about your school days. Great to put a face to the name."

With the distinct feeling that Almendra couldn't care less if she never met him, Aldrix replied, "It's wonderful to meet you too, Almendra, but I must admit, I didn't know you two were together. When did you meet?"

Almendra turned briefly toward Liam for a practiced smile that didn't fill her face before beginning her monologue, "Liam and I met at university. The Laurel League does have a way of bringing the right folks together, hmm? On a rainy day my junior year, I decided to frequent my favorite coffee shop nearby campus. When I finally got there through the pouring rain, I noticed a charmingly handsome guy chatting with an older man. I decided to sit and study at the adjacent table while I sipped my latte, and I couldn't help but eavesdrop on their conversation. I realized it was an interview and was extremely impressed with how composed the young man was. And did I mention how well he wore the suit? Still wears it well, honestly," she added, sneaking a look to her fiancé.

With his signature movie-star smile, Liam interjected to finish the story, "Anyway, after my Stonewick Investment interview was over—I got the internship that summer by the way—I purposefully dropped my umbrella under Almendra's chair. I had been sneaking glances at those beautiful green-flecked eyes since the moment she sat down and knew I needed to approach her. So, I walked out with my interviewer but excused myself to retrieve my wayward umbrella. I walked right back to her table, explained my umbrella just happened to be beneath her feet, and proceeded to introduce myself as her future husband."

Disgustingly, they both sighed to each other, clearly reflecting on the attractiveness of each other's money and social status.

Turning his attention back to Aldrix, Liam asked, "So, what about you, Aldrix? Is there someone special around here somewhere?"

Sterling stood tall as he said, "Actually, I've recently been on a few dates with a brilliant legal clerk. She's not here tonight, but I suspect we'll last a while."

Smiling widely, Almendra replied with, "Oh, a lawyer, what a cute profession."

Liam's eyes lit up at the jab. "I must admit I doubted whether your awkward self would be able to support a family with your Sterling salary, but I'm sure the two of you will have a good life on the combined income."

Aldrix remained silent, taking the jab. He was here for the conference. There was no point in making a scene.

With a hint of laughter, Liam said, "Speaking of which, I'm sorry to hear Sterling's stock took a dive after Carlson left. If you need, Onyx would be happy to lend you a little something until you guys get back on your feet."

Growing tired of the conversation, Aldrix said, "A generous offer, Liam, but I think we'll be just fine without your esteemed assistance."

Liam replied, "All right, suit yourself. But the hand's always extended if you ever wanna take it. I know you're about to take over the company, so Sterling will need all the help they can get, huh?" His hollow laugh was echoed by Almendra, and Aldrix managed a faint smile.

Fortunately, the sparkle of the crystal chandeliers dimmed in that moment, and the spotlights trained their aim on stage.

Aldrix took advantage of the moment, saying, "Well, it was nice to meet you, Almendra, and thank you for organizing this incredible event. And of course, I'm glad we ran into each other, Liam. I hope you guys enjoy the rest of the evening."

"You too, buddy," came Liam's reply as the couple began to walk off.

But Liam swerved back, grabbing Aldrix by the shoulder and leaning in. "You better get over that good guy act quick. You know my family takes care of everyone in our league. We make sure nothing goes sour in this town. And you better start playing the game as well as your old man does. I wouldn't want to have any disagreements."

Then Liam's charm returned, and he joined the side of Almendra, the two disappearing into the audience.

As Aldrix wove his way back to his seat, his world rocking from the impact of Liam's threat. He moved through the throngs of the influential elite, playing the interaction back in his head.

He couldn't help but feel Liam had become the man Aldrix's father had always hoped Aldrix would become. Arrogantly confident but entirely at home among the sharks.

He was clearly on a winning path, and from what Aldrix had heard regarding Onyx, they continued to be ruthless in their financial dealings. Liam was the perfect executive, but what Aldrix had always known was how flawed he was as a person. Clearly, that didn't matter now that Liam was undertaking his father's full dealings with the dark. He had no doubt Liam would look right at home surrounded by a horde of men in trench coats.

Aldrix rewound the conversation again and again. The conference flew by as blurs fluttered across the stage, each one proposing another tip to make them fiercer and more aggressive leaders.

They passed as if through frosted glass in front of Aldrix's glazed eyes. He simply dove deeper into analyzing Liam and more determined to carve his own way to the future. They would not laugh when it was his turn to lead.

Aldrix watched from backstage as his father gave his final speech to all the leaders of the company. He thought about their chess sessions. He remembered practicing by himself in his room and reviewing every move he could think of. He remembered his father weaving his business advice into the strategic tips he gave.

As a child, he was so eager to do whatever it would take to ensure he got to say a single word at the end of the day: "checkmate." His father raised him to knock aside others' queens, sacrifice his pawns to take others' bishops, and do anything necessary to win. But there was also a time when his father was loving and kind. When their relationship was more than spreadsheets and money.

As he stood in the shadow of the stage wings, Aldrix questioned whether his divergence from his father's set path had been worth a lifetime fissure in their relationship. Whether Aldrix's success would bring back the laughter, or only deepen the divide. Whether Aldrix's attempt to push away the Wellsworth would even be possible.

Aldrix was ready to play with the best. He was ready for the glares and the criticism and the barely hidden jabs of the Liams of the world. And he was prepared to do it by taking care of those around him. Protecting his own by whatever means necessary. His father taught him to be ruthless, and he knew that was hardwired into his nature. However, he had learned by himself that the numbers will never work if the people don't. He was determined not to forget that lesson when he saw his name etched into the mahogany desk at the top of Sterling Tower.

The room burst into applause, ejecting Aldrix from his thoughts. As his father walked offstage, Aldrix's ears tuned into the pitch of the noise. The clapping was polite and appreciative but not loving. His father's audience knew he had advanced the company, but they did not care for him because Alfred Sterling Jr. did not take the time to care for them.

As his father approached, Aldrix made a promise to himself. When he finally stepped out of the spotlight on his final day as CEO of Sterling, his colleagues' applause would echo with a resounding appreciation for the way he had changed their lives for the better. When his father arrived in front of Aldrix, he gave his son a doubtful glare. He said two words, "family first."

With only a nod of acknowledgment, Aldrix stepped past his father and into the unknown.

34

LIGHT READING

Nick walks down the street toward the metro, weight lifted from his shoulders after exiting that prison of a workplace for the last time. In the station, there are several street vendors along the side. Candy bars are stacked next to soda and newspapers, everything a person could need for a commute. He glances, skimming the headlines, but one sticks out immediately.

The Many Sins of Sterling Energies

He's never bought a paper newspaper in his life, but he runs to the vendor nonetheless. He grabs for his wallet and realizes he forgot to hand in his badge. *Whatever,* he guesses, *I deserve a souvenir.* He pays and hops on the train back to Aunt Stacie's while reading.

After several months of investigation, it now seems apparent Sterling Energies has been illegally dumping dangerous chemicals in minority and working-class neighborhoods across the city for decades.

Nick flips through, scanning until he hits one particular line. *Some of the affected areas include: Elm Park, Forest Heights, Stone Hill, and Piermont.*

As the train pulls up to Nick's station, the automated announcement rings out, "This is Piermont. Next stop, Forest Heights."

Nick purchases a large package of bottled water on the way home from quitting, heart pounding as he fumbles with his cash at the corner store. No more tap water until he gets a better idea of what they're really dealing with. Until he understands how far this contamination goes. His mind races through all the implications of this. *How could this have been hidden for so long? What does it mean for Aunt Stacie? For his own future health? Jamie?*

He does his best to act normal as he prepares dinner for his aunt. She asks him the same questions she always does. He gives the same answers, but the words feel different as they roll off his tongue. Nick isn't hungry. So, while his aunt eats, Nick walks out into the backyard. He pulls his phone from his back jean pocket and dials his brother's number.

He picks up on the third ring. "Hey, Nicky. What's up?"

Nick dances around the issue. "Jamie, I had an appointment with Aunt Stacie and her doctor last week. And then I found out something new today."

"Okay," his brother responds. "I'm guessing it didn't go well."

Nick tries to joke, "Right you are. That's why I call you a genius, bud." It falls flat.

"Ha. Well, it must be pretty bad if you're delaying telling me this long." Jamie senses his nerves and cuts to the chase. He softens his voice, "How much time do you think she has?"

Nick clenches his fist as he says, "The doctor didn't know. But J, she thought I was a little kid. She asked me about school. That's the first time she's confused anything about me. And when I asked the doc about it, he showed me some brain scans. The disease has advanced. I… I don't know Jamie."

Nick can picture Jamie's pained expression. He knows Jamie is grasping for solutions when he asks, "Man. So… she's gone? Like, her mind isn't hers? And there's nothing else they can try?"

"Yep. She's pretty far gone. There's nothing else they can do about it. But the worst part is I think I know how this whole situation came about now." Nick bites his inner cheek, uncertain how Jamie will react to his involvement.

Jamie responds, "I'm guessing you don't mean you've figured out how Alzheimer's comes about, right? Just how Aunt Stacie's did?"

Nick takes a deep breath and confesses, "Yeah, I was just on the metro, and I read this article in the paper. Sterling… the company I work… used to work for… it seems to have contaminated our neighborhood with chemicals. So uh, they're possibly to blame for Aunt Stacie, and that means we're probably at risk of developing health issues as we age too. They don't know how long this has been happening, but no one knows how long they've been dumping in the area. Could've been there forever. We'll have to stay on top of this."

There's a long pause as James digests this information. "So… you're telling me the company you just quit working for poisoned us and cut our aunt's mental awareness by thirty years?"

Nick's throat tightens at his brother's tone. "Um, yeah. I guess that about sums it up."

Jamie is logistical in his response. "You have to move. What are you even doing right now? Have you gotten some prepackaged water?"

Nick lets out a silent sigh of relief. His brother's anger would have made this day even worse. He responds, "I got some bottled water on the way home from resigning. Still, I don't have all the facts, but I know I have to do something. And I'm going to look up apartments tomorrow. We definitely have to move now."

Jamie sounds distant when he says, "I can't believe this is happening. Do you need me to fly in?"

Nick wishes he would visit but doesn't want to inconvenience his brother. He paces the backyard as he says, "No, I've got it. Don't worry. Thanks for the offer, though, Jamie. I'll talk to you soon."

"You can't hang up on me like that, Nicky. What are you going to do?"

Nick looks up at the sky, the final glow of sunlight fading. He lets himself be honest, "I don't know, Jamie."

Nick's phone buzzes again only moments after hanging up with Jamie. "What a cowardly way to walk away," Sterling's familiar voice says from the other side. His voice has an edge that Nick's never heard. It makes him feel like prey, a shiver running down his spine.

Sterling continues, "I made you. Your entire professional life exists because I saw your talent. And now you're just leaving because of a leak no one could control?"

Nick pauses. His eyes bounce around the yard as if the correct reply is hidden somewhere in the grass. He doesn't know which lie to tell, so the truth comes out. "I left because it was the right thing to do. I can't work for you anymore when there are so few environmental precautions that you take. I have warned you several times to listen to the calls for environmental change, and you never listened. But that doesn't matter. What really matters is what I suspected was immediately confirmed by the *Chronicle* the minute I walked out of that ego temple of yours."

Sterling's voice has entirely lost its charming warmth. "Why are you reading that garbage?"

Nick quips back, "Because they are telling the truth about why my aunt thinks I'm twelve. Because they are exposing how you have poisoned communities you've seen as irrelevant for decades."

For the first time in nine years, Nick doesn't think Sterling has anything to say.

The man manages to mumble through a response nonetheless. "I'm sorry to hear that, Nick. And I assure you I've never intentionally done anything of the sort. Plus, I was not CEO more than ten years ago, you know that. Your tenure here is practically as long as mine. How can you blame me for the acts of my father?"

Nick releases all of his pent-up anger, "Liar. You aren't sorry. You just want me back so I can help clean up the massive mess you made. If you were actually sorry, you'd acknowledge it and help these neighborhoods where the rates of birth defects, mental illness, and cancer are through the roof!"

Sterling seems unfazed. "Don't listen to the tabloids, Nick."

Done with his excuses, Nick says, "The *Chronicle* is literally the most prestigious outlet in this city. Actually, whatever. I'm not going to fight. Thank you for your call, Aldrix. But like I said, I'm out. And I'm not coming back. Goodnight."

Nick stares at the overcooked pasta in front of him while Aunt Stacie watches TV in the next room. He picks at the broccoli before tossing it back onto his plate. His stomach swirls as if he just hopped off a carnival ride. He hates everything.

He hates that he fought with Sterling, who, despite being a terrible human, certainly did keep Nick from drowning for the past nine years. He hates his situation. That his neighborhood got screwed. That he's to blame. That he played a role in this mess. Most of all, he hates that his aunt sits on the couch like nothing's happened.

Walking up to his bedroom, Nick gets out his laptop. He climbs into his old twin bed, having never bothered to replace it. He begins searching. He reads more and more into stories about contaminated water and "one-off" health reports.

He doesn't stop until his eyes close in surrender to sleep.

35

WICKED

Nick is exhausted as he cooks breakfast for Stacie.

It's his fault.

They sit down together, cardboard boxes in the corner of the room. He has already begun getting organized for the move. Aunt Stacie picks at her eggs. Her face is peaceful as she sips some orange juice. Nick clenches his jaw. He looks at his aunt. Her graying hair.

It's his fault.

Nick opens his mouth, "I—"

It's his fault. It's his fault. It's his fault.

He's not sure what to say. He reaches for the words, but he doesn't know how to convey his sorrow and his grief, and the pit growing in his stomach. Stacie looks down, focused lazily on her eggs. She's not even paying attention, but Nick lets it all out. "I… I'm sorry. I'm so so so sorry. I hate this. I worked for a company for a decade. I worked for a charming, cowardly, wealthy man for a decade. So I could take care of you. And I failed. I didn't take care of you. I just contributed to the thing that was making you sick. I made it worse. For years. I've been making it worse. And I love you, but I messed up, and now we'll never be able to have a conversation. Not like we used to. We can't laugh like we used to. Not like when Jamie would..."

Nick breaks down, the tears stream down his face. "Like when Jamie would do that ridiculous dance when he was washing the dishes. Or when you burnt the casserole so badly, I thought there was a fire in the house. And we didn't just laugh. We rolled on the ground."

Despite his words, the memory forces a smile to Nick's face. But soon, the dark thoughts return, "I thought I was so smart. So righteous for sacrificing for you like you did for me. But I was hurting you the whole time. I was a fool, and I was so content. So complacent. I—ahhh! I can't believe how stupid I was."

For a moment, silence fills the air. Nick takes a few deep breaths. "I... I'm so sorry. I'm—"

"I forgive you," comes Stacie's response.

Nick looks up, eyes red and puffy from emotions, and finds his aunt's gaze crystal clear. A tear slides down her face.

"Honey," she says, her lucid eyes staring directly into his soul, "I forgive you."

Nick wraps his arms around her. His entire apology conveyed through the embrace. She wraps her arms around him.

When he pulls back, though, her mannerisms have changed. And her eyes are darkened.

Stacie blinks for a second. Then looks at him and asks, "Honey, why... why are you, um, why are we crying?"

It's *Sterling's* fault.

36

REUNION

Emerald sits at her desk, her clothes sweat-stained and her coffee mug empty. The room is reflected in the windows at her back, the daylight long having given way to the night. The cleanup is going okay, but there is still so much to do. Her mind continuously replays Sterling's words over in her mind, his games messing with her head.

There's a light rapt on the door. Emerald looks up. Amelie hobbles through the door, her nose, shoulders, and arm covered by bandages. Even where no bandages are, her skin is raised with burns. She moves on crutches, and she looks absolutely terrible. When she sees Emerald, though, she smiles. Emerald rises and moves forward but pauses, not sure how or if to embrace her.

Amelie says, "Go ahead, can't hurt more than the crash."

Emerald hugs her friend as tightly as she dares. "God, I'm so glad you're alive."

Amelie responds in kind, "Same to you, glad you were the lucky one of us."

Emerald's smile falters for a moment, but she doesn't dare give anything away. Her mind wavers between telling Amelie who is behind her bruised, burnt body and not wanting to involve her precious friend in the darkness swirling around her.

"So," Amelie says, "are you all set for the night? I just wanted to stop by and say hi before going home."

"Are you honestly suggesting you do work right now?" Emerald says with a chuckle. At the same time, her mind shuffles through the options. *What proof does she even have, even if she did tell Amelie? She knows her friend would believe her, but still... What's the point when Sterling hides behind his henchmen? She knows Sterling is watching her office. Would they go after Amelie?*

"No, I was just being polite," Amelie says with a light laugh. "I've gotta go see my boyfriend. We had dinner plans for the night of the crash, so... gotta apologize for standing him up. He's good though. I think he'll understand."

Emerald is amazed at Amelie's spirit. She can't help but smile back as she says, 'Yeah, he better."

Amelie turns to leave but pauses. "I know you don't have anyone at home right now. But do you ever get tired of going home to an empty house? Like, while I was in the hospital. My boyfriend wasn't allowed in. But he left me voice memos. And they're really sweet. And everything hurts right now, but I'm really glad my parents and boyfriend are going to be at my apartment when I arrive. And in the future, maybe, hopefully, I'll have some crazy kids to return to. And I mean, I guess what I'm trying to say is... are you lonely, ma'am?"

Emerald looks up and sighs. Setting her glasses and pen down, she looks Amelie in the eye.

When Emerald was a child, she owned three dolls. Each was the same size with the same features, just in three distinct shades and bearing three radiant eye colors.

Every morning as a five-year-old, she would rise from bed and check on her children. Their three small cradles lined the wall, casting irregular shadows on the floor. Emerald's small feet made their way over, and she peered into the plastic faces of her dolls. Each day she would pick them up one by one and rock them 'awake.' Their perfectly spherical eyes would widen and shut to the swing of gravity as Emerald gently hummed a lullaby.

When her mother would come to wake her, she would almost always arrive to find her daughter tipping a fictitious baby bottle into the mouths of one of her dolls and talking unashamedly to them. For whatever reason, she never gave names to any of the dolls. It wasn't important to her. She simply thought of them collectively as 'her babies,' and that was all there was to it.

Directly after kindergarten each day, she would go straight to her room and check on her babies. Before the fire, their old house had ample space. Her room was her refuge, full of imagination and exploration. She would carry the dolls to the living room and lay them on the couch as she ate her snack, filling them all in on the latest drama of the day. If the family decided to go out for dinner, Emerald would throw a tantrum, wailing to her parents about abandoning her dolls.

At night, Emerald would religiously tuck her babies in. Resting them on their backs and pulling their blankets up to their necks. Only then did her parents even have a chance of convincing Emerald to clamber into her own bed.

For years, her babies were always by her side. Emerald cared for them continuously with unconditional love and care.

Then, at age seven, something clicked. Her second-grade teacher, returning from paternity leave, introduced his new baby to Emerald's class. As she shoved against her classmates to gain a better look, Emerald discovered how much softer the baby's skin looked compared to her own dolls at home. Her babies' sticker eyes paled in comparison to the brilliance of this real baby's irises. A bit deflated, Emerald returned home, and for the first time since she could remember, she didn't run to her babies. When she entered her room later in the evening, she felt silly for ever thinking of them as real.

Frustrated, she took all three and threw them out of her room in a sudden rage. When her parents came to check on the series of thuds they heard, Emerald was seated miserably on her bed. For a moment, they simply frowned at their daughter's evident falling out with her favored toys before approaching Emerald on her bed.

Her mother finally spoke, "Honey, why are you upset with your babies?"

Quietly, she answered, "They're not real."

Her father responded, "You're right, they're not, but that doesn't mean you can't still love them."

Stubbornly Emerald said, "Yes, it does."

"Well," her mother said, "one day, you'll have a real one, and they'll have temper tantrums and sit on their bed with their arms crossed, but that doesn't mean you can throw them across the room. Now, does it?"

'That's not funny," Emerald replied, lips poked out.

Her mother's eyes crinkled, and her father stifled laughter as he said, "Oh, I thought that was a pretty good one."

The sound of her parent's laughter made her reluctantly crack a small smile. When her mother saw this, she said, "Go to bed, Emerald. Sleep tight, and we can talk more in the morning, okay?" Emerald calmed down enough to fall into her bed and doze into rest.

In the morning, Emerald arose to the sight of her once-beloved dolls still in a heap in her hallway. She walked over and scooped them up, traipsing to a shelf in the corner of her room. After a while, they just became another decoration in her room. One day band posters took the place above their heads, then a calendar, then a chalkboard. The dolls remained there, almost invisible in their ordinariness, but a silent reminder of the future she one day wanted.

Her silly hopes for the future turned to ash after the fire.

The dolls burnt alongside the home she'd once known. Emerald continued to appreciate the sight of a two-year-old toddling down the street. Chasing a rabbit or throwing a fit in the park. For the most part, Emerald focused on getting out of the poverty they found themselves forced into.

A poverty not just of money, but of land and family. She mourned the loss of her community and honed her focus on her studies. She was content to volunteer at the local after-school program and make playful faces with babies who happened to turn their infinitely curious gazes toward her on the metro.

Then, in university, Emerald was assigned a reading on the future of parenthood. She was confused, thinking she'd signed up for a course on the economics of environmentalism. To her surprise, the paper argued the economy must prepare for the societal impacts of fewer children as younger generations were deciding not to have children for financial or ethical reasons. For the first time, Emerald thought not just about the babies she pictured in her mind's eye, but also about the quality of their potential lives.

She visualized the world her children could inherit, a place of drought and war and anger. She asked herself whether she ever truly wanted a kid. How in spite of her success, she dreamed of an even higher performing child. How she'd always imagined her childhood dolls winning Olympic medals or peace prizes. How she had wanted them to love her and find community in her family. To not look at her on the street and puzzle at her appearance, but be proud of their heritage. She had always just wanted someone who would look at her and only think of warmth and unconditional love. Someone to look straight through her skin to her heart and simply say: 'Mom.'

For the first time, she thought about whether that was even fair for her to want. To demand of a future life.

She promised herself then and there if she ever had kids, she would only bring them into a world that she believed in.

"Yes."

Amelie looks back at her with pity in her eyes.

Emerald delves deeper. "Yes, Amelie. When I go back home some nights, and the only company is the black sedan of huge men out front, I feel a… heaviness of living a life alone. And I used to have dreams of a family as a kid. But right now, even if I had a partner, I'm not sure I could live with myself if I had kids. Because I don't know what kind of world they would be living in, so excuse me for a minute while I save the world. Then I'll focus on the other stuff."

Amelie looks at her with eyes of such respect that Emerald looks away despite herself.

“Have a goodnight, ma’am,” her friend says. “Thank you for everything.”

“No, Amelie, thank you.”

37

TROUBLE

At age twenty, Ezra was making his way home from a day of classes. He'd watched Nick go off to MIT, and Lucas had a destiny for greatness at the top state school, but Ezra had other things to deal with.

He made his way through the local streets alone, coming from the community college just a few stops away.

It wasn't a long walk to the metro, but today, for no reason in particular, he didn't feel like going straight home.

He meandered his way through the residential neighborhood. Piermont wasn't especially beautiful, but it wasn't downtrodden either.

It was just a modest community, and he respected that. Sometimes he even passed Nick's aunt's place, and she'd wave and ask about his day. It was a little awkward, but they both liked that the other reminded them of Nick.

Turning the corner, he headed onto the creekside trail that took him the long way to the train. The mud always got all over his shoes, but the scenic views of the colorful trees made up for it.

Whenever he got a chance to see some green in the city, he liked to take it. For a while, he just breathed in the fresh air, adjusting his backpack as it continuously tried to slip off his shoulder.

Then he heard voices. The next thing he noticed was the smell of pot.

Grinning, he decided to be nosey and see which of his classmates had decided to pop into the woods for a smoke.

As he rustled through the branches, muffled voices became audible.

Ezra also heard some banging around as he slowed his pace but continued forward, still curious to see what was going on.

He paused as the men came into view. Two workers in hardhats accompanied by a well-kept older man in a luxurious looking button down with an elegant tie. He sat in a truck as the two workers hauled a vat of some sort of liquid that smelled awful.

The man in the suit was smoking as he ordered the workers around, directing them casually as if being disobeyed was completely unimaginable.

The vats were dark and unmarked, but the truck had a logo. Despite being scratched and dirtied, the "SE" was clear, and now Ezra wondered what the same company that owned the immaculate tower in the city center was doing out in the woods of this snooze of a neighborhood.

Ezra ducked, crouching into the dirt, but his sneakers slipped on the grassy floor. The man in the tie stepped out of the truck, eyes searching for the origin of the noise. He scanned in Ezra's general direction, but his eyes were unfocused. Ezra sat absolutely statue still. There was nothing physically menacing about the older man, but all of Ezra's instincts told him he was dangerous.

The man in the tie nodded at the two workmen, and they immediately dropped the vats, allowing the brown liquid to ooze out of the opening. They began to move toward Ezra. His heart pounded as he began slowly backing up toward the path, rising to his feet. Everything in his body told him to run, but he knew it would just give him away.

He held his breath. His blood pounded in his ears. He continued walking backward as gingerly as possible, but a tree root had other plans. Ezra fell hard to the ground, his forearm shooting pain. Still, he held his breath, hoping the men hadn't heard. He didn't hear any pounding feet, so he began standing up again just as a voice at his back questioned, "Who the hell are you, kid?"

Ezra bolted, flying over the twisted roots toward the trail. He heard two pairs of feet behind him, but he felt confident in his escape. The pattering of their feet lessened as Ezra made it back to the path and ran along the creek toward the meadow and the subway beyond.

He burst through the tree line and peeked behind him, seeing no one in pursuit. He slowed, trying to be as casual as possible and calming the adrenaline racing through his veins.

He just had to make it to the metro. *If there were people around, he'd be safe, right? Plus, he could disappear into the rush hour madness. He just had to make it there. He was so close. Definitely wasn't trying to be the cat curiosity killed. What made him want to pry? Stupid. He was stupid. He should've just stuck to the main road. Okay, almost across the meadow. Just a little more of the trail, and he would be fine. Everything would be fine.*

Then a new noise pierced his thoughts, a growing hum. All Ezra had time to do was turn toward the headlights careening across the meadow and throw himself out of the way of the vehicle.

Completely stunned at the near miss, Ezra laid in the grass in disbelief. When he heard the car doors open and then slam shut, he scrambled back to his feet, beginning to sprint home, but a hand grabbed his bag and yanked him back down.

And then a boot smashed into his face, and the world went pitch-black.

Ezra opened his eyes to a starry night sky. His head felt horrendous, and his forearm had begun to bruise, but he didn't seem to have any new injuries.

Ezra slowly got up. He quickly realized both that he was completely alone and he knew exactly where he was.

His head still swam, and his whole body was completely tense. Recognizing that he sat at the edge of the creek's trail, Ezra was only a few paces from his usual route and a few blocks from the metro.

What had happened to the men? How had he escaped unscathed?

Ezra paced his movement to avoid an even more piercing headache. He was going to have a crazy story for his mom, and he'd definitely need a visit to the doctor. He was okay, though. He hobbled down the sidewalk, his backpack low on his back. Ezra felt confident he could make it to the metro.

When Officer Danielle Williams' patrol vehicle rolled to a stop, and she saw him, the world froze. Behind her eyes, she already saw the headlines destroying her reputation. The hate she'd get if she messed this up. Especially in this weird neighborhood she was called to spontaneously, she didn't know the streets. She had to stay calm.

She'd dreaded this since beginning her assignment three weeks prior. She was brand new, fresh out of the academy. No associate's degree in law enforcement could have prepared her for the simultaneous monotony and nerve-wracking anxiety that was part of being on the force.

She'd learned to master every inch of her weapon. She learned defensive techniques that she'd never dreamt of. She learned what to look for in suspects, and how to spot a lie, and how to think. At the end of the day, though, she had barely seen a pickpocket in the past few weeks of standard patrol.

Somehow, she had a feeling this moment had the potential to define the rest of her career. The male suspect hobbled along oddly. Definitely looked like he was under the influence of something. His steps were severely uneven.

Looking harder through the evening darkness, she realized he was likely just a few years younger than she was, scaring her even more.

Shaking, she got out of the car and walked toward the suspect as calmly as she could while also scanning him for any signs of a weapon.

She did not want to kill anyone that day, but she did not intend to die either.

The moment Ezra heard the squeal of the tires and heard a commanding voice order him to stop, his world froze.

Out of the corner of his eye, he identified the vehicle as a cop car and immediately put his hands up. As slowly as he could, he twisted in place, barely daring to breathe.

As soon as he saw the tall woman step out of the car, his adrenaline shot into overdrive for the second time that night.

He breathed. He wasn't doing anything wrong. Just trying to get his bruised body to the metro.

If anything, maybe this could be his lucky night, and he could explain the whole situation and get it straightened out. Find the guys who'd pummeled him and left him alone in the night.

So he was fine. She couldn't do anything to him. Ezra just turned off his brain, stowed away the fear racking his body, and got ready to comply.

Officer Williams approached the suspect slowly, calling out as clearly as possible, "Please keep your hands in the air and remain still."

She tried to keep her voice commanding and steady, despite the distinct lack of control she felt over the situation. Despite the past several months of intensive training, they never taught her how to truly speak to someone. Especially someone who looked like him.

The suspect didn't move, frozen like a painting except for the tremor of nerves that rocked his body. He looked just as bad as Officer Williams felt. At about five feet away, she stopped and demanded, "Now, lower your hands and empty your pockets."

The young man did no such thing. Remaining completely still, eyes wide in terror, he barely breathed.

"Come on! Do it, now." Officer Williams placed her hand on her holster just as she was taught, preparing for the worst.

Ezra was pretty confident he was about to die, and he didn't know how to stop it.

He saw the officer yelling, but at first, the words seemed to pass over his ears as if plugged with nothingness. All he saw was the cop putting her hand on the gun, a frown splitting her face.

He read the number written below the officer's name, cop 54821, and tried to commit it to memory.

Then, there was a small pop in his inner ear and the officer's shouts rung clearly.

She shouted at him, her voice sharp, "Arms down! Empty your pockets!"

Ezra hesitated. *Is this a trick? Would he be shot for lowering his arm? Would the police report say he reached for a nonexistent weapon?* In the nanoseconds these thoughts crossed his mind, he looked into the eyes of the officer and found them just as fearful as he felt. Coming to a barely reasoned decision, Ezra finally responded, "Okay, okay, okay. Doing it, right now." He lowered his arms, reached into his pocket, and pulled them completely inside out.

"Good. Hands back up."

Ezra immediately complied, raising them slowly. Still wincing from the pain of his battered body.

Taking tentative steps forward, the officer said, "Okay, I'm going to inspect your backpack. Do not move."

All Ezra could do while the woman moved around him was imagine the pistol that was likely directed at the back of his head. How unfathomably close he was to death at that moment.

Then the weight on his back suddenly became lighter. And to his horror, officer 54821 came back into view, holding a bag of cocaine.

Ezra's mouth fell open, but he knew better than to say anything.

Officer Williams looked blankly at the young man as she held the drugs in her hand. She knew she must now arrest this suspect, but the process of doing that to someone who looked like he did was a scene from her nightmares.

She held on to her gun a little tighter without drawing it. When she looked back up into his eyes, she realized there was no danger, no fight, only a brief gleam of light betraying his total fear. He did not pose the threat she was always taught. Not the suspicious male profile she learned about, but rather someone who could have been at a desk next to her at the academy just a few weeks ago.

Looking at his face, Danielle imagined his terror was the exact same expression on her face at that very moment as well. Without a word, Danielle simply took three steps, reached out, grabbed hold of Ezra's arm, and steered him back toward the vehicle.

She could feel his skin trembling under her fingers as she solemnly stated, "Please turn around and hold onto the roof of the car. I'm going to pat you down."

She paused, breathed deeply, and added, "Please, for both of our sakes, *hold on*. Please." She received no audible reply, but the young man placed his hands onto the roof of the car.

Over the next thirty seconds, neither of them breathed as Danielle glided her hands over the layers of the perpetrator's clothing.

She found nothing.

The door slammed shut, and Ezra was alone in the back seat of the vehicle. He wasn't angry or sad or frustrated. He was just relieved to be whole. As the car started up and Officer 54821 drove Ezra toward his altered future, he was just glad he'd held on.

They made their way far from the neighborhood he knew and onto a highway, which was weird. *Weren't cops supposed to patrol locally?* Ezra guessed it didn't matter now. He was in trouble, but maybe they'd hear him out. It was unlikely, but it was all he had now. Ezra settled back into the seat and tried to make himself as comfortable as possible even though the lumpy cushion was working against him.

Seeing the Grayson Tunnel was fast approaching, Ezra tried to get one last peek at what he could see of the city skyline before entering the pitch-black. At the moment before the tunnel engulfed them, a billboard caught his attention from the corner of his eye.

Suddenly he understood. On the sign, Ezra saw the older man in the truck. Alfred Sterling's name plastered in one-thousand point font.

He realized he'd been setup by the most powerful man in the city. There was no way out.

38

SCHEMING

"Your son needs to get in line," Branson Wellsworth commanded across the phone.

It was only a couple of months since Alfred Sterling had handed the company over to his son Aldrix. The boy was already causing difficulties. Alfred had thought his problems would be over when he retired. His naïveté was laughable. His son's stubbornness was angering the entire power structure of this city. Over the past few weeks, the issue had grown. The Wellsworths were involved.

Alfred responded to his friend, "I agree."

Wellsworth was not a man to shield the truth. "He must understand going it alone is dangerous. And if he does not fold, he will be made to bow. And if not bow, then, so help me, break. Do not let your arrogant son destroy what you have built, Alfred."

Alfred paced the tiled floor of his home, the sound echoing through the cavernous halls. He responded, "Absolutely, Branson. I've spoken to him several times, but his hardheadedness is impenetrable. You said he has continued to refuse your generous security team and the support of your associates?"

Branson's disappointment in his friend began to bleed through. "That is correct. And my patience is wearing thin, Alfred. Our families' partnerships have remained steadfast for generations. How did you fail to drill this into him? Liam has taken to it all quite well."

Alfred took the insult. Branson was right. He feared what falling out of favor with the Wellsworths would bring. "My boy has always been particularly insolent," Alfred agreed. "But there will be no more trouble. We will put some fear into him. Would you be willing to provide some assistance?"

"What do you have in mind?" Alfred ignored the twisted pleasure he heard in Branson's voice.

Alfred told Branson his idea. The man agreed. Alfred was about to end the call, but Branson interjected, "Alfred, if this does not work, I will not deign to call you before course correcting. We will try your way. If that fails, my family will address the issue ourselves. Is that understood?"

Alfred steeled himself to reality as he answered, "Understood."

"You're pathetic," his father spit, gaze digging into Aldrix. Only three months into being CEO and his father had invited Aldrix to his home. However, the conversation had quickly derailed as Aldrix asked his father for guidance and was met with a wall of frustration.

Alfred Sterling's contempt for his son was laid bare in his seaside mansion. The estate had too many rooms to count, but the two sat at one of the crystal dining room tables overlooking the street as people streamed toward the beach.

Aldrix kept his ego in check. "I am here for your advice, father. I come in goodwill."

Aldrix watched as luxury vehicles parked, their occupants exiting before their drivers continued on to somewhere else. Only disappearing to await their next summons. He brought his attention back to his father.

His father's tone was unyielding, "You come for advice, but you spit on the most important piece of advice I offer: call Liam Wellsworth. He is your peer, and you require his services."

A guard named Apollo stood in the corner. He introduced himself to Aldrix on the way in, but then he was quiet in the corner of the room, out of Aldrix's field of vision.

Aldrix countered his father, "No. I told you when I overtook this position, I would not operate like you. There is a new era for Sterling Energies untainted by your darkness and lies. Just this week, I was made aware some twenty-year-old is facing prison time because you did God knows what to him. And now it is *my* problem to figure out how to keep him quiet. I'm not going to pass messes like this off to my own kid. It ends with me. If the Wellsworths want to continue their tyranny, so be it. We will be moving away from that path."

The air hung heavy for several moments, his father saying nothing. Then Alfred began, "I thought you'd know better than to reject your own. I wish—"

Aldrix was tackled to the ground. The window erupted without any warning. Shards pummeled him, but Apollo's body shielded him from the worst of it.

The sound finally caught up with the bullets. The noise louder than anything he'd ever heard. His ears rang. The world had been orderly moments before. Firmly under his control. Under the weight of Apollo, eyes dilated in fear, Aldrix felt as though his world had fallen off a cliff. The room filled with an acute metallic smell. Aldrix saw his father cowering under the table as the three of them watched the dining room wall become ridden with bullet holes.

The chandelier above them sparked, the wires ripped free before the elegant illumination plunged downward to the table below. Its weight pounded into the table with a *crash*. Bullets continued to fly through the window, the aim sporadic. Bullets ricocheted around the room, cracking the pristine mirror and carving their way through the walls.

Outside there were shouts and cries as beach goers panicked, running from the violent noises. Aldrix shut his eyes and wished he could just disappear. At the same time, his mind raced. *Who was shooting at them? Why? What had his father done?*

Just as suddenly as they came, the bullets stopped. Apollo was the first to rise. His pistol in hand, he took cover against an adjacent wall and peered out the broken window, looking for threats. For several tense moments, there was no sound except for the heavy breathing of the three men. When Apollo saw it was clear, he leaned down and helped Aldrix up.

For the first time, Aldrix actually looked at the man, the towering beast that he was. Though his stature was looming, Apollo's face was handsome, and when he spoke, his accent was just as refined as the Sterling's. "Are you quite all right, sir? Apologies for the sudden seizure. I didn't have time to explain when I saw the threat." Fear had gripped Aldrix so badly that all he did was nod his thanks.

Apollo was barely flustered as he helped Alfred up as well. Apollo ushered the two Sterlings away from the windows and into the interior of the house. For a few minutes, the three sat in the kitchen, processing the event. Apollo returned to a quiet position in the corner of the room after calling for assistance. Not from the authorities, of course. From trustworthy associates.

Aldrix stirred his tea, his nerves only now beginning to calm. Then the fight started.

Aldrix began, "Who did you upset, father?"

Alfred's malicious smirk said it all. "Who did *I* upset? No. I did my four decades of work and maintained power without a single try on my life. How is it a coincidence that after only a short while of *your* tenure, my house gets blasted up?"

Aldrix shot back, "All I have done is treat people with respect. I have rejected the Wellsworths because they *use* people. They use people and toss them aside like they are worthless. Because they resort to violence to keep their power. I will not follow that."

His father's veins were full of ice as he said, "Boy, it is not about respect, it is about power. You have it. Others are desperate for it. Simple as that. This is why you need the support of the Wellsworths and others. The police will not keep you safe. Your 'standard' guards are useless. This game is deeper, and it requires you to don the correct armor. There is armor provided by collaborating with the Wellsworths. This is what happens when you do not play the game. People get word. Whispers spread that you are unprotected. That our family is weak. People come for our fortunes."

Aldrix simply stared at the table, hating his father's words but now hearing the wisdom from an enlightened perspective. A perspective informed by bullets and the sounds still pounding in his mind.

His father continued, "You do not get to pick and choose the pieces of our legacy you inherit. Like it or not, this city operates because of men like Wellsworth. Men like me. And many people don't like that. You are part of this family which means many people wish you harm. They will come for you whether you like it or not. The poor, the powerless, they have nothing to lose. No honor, no legacy. They understand only force."

For the first time since university, Aldrix heeded his father. He called Liam. He was determined not to let loose his grip on power.

They met, and when Liam extended him a weapon, the steel gleaming, Aldrix took it.

His family's influence would not end with him. He would ensure continued success.

As he aged, Aldrix learned how to navigate the world the Wellsworths controlled. His requests of Apollo grew in number and complexity. He systematically removed his enemies. Whatever it took.

Alfred Sterling called Branson Wellsworth long after his son had left the premises.

Once again, the man picked up immediately. "Has our young Aldrix changed his mind? I heard he went through quite a harrowing experience today." His voice is full of spite.

Alfred replied, "Yes. You do not have to take any further action, my son was swayed. He has reached out to your boy."

"Excellent. Apollo was the man on site today, correct?"

"Correct," Alfred affirmed.

Branson replied gruffly, "Good. We will assign him to Aldrix permanently. He will report to me. Your son is still on a tight leash, my friend."

39

ROSE-COLORED

Miserably, Ezra sat in the dark jail cell.

His court date was the following week. He already knew what the verdict would be, though. That is, if he were unable to get in front of the press or someone else he could trust the truth with. He had requested they allow his mother to visit, but she was denied entry.

So, Ezra was surprised when a guard appeared outside his cell and told him he had a visitor. He was shackled and led out into the cold, dark corridor. Walking through the narrow halls with cracked concrete walls, Ezra walked by other men with gaunt faces and little hope. They peered at him as if they questioned whether he walked to freedom or condemnation. Ezra wondered the same.

The guard let Ezra into a stark white room divided only with a bit of hardened plastic. A man sat on the opposite side, his shoulders as broad as his head was bald. A little red light blinked periodically in the wall adjacent to the plastic barrier, their conversation monitored by the guards. Ezra sat down, the escorting guard closing the door, keeping watch outside.

The man spoke as if they were old friends, "Ezra! So sorry to see you in here. Are they treating you well in that pigsty?"

Ezra played along. "Not bad, the food is terrible, no other complaints."

The man kept glancing at the red light. It continued its usual pattern. He replied, "Well, that's excellent to hear, excellent to hear. And how is your mother? Has she gotten a chance to visit you yet?"

Growing more nervous, Ezra answered, "No, unfortunately, she hasn't had the chance to swing by."

The red light stopped blinking, and the man's façade fell instantly. "Okay, Ezra, here's the deal. There are two paths for you to choose: the carrot or the stick. If you're patient and quiet, you will receive the carrot. This is in the form of a reduced sentence and comforts. My boss is feeling generous, so we would reduce the sentence by three to five years. It depends on your behavior over the coming years. On the last day of your fourth year in this disgusting rat hole, you'll get a notice, call it a judgment, the Caesar giving you the yay or nay. If you did as required, you would find out how much sooner you could leave. Along the way, if you behave, you might get a treat on your dinner plate. You might get a cellphone with internet. You might get some drugs to leverage over the others. You get the point. My boss is not a cruel man. You are in control of his mood."

Ezra's heart sank. There truly was nowhere outside of the Sterling family's reach. The man continued, "Now for the stick. If you even think of talking. If you ever invite a guest that is suspicious. If you ever look at a guard the wrong way, that will make my boss upset. And that will get you disposed of immediately. You will never walk out of these walls again. Is that understood?"

Ezra nodded.

The man was unsatisfied. "I need a verbal response, Ezra. Don't want any misunderstandings between us."

Ezra said, "Yes. I understand. I will be patient, but your boss better get me out of here."

On cue, the red light began blinking again, the recording restarted. The man stood up, gave Ezra a final mistrusting glance, and left the room. A few seconds later, the guard retrieved Ezra.

He was escorted back to his cell, and he began his countdown.

The prison was huge. Ezra got off the transport bus, shuffled along with a dozen others toward Fort Laurent Correctional Compound. The facility consisted of a guard tower encircled by three concentric rings. The innermost layer was full of cells, a panopticon allowing the guards to monitor the prisoners' every move. The middle circle housed the cafeteria, the gym, the library. The final ring contained the administrative offices, visitors center, and offered a small portal to the outside world. Here, they let his mother visit. The two spoke through a plastic barrier each month. A privilege Ezra was all too aware that Sterling could retract.

Ezra picked up the social dynamics quickly. He observed how individuals interacted. *Why were gangs divided by race? Whites, Latinos, Blacks, Asians. Those seemed to be the main ones. What happened to anyone who didn't fit well? Seemed like they just had to choose. Mixed dudes weren't mixed in prison. Prison was a place of black and white affairs, with no room for gray.*

Ezra sat with the Blacks for lunches. He worked out with them in the gym. He stood around them in the yard, the only time they could see slices of the city outskirts around them. He did not particularly like any of his peers, Black or otherwise. But, staying together was the only way to stay alive. Sterling's threats didn't include anything about protecting him until his fifth year. He had to survive on his own. So he sat at the cafeteria table and buried himself deep as the others chatted around the chow hall table.

"Yo, you see that Latino dude wit' the snake tattoo on his arm? He's so feral for drugs he tried to bribe a guard. Got smacked on his butt like he deserved."

"Aww nah, man. 'D'you see white Jamal? Thought he was slick, tryna pull some gay stuff with a guard. He didn't even last a second, his own took care of him. Beat him good."

Ezra kept his head low and his heart cold—Or at least he tried.

At the start of his fourth year, a new guard joined the ranks. He had wavy blond hair and a perfectly kept beard. He stood tall and had kind brown eyes. His name was Sam, and he let Ezra out of his cell every morning for breakfast.

Where the other guards were rough and hostile when pushing Ezra toward the chow hall, Sam was gentle and considerate. Sometimes Sam's shoulder brushed against his, and Ezra's skin tingled with delight. Ezra felt Sam knew his secret, but he didn't care. Ezra had polished his image as a hardened prison vet over the years, but Sam looked straight into his soul. Soon they established a morning ritual. Sam named a city of the world, and Ezra would name all the foods he'd like to try there. If Ezra had never heard of the city, he had to make it up, listing everything from dragon stew to leprechaun fruit.

They went through Paris, London, São Paulo, Rabat, Montreal, Tehran, and dozens more. Over the weeks, the cities became more obscure and Ezra less knowledgeable of the cuisine, but that wasn't the point. Ezra's main aim each morning was to make Sam laugh. Every time Ezra interacted with the guard, his eyes lingered on the man's lips. Sam was handsome and caring. Something Ezra never saw in anyone else within the prison, especially his evening guard.

Jazer let Ezra out of his cell for dinner chow. When he wasn't shouting at other prisoners or brandishing his club, he did his best to make Ezra's life a living nightmare. Jazer pulled the cuffs until Ezra's blood flow was cutoff, his skin chafing under the metal. If Ezra walked too slowly, Jazer took pleasure in kicking him in the calf, often throwing Ezra to the ground and faking innocence. The guard never called him by his name, always 'prisoner 1008' or 'inmate' or 'worthless meat.'

The guard had a severe look, his eyes beady and his smile twisted. He was a war vet, and he'd clearly seen some messed up stuff. Ezra hated that the man's anger was taken out on him every day. While Jazer enjoyed spreading his anger around, the man tormented Ezra with special treatment. In the chow hall, Jazer stood in the balcony above, hand on his pistol, eyes digging hawkishly into Ezra.

Ezra quickly developed a sense for when Jazer was near, and his skin pickled as though he were prey tracked by a white wolf. Ezra just minded his own business, though. He withstood Jazer's taunts and dreamt every evening of Sam's soft hands. Until the fight.

Brawls occurred with a certain frequency at Fort Laurent, a simple reality of life in the pen. The guards were always supposed to be mediators, though. They weren't supposed to take sides. Ezra sat at the Black table in his usual spot, eating a boiling brown slush of a meal. The others talked their usual trash, but Ezra drowned them out. He watched as a tall Latino man with a bear tattoo marking his shoulder got up from his table. He made his way over, stalking toward the Black table.

His pace was slow, but his steps held purpose. All Ezra could say was, "Look out!"

The Latino man dug a glass shard into a Black man's rib. Or at least, a Dominican man who'd allied with the Blacks. Apparently, the Latino guy didn't like that one bit. At least, telling by the glass sticking out of his side. The entire chow hall burst into action, the Black table jumping all over the Latino. The fallen Dominican was forgotten in the fury, guards rushing into the madness to pull him away.

The Latino table sped over, defending their brother with furious fists. Then Jazer entered the mix. He did not try to calm the brawl. He did not break up the fight. He just tackled Ezra to the ground, fists raining down upon him.

Ezra could do nothing except throw up his hands in a weak defense. In the chaos, no one noticed Jazer's attack. He knew no one would even care if they did see. The authoritative whistles pierced the air, and a new wave of guards rushed in. Jazer leaped off Ezra and threw him against the wall as if Ezra was the one putting up a fight. Sam came in with the new wave, briefly noting Ezra's bruised body. Sympathy flashed across his face, but he could do nothing but help the others reestablish order.

When Ezra was escorted back to his cell, he limped there in pain.

The promised day arrived—the last day of Ezra's fourth year. The day Sterling's fixer had promised. It began as a standard day. Sam walked up, entered the cell passcode, and said a single word to Ezra, "Djibouti."

Ezra had never heard of the place, "What?"

Sam responded, "Doesn't matter. What am I eating when I visit?"

Ezra held out his arms, Sam lightly doing the cuffs as Ezra answered, "Well, they better have Pirate's Booty with a name like that."

"That's a pitiful joke," the guard replied with a quick chuckle. The sound was calm and melodic.

Ezra walked forward, Sam's steps only a second behind him. They stopped following him only when Ezra entered the chow hall, Sam taking his place among the other guards by the exits. Ezra grabbed his food and sat down. He looked around. He had no clue what he was looking for. *Would another prisoner tell him? Would Ezra be escorted back into the visitor's room, the shady henchman awaiting with Ezra's fate?*

Ezra kept his eyes peeled the entire day for a sign, but none ever arrived. He walked the halls, looking at everyone, scouring everything, his stomach sinking further and further as the hours passed on.

When Jazer threw him roughly into his cell for the evening, and the bars slammed shut behind him, Ezra finally gave up hope.

It was early morning the next day when Ezra called out to the guard stationed near his cell. At first, he got no response.

He tried again, louder, "Ay! I have a request."

"Shut up," is what Ezra got in return.

For the first time, he did not comply. "It's important, man."

"Fine." The guard walked over, staring at Ezra through the bars, his dark gray uniform as drab as the man himself. "What are you whining about?"

"I am requesting an escort," Ezra said as confidently as he could.

'Where?" the guard questioned.

"To the admin office."

"Why?" the guard was still unmoved.

"I have a crime to report."

That got the guard's attention, but his response was still gruff. "Do you?"

"Yeah."

"Okay, lemme call for back up. I'll get Jazer, and we'll go for a walk."

The guard reached for his radio, but Ezra stopped him, "No. I'll only go with Sam."

The guard's face distorted in a wicked smile, "Aww, look who's got a crush on Sammie, now."

Ezra's heart pounded. He wasn't going to be stuck with Jazer tonight as he made his most consequential move of the last five years. He looked up to the guard, softening his voice. "Please."

Ezra will never know what the guard saw, but the man saw his desperation. After dehumanizing him for years, the man saw a shred of Ezra's personhood. He took pity. "Aight, I'll call for 'em."

The guard spoke into the radio, and Sam came a few minutes later.

His face was full of worry, "I heard you called for me. It's way too early for chow."

Ezra was honest. "Yeah. I know, but I'd like you to take me to the admin office. I have a report to file."

Sam's eyebrows raised. "You sure you want to snitch? Ez, I know you know, but that's pretty dangerous. Plus, we guards don't like trouble. Are you going to stir the pot?"

Ezra looked into Sam's concerned face. "No trouble here. Trouble with the outside. I've been quiet too long. I've got a story to tell."

Sam shook his head, entering the cell passcode. "Okay, suit yourself, man. I'll walk you there right now."

He unlocked Ezra's cell. He just held out his wrists as Sam shackled him. He knew the drill. Ezra walked out, nodding a brief thanks to the guard stationed in the hallway. Sam walked behind him, through the halls, out of the first ring and into the second layer. The two passed the gym, yard, and infirmary. The sound of another set of lumbering boots rang out from an adjacent hallway. Ezra's mouth dried in terror.

Jazer turned the corner and entered their hallway. Ezra's chest throbbed with anxiety.

The cruel man's eyes filled with mischief when he spotted the pair. As though he couldn't wait to hurt Ezra however he could. Ezra hoped Sterling hadn't given him orders to put him in a casket. Ezra tried to stand tall, defiant as Jazer spoke up, "Looky here. Looky here. Where you taking 1008, Sammie boy?"

Sam responded, his voice calm, "We're going to the admin office. Apparently, he has some business there."

Jazer looked Ezra up and down, stepping forward, his face inches from Ezra's, "Do you now? And what, pray tell, d'you have going on in the outer ring? Hot date?"

The man's breath was horrendous, but Ezra kept his mouth shut. He knew answering was a trap.

Jazer rubbed his own eye and said, "Ah, feeling quiet in the early morning, I see, huh worthless?"

Sam spoke up, "Jazer, keep moving. Get some rest."

Ezra closed his eyes, quietly begging the man to keep moving.

Finally, he did. Jazer said, "Aight, aight. No worries. Better not give Sam any trouble, 1008. I'll see you in the evening, at our usual time. Don't miss it."

Jazer walked on. Ezra couldn't believe it. Sam pushed Ezra lightly forward, and the two made their way nearer to the admin office. They moved into a deserted hallway, only a couple of lockers lining the wall. They were only a few turns away from the office. The lights were dim for the night shift, but the linoleum floors still squeaked beneath their steps.

Ezra's face smashed into the unforgiving steel lockers. He saw stars, confused. Then he was thrust around, his back pinned, the locks digging into his ribs.

His eyes widened as he looked at Sam, a shiv angled toward Ezra's side. The sweet guard's eyes were no longer kind. They were those of a man with only vicious intent. Sam's voice was different, a roughness bleeding through. "Aldrix Sterling sends his regards, Ez."

That was all he said before burying the knife into Ezra's gut.

Sam's footsteps echoed on the floor. Leaving behind only the shock of his betrayal. Ezra laid crumpled on the ground, face blanched. One hand desperately tried to block the blood seeping out of him. He dragged himself with his other hand, crawling along the ground toward the main hallway. He pulled himself, every drop of his energy focused on making it a few more feet—a few more inches.

Finally, under the harsh lights of the larger hallway, Ezra saw his goal. Sliding himself against the wall, he reached up, two fingers slamming into the emergency assistance button. Ezra knew then his fate was out of his hands. He let his body fall to the ground, his only aim to stem the bleeding.

The guards outside the infirmary whispered loudly to themselves as Ezra laid on the gurney.

"I heard the med team is almost out of blood for all the bags they put into 'im."

Ezra's mind came in and out of consciousness.

"Ridiculous, why are we even trying to save 'em? What good are their lives anyway?"

"Eh, good point, they just gonna end up here again in a few months."

Ezra tried to ignore them, but their voices were the only things keeping him awake.

"Yeah, exactly. What happens if one of us gets injured today? The docs gonna let us bleed out cause this fool took all the blood?"

Ezra couldn't believe he was alive.

He couldn't believe it was sweet Sam.

Sterling owned Sam.

Ezra fell back into unconsciousness.

He never tried to snitch again.

He never tried to love again either.

40

MOVING ON

Stacie wakes up this morning with a strange feeling. Her room is unrecognizable. There are varying-sized cardboard boxes stacked on top of each other in the corner. Her entire wardrobe is folded neatly in rows at the foot of her bed.

She's confused. I *swear everything was normal when I went to sleep,* she thinks. Furrowing her brow, she walks into a similarly empty kitchen and finds Nicky cooking breakfast. *What a nice surprise.* She's glad Nicky is finally taking care of things himself. She's sure he'll grow into a marvelous, independent man one day.

With a "good morning," Stacie takes a seat at the bare kitchen table, determined to supervise the young Nicky. *Never can quite trust kids not to burn themselves, you know.*

With a brief clearing of her throat, Stacie calmly asks, "Nicky, what's happened to the… um… what's the… house?"

He turns to her with two platefuls of eggs and places the dishes down on the table as he says, "We're moving, Aunt Stacie. The movers have been coming this week to pack us up."

Surprised at this news, Stacie replies, "Really? Are we going? Where are we going?"

Then Nicky picks up a rather large box from the chair that she's frankly amazed a child of his age can handle. He takes a seat with her and takes a bite of his breakfast. Only then does he say, "We're moving downtown. There's a nice apartment I've found. I think you'll like it."

Curious but sensing the conversation was over, she takes a bite of her still slightly wet eggs.

Every morning this week, Nick's aunt has woken up and asked him, "What's happened to the house?"

The same exact words. Never varied except for maybe a 'Nicky' in front or a couple of stutters. Every time he tells her that they're moving. It's no longer safe to live here. He patiently explains and reexplains the situation over breakfast, but when she wakes up the next day, she still poses the same question. Today is their last day in the house. Stacie hasn't been to the new apartment yet, but Nick's been back and forth all week.

It's small, but it's right next to the commercial downtown area. Located on the second floor, it has plenty of sunlight and is unfurnished. Nick purposely chose an empty space so he could use his aunt's furniture. Hopefully, that'll make her feel more at home. She'll be confused, but at least she'll still have the reassurance of her ugly brown couch.

The new place isn't perfect, but it was the best place he could get in the quick turnaround. His aunt's house sold in the blink of an eye, but finding a suitable place for her was tricky. He hopes that she likes it. Nick looks at the checklist on his phone. Almost everything's complete. He's just missing two items. He has to turn in his keys to the new owners after cleaning out the basement.

Arriving at the new apartment, Nick begins unpacking the boxes the movers left in the living room while Stacie wanders around and explores. Over the next several days, he feels liberated by his resignation. Nick spends his time looking up other engineering jobs and organizing the new space.

It's still nowhere near complete, but within a week, he's made it livable. He and his aunt are sleeping with sheets on their beds and plates in the cupboard, so they can save the art and rugs for later.

Still, he can't believe his aunt will live out the rest of her days outside of the comfort of her home. Nick is glad he will have the buffer of the house money to take care of the new rent and meds for his aunt, but he knows she had wanted to die in that house.

Nick reflects on how odd homes are. People live in them for years but abandon them on a whim. They are simply shells, shelter from the rains and wind. Over the lifetime of a house, several inhabitants will make memories there. It may bear the marks of these inhabitants—a new paint job, a pockmark in the brick, or a stain on the wall—but these can always disappear with repairs. However, the memories of the inhabitants will always be inextricably linked to that physical place.

When Nick went to close the door to his childhood home once more, the ghosts of a lifetime's worth of memories waved him goodbye.

41

NOTHING TO WORRY ABOUT

John knocks on his boss' door and hears Mr. Sterling's voice call, "Come in!"

When Apollo swings the door open to let him in, it makes a small screeching noise that John feels perfectly expresses his anxiety at this exact moment. Before even forming the words on his lips, Aldrix Sterling sighs. "What's wrong this time, John?"

John is unsure of what his boss' connection between concerning events and him means for his job security, but it certainly isn't good. So he begins by trying to soften the blow and thus change the narrative. He tries to massage the story. He isn't the bearer of bad news, simply the diplomatic messenger.

He opens with, "I have been made aware of a report there is another large demonstration planned this weekend, sir." He swallows hard and continues, "The estimates are that it will be double the size of the last two."

"And?" Sterling replies, eyes still on his laptop screen. "It's just a few people yelling to themselves in the streets. Why does it matter to me how many of them there are?"

"Well, sir. It seems it may not be a peaceful interaction," John says, voice unsteady.

Exasperated, Aldrix looks up at John and asks, "Why not? A few months ago, those fools of security guards botched it, but it wasn't too bad. A few bodies and a couple of injuries, but nothing alarming, right? Plus, the protesting idiots started it, so it wasn't our fault."

John nods in agreement, "All strong points, sir. But this time, there seems to be a third side of the engagement. There has been internet conversation regarding a group of Sterling employees who are supportive of you and the company. They plan on conducting a counterprotest at the same time and location in front of the gates."

"That's excellent news, John. We finally have some people with some spine around here."

"I—um, yes, sir. That is one interpretation, but it just makes things... likely less predictable, sir."

Aldrix turns back to his work, unbothered. "Understood. But it doesn't have anything to do with me, John. Just tell the guards to protect the front gates and let the weak do what they must."

"Of course, sir."

Sitting in his high-backed leather chair on the seventy-fifth floor of his empire, Aldrix Sterling is trying to return to his work, but the report continuously latches onto his mind.

His request to Liam was to ensure another protest like the one weeks ago didn't happen again. He hopes his counterpart is more cunning than John's concerns make him sound.

He has built his business on security. He has always perceived himself to be quite safe and his business quite stable. The winds of fate may toss and turn him, but his personal safety is carefully guarded. The security of his business is too.

Although, in the current circumstances, he can't help but question the objective security of a tower made of glass.

Aldrix Sterling closes his eyes. There's work to be done. He can't dwell on this. As if trying to convince himself, he mutters, "It's nothing to worry about."

Picking up his pen once more, he continues working while the wind howls outside.

42

OUR MOMENT. OUR CITY. OUR FUTURE.

The spotlight was brighter than anything Emerald had ever known. It was as if the night sky had opened up and angels pointed all the starlight directly onto her. The crowd was deeper than she'd ever seen. The rows were seemingly infinite, a sea of supporters she could never hope to fully thank. The noise was sharper than she'd ever heard. The cheers rose to a decibel level beyond most concerts.

In spite of it all, she felt like a goddess.

Silva! Silva! Silva! Silva!

The energy in the arena was incredible. Tonight was her last chance. Her last attempt to sway voters for tomorrow's election. The final opportunity to prove they should not discount her. Her face was projected across the stadium. She tapped the mic. Many prepared to listen to their candidate, but still, the shouts of excitement rang out.

"Thank you. Thank you. I'm so proud to be in front of you today."

Thousands called out their love, a sea of camera phones bobbing before her.

"My dear friends, I am here before you today not for want of power or privilege. I have no desire for prestige, nor do I hunger with greed. I am here because I am one of you. I claim no divine right or superpower. I simply dare to see beyond the present in favor of a bold future.

My opponent wishes only to further institutionalize the status quo. He has grown complacent, his pockets swelling to the tune of the corporations and his pen beholden to the whims of the elite.

Our movement rejects that model. We reject the idea wisdom only comes from the top. That money is equal to worth, that competence is a market cornered by those with power.

Our vision offers something greater.

Tonight is for Marianna, an educator who funded her class library from her own pocket. The library from which dozens of children learned to read.

Our movement is for Horton, the fisherman who was denied loans to expand his business. Not for lack of success, but because his address had the wrong zip code.

We work together for Celeste, a brilliant Laurel League student who interned for this campaign. Someone that many may say has it all, but who has a loved one struggling with addiction. We fight for a healthcare system that will treat her loved one with respect, not as though they are a plague on this community.

We advocate for an education system that will find the talent inside each of us and promote a labor market that rewards us equally for those skills.

So tonight, I invite you to dream. And as we dream together, I ask that you see our city's thriving future.

Imagine a sea that shines, its waters crystal clear. Envision a city of stars, glittering in a night sky free of pollution.

Let us dream of a city where regardless of where you come from, anyone can succeed. Where automation and energy transition are not a threat to jobs, but an opportunity to climb higher.

Let us believe in a system of carbon taxation, one that reduces our emissions and is used to invest in our neighbors. Imagine a time where no block is red-lined, and no one fears for their life walking home.

Let us create this vision together, not out of spite for the generations that came before us, but out of hope for the generations ahead.

In our future, wealth will not dictate potential.

Addresses will not be determinants of a lifespan.

Nature will not be something to subdue. It will be a friend we embrace.

As many of you know, I was not born in this city. Many call me an outsider, a Droughtie, a fraud, and many more unspeakable slurs. They cast doubt on my experience, saying I'm too young. They slander me for the sole reason that my gender differs from many of their own. So let me set the record straight.

They are right. I was not born in this city. A drought-caused fire destroyed our home, forcing my family to move here. A drought made more likely by the very smokestacks allowed to spew their venom into our skies day in and day out. So yes, I was not born here, but I have made this place my home even when it has not wanted me.

They say I am too young, so be it. My elders are wise, and I keep astute advisors, but I have never accepted the idea that innovation has an age requirement. I have served in our proud state government for years, and my age has never been a barrier to empathy. To respect. To meeting people where they are and believing them when they share their stories. Those are the skills that a mayor needs, not a lifetime spent crunching numbers for billionaires. Our leaders need to be listeners first.

I am here because I listened. I listened all the times my parents' dreams went dismissed. I listened to the fictitious reasons they cast my community aside. I listened to every one of you who was brave enough to share a memory with me.

I heard when you cried, hospital bills stacking up. I heard when you called, fear in your voice as you watched job prospects dwindle. I heard when you laughed, smiling at your incredible children who beat the odds.

After all this time listening, I am ready to speak. And I say it is time for a new generation of leadership, one lead by the values of love, kindness, and creativity. This city is long overdue for a period of unity, inspiration, and opportunity.

Everyone I meet asks me the same question: *who am I?*

For me, that is simple.

I am a mosaic of my memories, a patchwork of stories spanning generations, the aspiration of everyone who has paved my path. And so are all of you. Together we represent not just ourselves, but all those whom we love, whoever loved us. We are made of shared sunrises, reckless days, and tearful nights. In each of us is a mixture of fears, and hopes, and failures. We all consist of the sweat of our forebearers, the hopes of our parents, and the gratitude of our children.

This great city was nothing just a hundred years ago. And then, one day, someone decided to put down their stake. They built with a vision in mind, seeing beyond a couple of brick houses toward a bright future that we now live in. Over the past several years, this vision has been lost. Our city has strayed from the path ahead. We are indebted to those of the past whose shoulders carried the weight of despair. Who built our beautiful city in the hope we would realize the utopia they had in their mind.

Those now in power spit on that vision. They want to deny us that future, that shining hill. History will prove them wrong.

This is *our* moment.

This is *our* city.

Together, we will build *our* future."

Though Emerald said the words, thousands of voices echoed her. Together, they repeated the line.

"Our Moment. Our City. Our Future."

They repeated the words over and over again, the sound rising up into the night.

Their collective chant became one voice, one hope, one prayer calling out to the universe.

Emerald closed her eyes, and for a moment, she let herself feel invincible.

Emerald wakes up, the memory fading in the morning light. She will never forget her triumph, but now it feels so out of touch. Her city is falling apart, and she is so incredibly powerless to help. She thought she could make a difference, but she knew nothing of the puppet she would become. How much others would challenge her values.

When she came in, the city didn't understand how to care for people. They let their own walk the streets at night, without food or housing. They discriminated ruthlessly, the powerful dictating everyone's portions. It is different now.

Her housing policies are earning more people reasonable loans. Her community policing initiative and mental health units are decreasing deaths of despair. People look at her with gratitude in their eyes.

But now Emerald understands, she only finds success where it is allowed. Where Sterling and her other faceless masters have already paved the road. She is the one who makes the city hope. They want the people to think that progress has come. That a woman mayor and a new generation can hold the threads of power. She is just a pawn.

As long as she is under their thumbs, nothing will change. She needs a way out.

43

FREEDOM

Rodrigo sits on his usual bus, watching the lives of his neighbors through the window. Even though his eyes are seeing them, he isn't as engaged by the everyday miracles as usual. Today his mind is too busy thinking about how quick people have become to judge. As he ate breakfast, he watched the continued coverage of the leak. It still dominates the city's papers and TV stations. But, he watched as Aldrix came on TV and addressed the city. Unlike so many, Rodrigo believed him when he said he was sorry.

Aldrix apologized. Why can't people give him a little mercy? Sure, he's a bit arrogant, but he has the right to be. He manages one of the most successful businesses in the history of the city.

If you ask Rodrigo, all the protesters are just jealous. He understands accidents happen. It's the fault of the maintenance crew, not Aldrix. The city just wants to use anything they can get to criticize one of the wealthiest men in town.

His friends online think the same. Those who haven't lost their loyalty to Sterling have been posting their support. Aldrix has provided for them. They're ready to step up for him. So, here he is. On his way to work. Looking at the houses powered by Sterling Energies. The cars fill up with gas from the very oil pipeline they're calling to remove.

Rodrigo has liked living in this country because of the freedom it provides. *If the protesters had their way, wouldn't that restrict the liberty they so desperately love?*

Rodrigo isn't a lawyer, but it seems that limiting the resources people are allowed to use is restricting their rights. When Rodrigo gained his citizenship, he had to learn about the constitution of this country. It fascinated him, and he came to love it. He came to love the guarantees it provides. The protections it outlines. He appreciated how passionate this new society was about remaining loyal to its principles and honoring its words. It pains him to see those words don't matter quite as much as he thought.

The protesters are the ones breaking the rules. They're the ones questioning the freedom to use any means necessary to progress society. Why isn't that the breaking news?

As he gets off the bus, he sees the signs outside of the building have grown ever more vicious. "Sterling deserves death" and "Tear down the tower" are plastered in large font nearest the entrance. He can't help but take the insults addressed to Aldrix personally.

At the end of the day, he is going to retire soon. This job is still providing him with a strong foundation for the rest of his life, just as it has given him stability throughout the last four decades. Soon, he'll get to walk away from this mess. The protestors can continue attacking Sterling Energies for all he cares. The climate can change. By the time any of this comes to a head, he and his wife will be enjoying their liberty from work and looking forward to spending time with the grandkids.

He loves his children and his family more than anything in the world. He didn't come all the way to this country to have them living their lives under a state so regulated that accidents become criminalized. *Why can't people just be grateful for the amazing services Sterling provides?*

Now entering the locker room, Rodrigo looks around at his fellow coworkers. They aren't the monsters they're made out to be. They're just working hard to attain the futures that they want for themselves. They're just playing by the rules.

44

BATTLE LINES

Nick finds himself back in front of the looming skyscraper he called his office for too many years. This time, he's not here to flick a few switches or fix any machinery. He's here to protest, and he isn't alone. Nick squeezes his way through the crowd under an overcast sky, the yells incoherent, lacking a leading voice. He can see the unremarkable door he used to enter, bile rising within him in disgust.

People call out random phrases.

"Down with Sterling!"

"He destroyed our sea!"

Nick continues forward but trips right as he makes it to the front.

Boom. Boom. Boom

Nick scrapes his palm on the ground, but he shakes it off, pushing to his knees.

Boom. Boom. Boom

The ground rumbles. And then he is slammed back by a riot shield.

Dozens of people in black pummel the front line of the protest, not police, but armed just as heavily. In unison, they stomp on the ground.

Boom. Boom. Boom.

The newcomers scream profanities at the initial protestors, and a man looms over Nick, spitting at him. He shoves Nick to his knees.

A new line forms, protestors on one side, Sterling supporters on the other. The guards take it all in stoically from the top of the marble stairs.

Nick gets up, pushing back against the man's riot shield. "What was that? Why are you defending Sterling?" Nick screams over the din.

From behind the safety of his plastic shield, the man replies, "Get out of my face, man."

Nick does no such thing. "Tell me right now. Why the hell are you supporting a multimillionaire that doesn't care about you one bit."

The man thrusts his shield at Nick, but he stays on his feet. He was ready that time. "Tell me. Why are you doing this?"

Finally, the man responds, but he does so in rage. His veins pop from his neck as he roars, "Because Sterling is the only one who seems to understand how this city works. He provides jobs for everyone I know. So why don't you take your snob self back to your mansion? Sterling is a man of the people."

Boom. Boom. Boom.

The man hits his palm against the shield once more, along with dozens of others who are clearly outnumbered but far more organized.

Nick glances down the line and watches hundreds of more protesters engaged in similar one-to-one battles of rage. Some pushing one another, punching, screaming slurs.

A man next to Nick crumples to the ground. A bat flies by Nick's head as one of the men clad in black beats the protester with his baton.

And for a second, everyone in the crowd pauses and looks at this one encounter. This one middle-aged man, in shock but shielding his daughter from the merciless blows of a man dressed black as night. Then finally, the middle-aged man collapses fully. His daughter kneeling over him with tears streaming down her face. The reaction is ballistic. Nick scrambles away as glass is thrown all around him. A rock glides in front of his face, barely missing him.

With a glance, he looks at the staircase of guards. They stand aside, doing absolutely nothing. He watches as a protestor leaps onto the back of a man in black, punching his head furiously. Nick runs to the only place he knows, the side entrance of Sterling. He fumbles for his wallet and thanks God that he kept his ID. He frantically places his badge on the scanner, praying that it'll work.

The machine only takes a moment to process, but as the wails and fighting grow at his back, it feels like forever. The green finally flashes, and Nick throws himself into the building, the heavy metal door muffling the sounds of the outside. He slumps against the door, his nerves unable to calm as he hears the crowds outside begin to reform. The chants reemerge on both sides, still muffled but relentless.

Nick moves deeper into his old building. He tries to put as much distance between him and the roars outside as possible.

45

LESSONS LEARNED

John enters Aldrix's office more scared than he usually is. He just focuses on getting in and out as fast as humanly possible. He greets his boss, crossing the room to hand him the report. "Sir, I have this quarter's earnings readout for you."

"Excellent, thank you, John."

Taking the elegantly printed package, Aldrix pauses for a second to open the folder. John whirls on his heels, heading back to the door. Aldrix senses his discomfort and asks, "Anything of note?"

John's heart drops to his stomach as he turns back toward Aldrix and says, "Ah, um. Yes, I do believe you'll find it… informative, sir."

Aldrix's eyebrows raise at that. "Is that right?"

"Yes, sir, if you'll excuse me," Johns says, trying once more to take his leave.

Aldrix's voice booms back, "Tell me what is so informative about the contents of this package, John, before you slink off like the spineless swine you are."

John blanches. He answers and does his best to remain calm, "Flip to page four, sir. It lists our revenue against our estimates of top competitors… and, well, Alteryn, the clean um, the alternative energy company. Their revenue has grown significantly this quarter."

All Aldrix said back was, "I see. What else?"

Not daring to move, John says, "Of course, we are still investigating whether to purchase them, but by the time that tech company finishes the algorithm, it might be too late."

Voice steady but face tight, Aldrix asks John one more question, "How screwed are we?"

John has no clue what to say to that, but he evidently says the wrong thing. "Well, it seems... it seems an increasing number of our customers are deciding to transition to their services. Their stock has soared after the leak. We are, um, losing—"

"Get out, John."

"Yes, sir, right away."

From this height, only the mob below is visible, not the countless individual faces betraying him and his family after relying on them for decades. Aldrix looks out from the seventy-fifth floor once again, at the energy pulsing through the city's veins as the afternoon light fades and the night takes over. Clouds cover the sky. The days have grown short. So has his patience. He makes a decision.

Aldrix grabs the intricate key card that lays in the glass box beside him. Then he slides open his desk drawer, grabbing the item inside. He makes for the basement. Apollo instantly falls in line behind him. Aldrix waves him off. "Give me five minutes before you follow. This I'm doing myself." He startles the other executives on the floor as he bursts out of his office. He marches past their inquisitive faces, determined.

He presses the elevator button. And when it doesn't open immediately, he jabs it again and again. The elevator doors finally cleave open as his rage builds. He presses the basement level and paces the elegant box as he plummets down. He arrives to a normal scene, his workers going about their business as they ought to. Except here, he can hear the crowd gathered outside, the roar of their cheers. Their ignorant defiance. Their ungrateful, spiteful whining. But also his supporters, railing against the others.

"Tear down the tower!"

"Tear down the tower!"

Then come the responses. "Sterling forever! Energy's a necessity!"

He scans the room of shifting gears and mechanical marvels, strutting into the control room. Rodrigo greets him, but Sterling ignores it.

"Tear down the tower! WOOOO!"

Sensing the anger, Rodrigo simply shrugs.

"Get out of this room, Rodrigo. And tell everyone to go home right now." Tentatively, the older man rises, leaving the control room.

"Tear down the tower!"

Sterling taps his key card to the main monitor, and the map of the city's power grid appears on the screen. It is a sight to behold, the enormity of power being generated at any given moment, and all because of him. Not the idiots outside.

"Sterling! Sterling! Sterling!"

With that last despicable cry, Sterling grabs the keyboard and types in the command he's always kept in his back pocket. Just in case.

Sterling takes a deep breath, then presses enter.

The roars outside turn to screams.

Even from inside, Nick knows something happened. The shrieks from outside chill his blood as they increase to a wholly new level. He continues away from the door, hoping to barricade himself in his old office until things calm down. Nick walks down the corridor and hears dozens of feet running up the stairs. He flattens himself against to side of the hallway, waiting until they all pass by. Only after a few seconds does he keep moving, the basement level now seemingly abandoned.

Nick is greeted by a familiar face when he walks into the control room. "Mr. Sterling?"

The man whirls around, releasing his grip on the master keycard.

Apollo now appears behind Nick, instantly shutting the door behind him. The huge man stands right behind Nick, his presence lurking.

"No way," Nick begins in disbelief. *That's what must've happened.*

Nick has never seen Aldrix without his cool demeanor. Now his face twists with rage. "This is what they deserve. Let them fumble around in the dark. Let them have a taste of life without their comforts."

Nick shouts back, "You're insane! Did you see that crowd out there? They're going to rip each other to pieces."

Aldrix turns to look directly at Nick, his motions terrifying in their composure. "I didn't need to see the crowd. I know what the masses look like."

Nick takes a step forward as he says, "No, you don't. You have no clue what your actions do to everyday people. The harm you cause to people like my aunt."

"Oh please, Nick," Aldrix says dismissively. "There are a thousand reasons why your aunt could have developed dementia. It happens every day."

"Not to hundreds of people in the same neighborhood you dumped waste in. That's not a coincidence."

Aldrix shows no sympathy. "I'm sorry, Nick. But even if your aunt unfortunately felt the impact, that was my father's doing, not mine."

Nick shakes his head, refusing the excuse. "Just cause you didn't do it to her doesn't mean you're not harming others. And I already told you I don't accept your apology."

Aldrix looks at Nick with a pained expression, "You were an excellent team member and a strong manager. Why did you have to throw that away? And why did you sneak yourself in here tonight."

"I did both for the same reason, to escape your messes," Nick quips back.

"Well, clearly, it didn't work," Aldrix says.

Nick's words are bold, his gestures brash as he says, "It'll work when I tell the press you purposefully shut down the city."

"That's not how this is going to go," Aldrix says with the surety of a king.

Nick twists, pointing to Apollo as he says, "You always say that because you have your henchmen to do your dirty work for you. Are you going to have Apollo beat me up? Roughen me up, so you don't have to bruise your precious knuckles?"

Apollo steps forward to seize Nick, but Aldrix raises his hand.

With searing sarcasm, Nick says, "Thank you. That's what I thought. Tonight it's just you and me. There's no one to hide behind. And you'll finally have to face the music."

Nick turns to leave, but Apollo blocks his path.

"Don't turn your back on me, Nicholas," Aldrix's voice commands. "I made you."

Nick looks Apollo dead in the eyes, and the larger man moves aside. Nick goes to grab the door handle, but Aldrix has one final thing to say, "Well, then I guess I still have one option..."

The bullet blows through Nick's back before he even knew it was coming.

Sterling hands the weapon to Apollo and walks out of the room.

From this height, Sterling can't see a thing. Back in the comfort and safety of his office, he looks out over the normally familiar view and sees a void of his own creation.

He hopes they learn their lesson.

PART III

INTERLUDE II

HOME

"Artemis III, set for launch in T minus ten, nine, eight…"

The Commander closes her eyes. In a few minutes, she and her crewmates will either be dead or their dreams will come true. She rubs the torch tattoo marking her wrist. The ignition sequence begins, the rumbling shaking her body.

"Seven, six…"

She looks toward her Mission Specialist next to her. His expression is complete determination.

"Five, four…"

On her right side, the Flight Engineer's face is at peace. He is at home among the rattling.

"Three, two…"

The Commander looks out the window and takes in the light blue. She glances at the mountains in the distance.

"One, launch."

She is thrown back in her chair, her limbs suddenly weighing a thousand pounds. All of her focus is on the dashboard, projected onto the fortified glass in front of her.

All she sees is the blue sky above her. It steadily becomes darker.

Light blue.

The engine rages around her, the sound incredible.

Royal blue

Her entire body vibrates.

Cobalt.

The Commander jolts as their ship pierces the sound barrier.

Navy.

She tries to take a deep breath.

Midnight.

Pitch-black.

The engine cuts out.

Silence.

Simultaneously, the entire crew unbuckles. They push off their chairs and float around the room. The Commander picks her pen from the air and places it on the Velcro of her dash.

She moves into the interior of the ship, followed closely by her two counterparts. The Flight Engineer does a flip in the air and lets out a laugh. The Commander smiles at his jovial spirit, then looks at the Mission Specialist. He does not smile. He just floats next to the glass of the exterior dome, his body silhouetted, awe on his face. The two others join him, and they, too, are enraptured by the magnificence below. For the first time, they all truly see their home. A single blue speck among an expanse of darkness.

The sun peeks over the horizon, bathing the edge of the earth in an orange tint, the light blue of the atmosphere as thin as a razor.

Then the indescribable happens.

Green and blue dance around the earth, swinging toward their ship. It looks as though wind spirits dance with one another in the heavens.

The aurora borealis fills their view, the Commander's eyes well. The unheralded majesty that moves above them is unmatched by anything she's ever seen.

No one speaks.

Reverence hangs in the air.

Minutes go by, the crew simply stunned.

The colors swirling in the sky.

The lights almost look like a hologram, something so perfect they must be artificial. Nothing humanmade is this spectacular, though. The blue marble that hangs suspended above them is gorgeous. She can barely believe it is home. Finally, one of them speaks, barely a whisper of a question, "How are we ever going to convey this to everyone down there?"

The words hang in the air for several seconds before another dares to answer. "We never will."

The Commander stays quiet. The view is extraordinary.

Breathtaking.

She has been preparing for this moment for months. Now, for the first time in a while, she thinks. Not about logistics or systems or astrophysics. She relaxes her body and tries to fathom how unbelievably miniscule she is.

Their mission is simple: prepare the moon for the next generation of explorers. They will set it up as a hub. The future dock for launches to Mars. To build a bridge into the future. To tame the immaculate hostility of the darkness around her. She believes wholeheartedly in that mission. She believed in it when she was still just a kid playing with toy rockets, with an oversized helmet on her head. When she first envisioned the world, not as it was but as it could be.

Her team will achieve the extraordinary. She will contribute to a legacy of interplanetary humans. It will be an accomplishment shared by all of humanity.

But now that she's here, floating above the highest mountains and looking down into the deepest valleys, something else becomes apparent.

No matter how many future planets humanity finds, there will only be one home.

46

ALONE

Stacie wakes up in a strange place surrounded by familiar things. Her bedroom is not the one she has always known, but the sheets are her own. The kitchen is different, but her beloved mugs are the same.

This is definitely her home.

Maybe I just had an odd dream about spending a lifetime in a house with a porch and a backyard where the boys used to swing. That always had been a goal of hers.

Speaking of which, where are the boys? Maybe Nick's around.

"Nicky!" she calls.

No one responds.

"Anyone, um… um… home?"

Ah! Why is it so hard for the words to come out! Why don't they sound the same as they do in her head? She's so tired of reaching for the ghosts of words she once knew.

Stacie leaves the kitchen, padding over to the bedroom, but finds it empty. The bed has pillows tossed to the side and a sheet hanging loosely off the mattress.

Ugh. Nicky left his bed completely a mess. She'll have to talk with him when he comes back from school.

Until then, she intends to enjoy the peace and quiet. Before he comes home and she has to fight him to make the bed.

He's such a mess, her sweet boy. Her love. Her, N—Ni—hmm. What's the name? Ugh, well, him.

So, she just puts on some tea and sits in her usual seat, waiting for *him* to come home.

47

TAP. TAP. TAP.

Tap. Tap. Tap.

Rain falls across a city engulfed in darkness. The droplets beat against windows and crash into the asphalt below. From the air, it is beautiful. But right now, no one stops to recognize the beauty because of the danger in the streets. The splendor of nature does nothing to stop humanity from tearing itself apart.

Tap. Tap. Tap.

Ezra bounces his foot against the floor as Meg once again steers them violently to another call in the darkness.

He fidgets with his backpack, checking each pocket again and again. According to Meg, "Anyone checking their materials last minute is bound to be missin' somethin'." After triple-checking the flashlight batteries, he tries to calm the nerves. He can't do anything to turn the lights back on. Nothing except for rotating between stress snacking, staring at the walls, and trying to care for everyone who has been injured in the blackout. There are plenty. Everything from people in the fight at Sterling Square to people falling down stairs and getting into car crashes. Meg warned Ezra tonight would be a long one.

Ezra does his best to keep himself alert. He just needs to get through the night. He has more important things ahead.

Tap. Tap. Tap.

Emerald watches the rain hit the glass.

She has been instructed by her security team not to leave her office. The whole of City Hall is on lockdown. The power generator is up and running, though. Someone informed her the situation outside was "unpredictable and too risky."

How is she supposed to just sit here dry, with power flowing through the outlets while peering out across dimmed houses?

So fine. If security won't let her out of her room, she'll take another route. One that hopefully ends this whole mess. She picks up the phone.

When the voice answers on the other end, she tells them the truth—all of it.

Beep... beep... beep

The steady rhythm of the lifeline led to Sierra nodding off almost immediately, and Lucas can see why.

The hum of the machine next to his arm and the reassuring pulse of the EKG is calming. Sierra cuddles next to her mom on the gurney, Lucas dozes in the side chair.

Humm...

When he turned off the lights and pulled the curtain a few minutes ago, it really was very easy to nod off. The only thing keeping in awake is the soft vibrations of the life-support against his arm.

Humm...

He just relaxes in peace, eyes closed. He picks up Sierra from Suzuka's bedside. Placing Sierra on his chest, he feels his daughter's heart beating against his.

Humm...

Lucas' eyes feel heavier. Something makes Lucas pause. Eyes still closed, he feels like something's missing. The hum is gone. Lucas snaps his head up and finds the monitor blank. Suzuka lies just as peacefully as ever, but Lucas jolts to his feet. Sierra bursts awake and screams in his arms. As gently but quickly as possible, Lucas places Sierra in the cradle next to him. Then he rushes to throw open the curtain of Suzuka's room for help and finds pitch-blackness.

A few other forms are moving around in adjacent rooms, clearly desperate to save their own loved ones. But there is nothing to see. The entire hospital is absent of life. Lucas runs. *There must be a backup generator. Aren't those supposed to come on after a few seconds? What's happening?*

The lights flicker back on, and for a moment, the hall sparks to life. Lucas sees a group of nurses at the desk ahead of him.

Then it all shuts off again.

Lucas races forward, bumping into the nurses' desk. There is nothing they can do.

The lights flicker, but in an instant, they're gone.

It takes four minutes for the generator to kick in. Suzuka's heartbeat never does.

48

DREAMSCAPE

Suzuka's body lies in the darkness of a hospital room. Her daughter snuggled next to her and Lucas at her bedside.

Her breaths are shallow.

Though her mind registers Sierra's movement, Suzuka cannot react. She falls into her dreams. The landscape in her mind is as vivid as any of her paintings.

She pictures a young woman dressed in a plain white blouse, a bracelet studded with blue stones around her wrist. The young lady stands straight-backed and proud before a skyscraper, the top obscured by layers of clouds.

Suzuka's breath hitches.

A vision of Sierra, no longer a child. She is the woman Suzuka has fought her whole life for. Surrounding her daughter is a world of green. The sea sparkles under the morning sun as electric vehicles roll beneath the crisp, clear air.

Trees line the streets, their flowers bright. Parks weave through the blocks, the city leveraging both the ingenuity of humans and the gifts of nature. People stroll calmly down pedestrian paths, bikes zooming by on a curbside track.

Suzuka floats above, admiring the future she imagines for her daughter. It is a scene she longs to paint, the cityscape embedded within nature.

Suzuka stops breathing.

She begins to pull away, climbing higher into the air. Desperately she tries to claw her way back to the ground, toward the image of her daughter.

The world goes dark.

49

WINDOWPAIN

Lucas sits in front of the window of the hospital's cafeteria. The lights are now back on. He sits with Sierra in his arms, staring out at nothing. He is aware of the plumes of smoke that rise from the city center, a glow of orange beginning to fade near Sterling Tower. He sees the red and blue lights reflect in puddles as ambulances come in and out of the hospital entrance. He doesn't process any of it. All he can think about is the silence. The absence of the hum. It's the deepest silence he's ever heard.

Sierra cries. She may not know what happened, but she feels the weight on her father's shoulders. He vows to honor his wife. He quits. With just a few taps, he sends the email to his boss. It's over. Forget project RENEW.

With just a few more, he writes to Alteryn:

My name is Lucas Maamoun, and you need to believe me. Please. I don't know everything, but these words are important. I did not believe someone who told me while she could. And now, you have to believe me.

Lucas tries to sound professional, to be convincing, but his desperation shows through.

I have been made aware that Sterling Energies may approach you offering to purchase your company and expand your services. Don't believe them. That corporation is vile. Their words are worth nothing. While they may offer to invest millions to scale your company and bring renewables to the city, I don't believe it for a second. I have no doubt they instead mean to slow your operations, control your board, and obliterate your vision.

His words are part drive, part anger, part hope for what is to come.

If Sterling's recent speech is any indication, I wouldn't be surprised if he blamed the failure on shortcomings with your technology or limitations of cleantech. But I won't let him.

For the past few months, I was contracted by Sterling to assess your company. I weighed your chances for success using a machine learning algorithm. Sterling wished to acquire your company and bring our city into the future. But here's the clearest warning I can give: your chances are zero if you accept his offer.

Lucas' fingers tap furiously on the screen as he finishes the note.

Between the oil spill, blackout, and my personal experiences, I have not found a single redeemable quality in the corporation or the man. Where you are energized by a shared future, a healthy future, Sterling is fueled by greed. That company must be eviscerated.

I am frustrated. I have been lied to. And I have been personally devastated by that twisted organization. Please give me a chance to fight back. I'll do whatever I can to help. Though, I will fight for that future regardless of your help. I will do absolutely whatever it takes to build a better world for my daughter. For the future my wife believed in.

Lucas Maamoun

50

GHOST TOWN

The lights have returned the morning after the blackout, but the remnants of the damage litter the avenues. After a fourteen-hour shift, Ezra leaves the hospital and passes Sterling Tower to the metro. In the street, there are dozens of firefighters helping to clean up the mess out front. Burnt out trash bins and discarded metal fencing, glass covering the ground, and some blood splattering the way. They will clean it—one piece at a time.

That is not the case when Ezra emerges from the train and walks through his mom's neighborhood: His home.

A stalled-out car sits on the side of the road, the front clearly wrecked. A few of the storefronts are busted, glass dotting the sidewalk. Some smoke still rises from smoldering fires from tires in the street. There is no help.

Ezra arrives at the door of his mom's apartment, swinging it open with anxiety.

"Mom?"

The news plays in the background, images of fires and ambulances displayed on rotation, "**The cause of the outage is still unknown, but Sterling Energies is set to give a statement in the coming minutes, detailing the incident.**"

His mom answers, "Ez?"

Ezra hugs her tightly. "Thank goodness you're okay."

Mumbling into his shoulder, she says, "Yep baby, I just stayed in the house, but I heard Carla down the street done got her knee messed up, banging it on sumthin' in the dark. You think you could give her a visit? Work that medicine magic? You know none of your colleagues were rolling through here last night."

"Of course, mom, just glad you're okay," Ezra replies.

"Oh, you'd know if I wasn't okay. I wouldn't be quiet about that," his mom says with a chuckle.

Despite his complete exhaustion, Ezra has to smile at that.

Right as he is about to turn to visit Carla, the TV begins displaying the faces of some who passed away in the night, a hastily made *in memoriam*. Ezra pauses, taking a moment to think about some of the people he treated that he doubts made it through. Sure enough, he recognizes two of the faces that fade onto the screen. But then Ezra's stomach drops.

Nick's piercing blue eyes appear on the screen, and Ezra's knees go completely weak. He begins shaking uncontrollably.

He obscures his face from his mom as the image fades and a camera pans to a stage inside Sterling Tower. Keeping his voice as controlled as possible, Ezra says, "Mom, turn up the volume, please."

She does, and the moment Sterling opens his mouth, Ezra feels something is deeply wrong. He has no proof, but when he looks into Sterling's eyes, he sees the same steel as the day he met Aldrix's father in the forest.

Aldrix has always hated the lights at these ridiculous press events. Sweat drips down his back as the heat beams down on his suit. It's unbearably uncomfortable. He gives the speech nonetheless:

"My fellow residents, last night our city experienced a tragedy. Dozens of lives were unnecessarily lost, thugs vandalized our beautiful streets, and fires were set to the homes of the innocent. This was a complete disaster, and it came about as a result of the dangerous mob that came with violent intent against Sterling Energies last evening."

Sterling scrunches his face in exaggerated anger for the cameras, "In their chaotic and vengeful fury, this group of spiteful individuals threw projectiles at our complex. As always, the professionalism of our guards and the city's authorities shone through, and they practiced restraint. However, several individuals launched flaming objects toward the building, shattering glass and setting a fire inside our halls. Unfortunately, this happened to damage some of our key grid computational infrastructure, resulting in the outage that we all witnessed last night."

He relaxes, calm returning and gratitude entering his voice. "It is only because of the expertise of the Sterling staff we were able to bring the entire grid back online at 3:26 a.m. These hardworking men and women toiled through the night to undo the damages of the mob and restore the light to our town. They are the heroes."

He continues, his tone reflecting the warning he seeks to give. "The villains are those that would seek to package their hate under the guise of progress. Those inspired by our competitor Alteryn, who point fingers at this company that has provided power to our city for decades. Now, I would never go so far as to blame our competitors for what were clearly the actions of a few wayward actors. However, those who advocate for radicalism must understand the weight their words hold."

Once again, he pivots, softening his eyes in understanding. He brings the audience into the conversation, sharing their pain and humoring those sympathetic to the fools who attacked his empire. "Sterling Energies is not opposed to progress. We innovate every day so you as a consumer can enjoy warm meals with your family and enjoy a movie night with your friends."

Sterling speaks with confident conviction, knowing his words must placate millions. "We accept change must come. Sterling is proud to be developing energy sources that will bring our city into the future, but it cannot come at the cost of lives today."

Wielding the full force of his charisma, he looks directly through the camera and into the hearts of those watching. "So please join me in thanking our first responders, Sterling staff members, and good Samaritans who showed their bravery in the midst of chaos last night. But, let us also condemn those who brought our city to its knees yesterday and whose ideology must not be spread.

"Thank you."

51

A CANDID CONVERSATION

Rodrigo is driven home by his daughter in the morning light, having spent the blackout in the comfort of her electrified suburban home. The road is slick with water, so Lucia does her best to drive safely. Her eyebrows furrow with the concentration required as she avoids glaring puddles. The wind blows lightly outside, and small raindrops drizzle around them. The windshield wiper swings back and forth, clearing a line of vision for Lucia.

Rodrigo takes a second to admire his grown daughter. Even though he sees her monthly for dinner, he often feels her guardedness during those visits. That she steels herself each time to give the precise answers that she imagines they want from her. He sees how her shoulders are tense around him. Her movements are always so precise, never relaxed as she was in her younger years.

Maybe it's the setting. Maybe being in her childhood house causes Lucia to revert back to her old desire to please her parents at all costs. Or maybe it's him. Rodrigo often wishes they could have more heart-to-hearts or at least more honest conversations. He just doesn't know how to break into the shell of the woman who reminds him of a two-year-old he once knew.

In an effort to take advantage of this opportunity for a father-daughter chat, Rodrigo begins, "Quite the event, this blackout, eh?"

Eyes still pinned to the road, Lucia replies drily, "Yeah, Sterling should be proud."

Not having expected that answer, Rodrigo responds, "Mija, Sterling has fed you your whole life. It is a good company."

Lucia laughs hollowly, "Sure. Sterling has paid your checks for decades, Papa, but that doesn't make them good. Just because a company benefits you doesn't make it good."

Rodrigo adjusts his place in his seat and defends his boss. "Sterling is a good man. There are good people at the company. We power the city."

Lucia speaks back, "I'm sure he is good to you. It's easy to be nice to people when they're making you a ton of money. I wonder if he's still such a good person in private. And okay, yeah. Sterling powers the city, but for how long? If they just decided to invest in green energy, the city would be less polluted. It would be cleaner for everyone now and long into the future."

Rodrigo tries to contain his rising anger. His daughter should be grateful for everything the company has done for their family. It allowed him to start anew here. They have never been rich, but it allowed her a good childhood. A good start in life. Lucia got to study because of Sterling. He knows the arguments she throws at him are from her university textbooks, paid for by his checks.

His voice gains a warning edge as he pushes back, "Lucia, making everyone use solar power and placing windmills everywhere isn't going to do anything if other cities and countries do not. Forcing companies to use those sources will kill innovation. This city is amazing because there is no limit to what people are able to create. The government does not keep people from making the most of themselves. There is no way the government should be able to restrict the freedom of businesses and take away people's rights to live how they want. That is why this Silva administration is a mess. I know what it is like without that freedom. You do not want to live in that world."

His daughter replies immediately, her grip on the steering wheel tightening, "Just because innovation stops in sectors that are contaminating the Aurietta Sea doesn't mean innovation can't grow in renewable energy, Papa. In fact, that's the whole point. We should be transitioning to a society that lives with the earth, not off of it. That won't keep people from making the most of themselves. People will always invent new things. It's just a matter of encouraging them to create things that are good for the world. I'm sorry, Papa. I'm not trying to attack you. You have worked so hard for mama and all of us, but you can't keep on thinking that climate change is inconsequential. It is complicated, yes, and it's going to be hard. We may not have all the comforts we're used to if we move sharply to new energy sources. Lots of hardworking people like you might suffer. I'm not saying it's going to be a piece of cake or that I have it all figured out, but we can't just shrug our shoulders while we continue to destroy the only home we have."

Rodrigo shakes in frustration. "You are not listening, Lucia." His voice rises forcefully, "It is a matter of freedom, do you not see that? No one should abandon their values because a few things we do are making it a little hotter outside!" Rodrigo hits his fist against the dash, and Lucia flinches, swerving abruptly on the road. They both experience a moment of panic before she course corrects. They continue to roll along smoothly across the asphalt.

Lucia drops her voice, compassion entering her tone. "Papa, I love you. I love you, but you weren't in that helicopter the day of the leak. I cannot tell you how disastrous it was. There were more fish than I'd ever seen lying dead on the beach. Is that freeing for the fishermen whose livelihood was destroyed? And it's not about every single little freedom now, Papa. It's about preserving the most freedom possible for the future. For my kids and me, if I ever have any. The planet isn't getting 'a little hotter.' We're completely changing how it operates. And what about other countries? Places suffering because of the lives we've led and then getting blamed when they try to have the same quality of life. Our actions are killing us, and Sterling, and other large businesses have a responsibility to do everything they can to reduce how much they contribute to that harm. I'll take a little bit of inconvenience now for a green future any day of the week."

Rodrigo opens his mouth to protest, but Lucia adds the words that reverberate in his mind. "Dad, you're not evil. I love you, but you're hurting me."

Rodrigo's stomach drops.

Lucia finishes, "Sterling knows about the problem, and he's apathetic. *That* is evil. He is harming people knowingly. Don't let him turn you into a monster too. Changing your mind isn't weak. You're not abandoning your principles. You're just loving your family and your neighbors enough to sacrifice a little. And if there's one thing I know about you, it's that you've never stopped sacrificing for us."

Rodrigo has no response. No answer except the tears that well in his eyes. For the next few minutes, they sit in silence. He replays Lucia's words over and over, hearing the conviction in them. Hear the fear in her voice.

I won't be the reason for my daughter's pain, he thinks.

Rodrigo has heard many of these points before, but never from his kids. Never with that same level of alarm. He thinks about the images he's seen on the news of crashing glaciers. He reflects on the future, and he thinks about his family.

He thinks about the look in Aldrix's eyes when he ordered Rodrigo out of the room. About the timing of the blackout and the *bang* he thought he heard when he was walking away from the control room hallway.

He makes a choice.

The next day Rodrigo calls the *Chronicle.*

A calm male voice answers, "Hello?"

Rodrigo pauses, *is he actually doing this?* "Hello, I would like to speak to a reporter. I... I work in the Sterling Engineering department. I have information about the blackout that is... eh... questionable."

The man's voice tries to remain calm, but his urgency spills through, "Yes. Absolutely, yes. What time are you available? I can meet you this afternoon."

Rodrigo responds, "Eh, we can speak after my shift today. I will get off at 8 p.m."

The journalist replies, "Excellent, excellent. I can meet you at the facility entrance. We will drive you to the office and I'd be happy to preserve your anonymity if you have any anxieties about privacy and employer retaliation and such."

Rodrigo only has the courage to say, "Yes. I think that would be good."

Rodrigo enters Sterling Tower and takes the elevator down. He moves into the control room and looks at the engineering lead chair that is now his. He thinks of Nick's face on his television screen, the reports of his murder, their only guess a crazed protestor who shot a stray in the dark. Rodrigo slides the chair out of the way and takes another seat. It is Friday. Sterling walks in moments later.

The man's smile is brilliant, "Rod! How's your week been?"

Despite himself, Rodrigo smiles, "Going well boss, how are you?"

"Good, good." Sterling says jovially. "Listen, I've been walking around and checking on everyone after the blackout. Is your family okay? Everyone safe and sound?"

Rodrigo replies, "Yeah, everything is okay. Luckily I stayed with my daughter in the suburbs for the night."

Sterling says, "Phenomenal. I'm glad it all worked out. Well, I just wanted to say that you'll get a notice from HR soon. Between the blackout and Nick's tragic death and the oil spill, everyone has gone through a lot recently. I really want to recognize the hard-work, and so everyone on your team will be receiving a raise. Additionally, we have our trained specialists if you'd like to speak with anyone about your grief in regard to Nick or your emotions over the recent months."

Rodrigo doesn't know what to say, "Thank you so much sir. I... I am very grateful."

"No Rod, you've all earned it." Pride is on Sterling's face as he states, "Like I said before, you've worked here forever now, you're part of the family. Please know that your job is secure. You've earned your tenure and I'd be honored to have you around until you decide the time is right for you to retire."

"Thank you so much, sir." Rodrigo says.

"Of course." Sterling squeezes his shoulder and walks out of the room.

The entire rest of the day Rodrigo asks himself a single question: *Can he betray a man like that?*

Rodrigo sits in a modern office surrounded by sound-proof walls and the journalist in front of him asks a single question, "What would you like to report here today?"

Rodrigo takes a deep breath and says, "I..."

His mind is still conflicted, his brain bouncing between responses. He isn't sure what he will say until the words tumble out, "I wanted to say how honorable of a company Sterling Energies is. Today, Aldrix Sterling visited all of the workstations and personally checked on us after the blackout. I am proud of my colleagues' work to repair the damages of the mob."

The reporter's face draws into a look of confusion, "Didn't you say you had some information about questionable choices inside the organization?"

Rodrigo stumbles over his words, but he answers, "No, just about the protesters."

The journalist is clearly disappointed, but he politely responds, "Thank you for your time, Mr. Martinez. We'll have you escorted back to the lobby. Have a wonderful rest of the day."

Rodrigo imagines Lucia's reaction to his words, and he is overtaken by shame.

52

TICKTOCK

Tick. Tock. Tick. Tock.

Ezra hoists his bag onto his shoulder and walks out of the metro into the daylight.

Today's the day.

This is for Nick. And his mom. And everyone the Sterlings have messed with.

The cars race past as he walks in pace down the block.

Ticktock.

Ezra sets his watch.

This is for his twenty-year-old self.

Ticktock.

His journey flashes through his mind.

Nick's eyes.

Ticktock.

Sam's cold, dark face.

Ticktock.

The confusion of this new world.

The trust Meg has in him.

Ticktock.

Sterling's face giving that ridiculous speech.

Ticktock.

Ezra checks his gun.

Ezra leans against a building across the street from Sterling Tower, dressed in casual clothes, staring at his watch.

Two minutes.

He scans the area, nothing out of place. The usual vendors and businessmen huddle around a coffee stand.

One minute.

John walks onto the scene right on time.

Ezra swears the man is a robot.

He's about two blocks away from Sterling's entrance, so Ezra leaves his post and goes to meet him.

A few paces away, Ezra reaches into his pocket, fingers grasping the incredibly fine point needle and readying it. He slams into John, jabbing the needle into the back of his neck before quickly sliding it into his bag.

John whirls on him, face red in shock and anger. "Ouch! Watch where you're going! Did you just stab me?" John feels his neck, but there's no blood.

Ezra responds in character, holding up his empty hands. "Yo, I'm so sorry. I think I just scratched you, bro. No blood or nothin'. I really apologize. Wasn't lookin' out." John glares at him, but Ezra knows he's now running late. And John is never late.

He rushes off with one more scathing glance and goes along his merry way.

Fifteen minutes later, Ezra walks straight up to the guard tower at the front gates of Sterling, dressed in his EMT uniform.

The guard stops him.

Ezra throws everything he has into his pleas. "I'm sorry, you have to let me through. I received an emergency call about someone suffering symptoms of a heart attack. Please, my partner is on the way with an ambulance. We've gotta get the patient help. You can check if you need, call up to the seventy-fifth floor. We got an urgent 9-1-1."

Scanning Ezra up and down, the man obliges by picking up his phone and dialing a number.

Ezra holds his breath. The guard speaks in hushed tones into his device, Ezra doing his best to appear completely concerned and steadfast.

Finally, the guard waves him in. "Thanks for coming. Head right toward the elevator bay on the left."

Ezra hesitates for a second. He's been planning this for weeks, but he can't believe it actually worked. He rushes past and hops in an elevator. The doors open to a beautiful lobby space with no one there. He hears fearful voices coming from the office in the back. The one with wooden paneling and the name Aldrix Sterling etched into the door.

Ezra double checks his gun then pushes into the room, steeling himself to commit the act he's thought about for so long. Only John is inside. Just John and another man who is performing desperate CPR. A man who is not Sterling. *How did he get this wrong?* Sterling is always in his office at this hour, he checked. And triple-checked.

When the elevator pings, Ezra has just enough time to watch Aldrix Sterling board as the doors close behind him. Ezra pauses at the passed out John, poisoned by his own hand, now completely unnecessarily. The man is pumping at his chest in vain. Ezra knows he could help him, but he turns back toward the elevators.

He is going to finish this today.

53

MEADOW OF STONE

When Emerald emerges from the trail onto the overlook, Sterling stands at the edge, gazing out across the city. The stones that speckle the ground are worn from years of people taking in the sunset from this marvelous nature preserve, a haven far from the reaches of the congested city center.

Sterling barely moves as Emerald approaches, not turning from his panoramic perspective.

She greets him curtly, "Enjoying the view?"

Sterling shifts his attention to Emerald. His face is hard, no inkling of his usual charisma. "Let's just cut to the chase."

Emerald happily obliges. "Are you proud of yourself?"

Sterling's mouth only curls into a fraction of a frown in response.

Emerald spits at Sterling. "I spent this morning reading about the millions in damages, people dying in hospitals mid-procedure, and riots from a protest that was already rough when there were lights on! Absolutely phenomenal. And sure, blame it on the protestors, but from the information I've received, the only way to shut the whole city off is from inside your control room. So I may not have the full picture, but I know you're even more selfish than I thought."

Sterling is composed in his response. "That's quite the small-minded view, Emerald. I did what I had to do. Did it benefit me? Surely. But I didn't do it for me. I did it because I have more things to worry about than playing princess in 'the halls of the people.' I have a legacy to secure. I will not be the one to ruin what generations of my family built. People had to learn their lesson. Their lives are dependent on *me*."

Emerald rages. "What your family built? Do you have any clue what building means? Have you ever done a day of real work in your life?"

Sterling continues, unperturbed, "I will not be the one to let all of the families who work for my company go hungry just because a few radicals want to replace reliable energy for fickle windmills."

Emerald moves closer, shouting, "Is that what you think? That everyone protesting your practices just woke up with a vendetta against you? You want to know the truth, Aldrix? It's not about you. Does that compute? This is way bigger than your company. I'm here right now because people like you messed up the planet so bad my family's way of life was unsustainable. I ran from a fire and got this beauty mark on my neck because of you. My home, Aldrix, is in ashes. I can never go back. That's what this is about."

Sterling begins to speak, but Emerald continues, "Tell me what you did."

Aldrix tilts his head and glances around. "And why would I do that? I have no crimes to confess."

Emerald loses her patience. She shoves Sterling, but it only results in him taking a few steps back. Her eyes widen as she closes the space between them and rages into his face, "You have too many crimes to count, Aldrix! You pretend to be honorable as if you have a shred of decency. And then you send reapers in the night. You have blood on your hands, Aldrix."

Looking directly into her eyes, Sterling simply smirks. "You are pathetically weak, Emerald."

With all the terror Emerald holds from the moment her car was thrust into the air, with all the frustration she holds from being trapped by manipulations, with the rage she feels from waking up to a world with a battered Amelie, all the grief she suffered when reading of Suzuka's death, and all the pain of a childhood turned to dust, Emerald swings a fist toward Sterling's head.

As her hand arcs through the air, Sterling's eyes widen in surprise. Power courses through Emerald, her one desire for him to feel an ounce of her devastation.

The blow never lands.

A bullet screams over their heads. Both Emerald and Sterling throw themselves to the ground. Standing and turning toward the source, they are greeted by the barrel of a gun and the eyes of someone with long-festering hatred.

The man looks past Emerald, eyes burning into Sterling. His voice is low, heart-wrenching pain mixing with unfathomable fury. "Aldrix Sterling, do you know who I am?"

Emerald's pulse pounds as she turns toward Sterling. He has nothing to say and despite the weapon pointed toward him, there is no fear in Aldrix's eyes, only loathing.

The man asks again, anguish on his face. "Do you remember me? Or was I a problem you just sent your prison henchmen to deal with?"

Sterling remains quiet.

Ezra takes one step closer, his words barely a whisper. "Aldrix Sterling, do you remember what you did to me?"

Then in a single blink, Ezra has moved only feet away, his gun set on Aldrix's forehead and tears now rolling down his face. With his free hand, Ezra lifts up the edge of his shirt, displaying his scarred side. The knife wound forever etched into his distorted flesh.

"*Look at me*!" Ezra roars. "You ordered my life away, and you can't even look in my eyes. Do you know what it is like to lose *ten years* of your life? Do you know how terrifying it feels to think you're going to die because a cop is pointing her gun at your head? Have you ever felt your own blood pooling around you as someone you thought was your friend walks away? Have you ever seen black pour out of your faucet? You might give the orders but don't have a clue about the people whose lives you are destroying."

Aldrix keeps his eyes trained on Ezra's, not daring to look away. He still refuses to open his mouth.

"*Answer me*!" Ezra booms. "What happened to Nick?" His hand fingers the trigger, but he wants answers first.

Sweat dripping down his forehead, Sterling finally responds, "You were in the wrong place at the wrong time. And so was he."

Emerald interjects, "How did he—"

Ezra whips around, training the gun on Emerald. "This is not your business. But I can't say I'm surprised you're here. I saved your life when you were passed out on the asphalt, but you've never come to my community's rescue, have you?"

Two more guns cock as two officers emerge from the tree line, pistols trained on Ezra.

Sterling doesn't miss a beat, arms wrapping around Emerald in a vice grip. The metal is heavy and cool against her head.

Sterling's breath blasts against her neck. "What did you do?" he hisses. At the same time, he notices the small wire that now peeks out from her pant-line, his suspicions confirmed. Aldrix grits out, "You're a fool."

Everyone pauses, Sterling with a gun to Emerald, Ezra still looking toward Sterling, and the cops focused intently on both.

Emerald is the first to speak. "I told the truth. I'm not going to let your dark money hang over me anymore. Sure, my reputation is done, and I might lose my office. But you're going to prison, and your precious legacy will be out of the way for progress."

Sterling relaxes. "Do you really think I came alone?"

One officer collapses, a shot reverberating through the air from a distance.

The second barely blinks before he joins his partner on the ground.

Ezra leaps aside milliseconds before a bullet whizzes through the space where he'd been standing. He sprints toward the tree line, turning back toward Emerald and Aldrix to fire a single shot. She recoils, but Sterling still holds her in place as the bullet flies far wide.

Emerald watches blood splatter across the stone as a bullet pierces Ezra's leg. He cries out, gun falling to the side as he crumples to the ground. He grimaces in pain, unable to do anything about the blood spilling out of him.

Emerald stumbles forward as Sterling shoves her away, ripping the microphone cord from her as she falls hard onto the gravel.

With a brief smoothing of this hair, Aldrix walks away, not even bothering to utter the threat that hangs in the air.

Emerald is left on her knees beside a half-conscious Ezra, the last of the sun's rays washing over the sky as the city lights come alive.

54

BREAKING NEWS

News Anchor, 7 p.m. Nightly News

"Breaking news, there has been a shooting at the Leafbridge Overlook. Official sources report two bodies, both police officers. There were also sniper bullet shells found at the scene. The officers were shot from behind. Sources say it was the work of a single attacker. No suspect or motive has been identified yet. The officers were seemingly heading home when attacked by the suspected lone sniper. Our hearts go out to the families of these heroes.

"This comes just minutes after a scandal embroiled City Hall. Mayor Silva disclosed to the press that Sterling Energies contributed to her campaign. Long-time supporters of the mayor are outraged, calling for her resignation. Aldrix Sterling himself has denied the allegations. The mayor has yet to provide any evidence of her claims."

Sterling Energies official statement on the Leafbridge Shooting

"Sterling Energies is horrified by the recent terrorist attack at Leafbridge. We stand alongside all other residents of this city as the authorities seek out the lone wolf who perpetrated such horror against our city's bravest."

Stratford Hospital Press

One of our own was injured today in what is speculated to be a drive-by shooting. No statement has been released from the young EMT who sustained a single bullet wound to the leg. From early reports, he resides in Bengelwood. If claims are corroborated, this would be the seventh gang-related incident in the area this month.

The *Chronicle*

"The shooter in the Leafbridge attack still remains at large as the city announces a vigil to honor the fallen officers. No motive has been found."

55

THOUGHTS FROM THE AIR

It is lonely in the dark flying tube.

James Myelin is surrounded by hundreds of people, but all he cares about is getting to one wonderful woman on the ground. He takes the hits from a particularly annoying kid kicking at the back of his seat, his mind in another place.

He has never felt more alone as his plane glides through the air. He considers what it will be like to pick up the pieces of his brother's smothered life. *What will it feel like to care for an aunt who barely remembers him while his fondest memories revolve around her radiant laughter?*

He's scared and numb and doesn't know what he's doing. *Is he the only one left in the world that can recall his brother's childish smile? Who remembers how Aunt Stacie would cover their birthday cakes with whipped icing, then dab their noses with the frosting? Is he the only one on the planet who remembers the kindness of his parents? Will he ever know what Nick's last moments were like?*

Jamie tosses and turns in the seat. He tries to close his eyes, for the penetrating voices to leave him alone. He's unsuccessful. When the wheels skid upon the tarmac, Jamie looks out the window at the skyline of his hometown. It is not how he remembers, darker somehow, even in the afternoon light. The towers he always found awe-inspiring fill him with discomfort now. When he hops in the taxi and speeds closer downtown, the grief only deepens inside him.

It only takes a few minutes for him to realize how this city was never his home. It was just the place where his brother's warmth and his aunt's laughter greeted him. They're his true home. When he knocks on the door and a familiar face answers, he throws his arms around her with joy.

Though when he withdraws and sees the confusion on her face, he knows that he's lost his home for good.

56

BEDRIDDEN

The moment the bullet pierced Ezra's leg, he thought he was dead. As he fell, the pain ripped through him, and he thought about what his life would have been if it had ended that very second.

He pictured his childhood, lunch periods surrounded by the kindness of Lucas and Nick, but the rejection of others. Of his loving father lifting him up to dunk at the basketball court, turned unrecognizable by a vicious drug. Of watching his friends excel while he walked retail aisles to keep him and his mother afloat. The pity in the eyes of some residents who walked the streets in suits and skirts, the disgust in others. The terror gripping him when cop 54821 gripped her weapon under the starry sky. He saw Sam at the moment he slid the blade into Ezra's skin. He felt the cold, dankness of the cells, the metallic smell everywhere. And he thought of how he'd buried his heart to survive. He wondered if he could have done anything different or whether his fate was sealed the moment he entered the world with darkened skin under the shadow of Sterling Tower.

Ezra hit the ground, writhing in pain.

But he also pictured the dawn-filled sky on the pier and the harbormaster's words. His mom's smile and the hardship in her hunch, the black water welling in her sink. The relief in her eyes when he came back home. He thought of Meg and her unwavering commitment to saving lives and mentorship. Her level-headedness with bullets flying and her fierce loyalty to him. He thought of his childhood self deep inside him still, longing to help others. And how that part of him radiated when he held his EMT certificate.

He thought about how willing he'd been to throw it all away for vengeance.

Blood welled in the gravel around Ezra. He closed his eyes and waited for a second bullet to turn his world to darkness. In those moments, he wondered whether he was good or bad. Whether acts of survival would receive judgment when he passed. Whether heaven would see his actions or just label him as broken as society did on earth.

What had his life been for? What would they say? A would be assassin, an inmate, a lifesaver, a friend, a son, a poor person, a young person, the cause of pain, the cause of laughter? Ezra isn't a saint. Ezra isn't a devil. He isn't a hoodlum or a Laurel Leaguer. He isn't a Sterling or a Sam or a Wellsworth. He's Ezra. And if he remained himself despite being battered by all the forces that sought to trample him, is that accomplishment enough? Would people remember the gray or just paint the black?

The second bullet never came. He does not know whether it was mercy from a ruthless man or simply the fortune of Sterling's hasty exit. The arrogance in Aldrix's belief that Ezra would never touch him.

So now he sits on an uncomfortable, lumpy hospital bed, grateful to be alive. His anger still rages but in a different way. When the day finally comes, and the reaper greets him, he refuses to have wasted any more energy on tearing down an impenetrable tower.

Though, as he sits wrapped in bandages, he is lost. The future seems hazy. He vows to remember those society forgets, but he's not sure whether he'll ever be able to give more than Sterling takes.

Ezra knows who it is before she even steps into the room. Ezra rises to his elbows, but the movement sends a burst of pain through his leg. Even with the meds, it throbs. He lies back down and prepares himself for the onslaught.

Meg begins speaking the moment she lays eyes on him. "Remember when I said we are partners and that you should call me if something's wrong?"

Ezra starts to answer, but Meg doesn't pause. "Remember when I told you to trust me?"

Ezra just nods this time, but he winces as his leg shoots another bout of agony across his body.

"Then why are you lying in a hospital bed, and I just found out about it a few minutes ago?" Meg asks, her words sharp.

"I'm sorry," Ezra says as Meg sits on the chair next to him.

Meg waves her hand and shakes her head. "Whatever. We're here now." Looking directly into his eyes, Meg asks, "What happened?"

Ezra starts, "I was just walking down the street—"

"Cut the crap," Meg responds. "Why aren't you telling people what really happened?"

"How do you know I'm lying?"

"I know you're not telling the truth."

Quietly, Ezra says, "I can't say anything, or next time I won't make it to a hospital. I've been betrayed by so many, and everyone comes in here and asks why I'm upset. I just want everyone to move forward together and not be completely obliterated for it."

Meg says, "It's fine to be upset. God knows I enjoy a good fume and fury. But we have an opportunity to do good here every day. Ezra, you have helped save dozens of lives since we met. Don't let them turn you into the caricature they spin on TV."

Lowering her voice, Meg drops her usual confident façade. "I don't know what caught you a bullet in the leg, but I know there is always more value in healing the good in the world than tearing the bad stuff apart."

Her words echo Ezra's epiphany lying on the ground in the evening light. But still, Ezra's anger smolders. Ezra pushes back. "And what if the bad stuff is so bad that it stops you from healing?"

Meg hangs her head and candidly says, "I don't know."

Ezra leans back in his seat and closes his eyes. For several moments they sit in silence.

Then Ezra says, "You're a good partner, Meg."

Meg responds, "Yeah, you're lucky to have me."

They both laugh, neither having found clarity, both committed to weathering the storm together.

57

A GARDEN AND A PROMISE

When the men and women clothed in black gather in the garden, there are more people than Lucas could have ever imagined.

Though the sky is dark with clouds, the droplets do not fall on the mourners. The glass covering of the conservatory shields this sacred remembrance. Lucas sits in the front row, Suzuka's casket laid out before him. Sierra cries in his arms. She can feel the distress of the day.

The space is filled with a crushing amount of love for Suzuka. Mourners pack every row. Family and friends crowd the front, Suzuka's sister Aina first among them. Other faces Lucas has never seen line the walls and fill the back benches. He didn't know how many lives Suzuka touched while she lived, but it is unmistakable now.

He hopes she can see the darkness did not smother her efforts. That she is looking down and basking in the warmth that radiates through the room. The proceedings are somber but also light. The occasion is one of sadness but also tinted with the joyous memories of Suzuka's laugh, the bravery of her actions, and the remembrance of her spirit.

After the ceremony and hugs and cards, Lucas returns to his doorstep. It's the moment he has dreaded. For a while, friends surrounded him, he had others to lean on, but now he is left to face an existence without his partner. His heart is as hollow as their home.

He places Sierra in her playpen, left amongst a mess of train tracks and stuffed animals.

Making his way down the hall, he pauses at the doorframe of Suzuka's refuge. He peers at the covered painting, natural light streaming through the windows of the room. For the first time, he crosses the threshold without her guiding hand.

He approaches the artwork as if it is an altar, reverence filling his steps with caution. For several moments, he simply stares at the tarp, weighing the morality of looking upon her unfinished art. Ultimately, the desire to see one of the final things she touched overcomes his doubts. Gingerly, he removes the covering.

He looks upon the landscape in wonder. He is instantly transported into a battle of hues, molded into the shape of mountains. A single fire crackles against the looming mountains as snow whips across the rocky range. Low hanging clouds move amidst the peaks, pointing toward an unfinished navy blue sky.

Lucas feels the tears begin to form, plopping softly onto his button-down. Taking in the scene, he can almost feel Suzuka's embrace. It is not a calming piece of art, but she wasn't a calming partner. She was the steel-laced wind. She was the unshakeable mountain. Suzuka was the swirling cloud overlooking the chaotic earth below.

The longer Lucas looks at the work, the more his eyes draw to the orange woven fire. A mix of crimson, golden, and vermillion cinders rolling off the edges. Because most of all, Suzuka was the flame, struggling in the face of ferocious forces and refusing to go out.

The torch teeters as if Suzuka never decided whether it was meant to go out or whether it would go on shining until the morning light. He wonders if she knew her own life's flame was just as uncertain. Unable to take his eyes off the fire, Lucas picks up a brush.

Hands shaking, he dips it in pearly white. Shifting his arms to the top of the piece, he writes out a promise amidst the darkened sky: *I won't let the torch go out.*

58

VIGIL STATEMENTS

The Seaside Times, Featured Article

"Pressure mounts for Mayor Silva as protesters demand that she leave office after taking money from Sterling Energies during her mayoral campaign. An independent investigation has been opened by the state into whether the contribution from Sterling occurred and, if so, whether it was legal."

The *Chronicle*

The completed tally of dead from the night of the Sterling protests and blackouts totals fifty-two. These were our mothers, caretakers, partners, and neighbors. Tensions remain high between environmental activists and supporters of the energy titan. Tensions that have only flared with the recent political allegations concerning the mayor. Based on our polling, residents have little confidence in the government's ability to bring about meaningful change regarding green policies.

Sterling Energies Official Statement on the Alleged Campaign Contributions

Sterling Energies has never and will never meddle in political affairs. The corporation's mission is to power our city, and we have excelled at this for generations. We will endure today, tomorrow, and long after Mayor Silva and her anti-energy agenda have left office.

City Hall official statement on Vigil for the Fallen
Tonight, we will honor those who gave their lives so that we may live in peace. They were some of our bravest and most loyal. We are seeking justice for the families of the victims. Mayor Silva gave this statement:

"If those responsible for this horrendous attack are not brought to justice today, that will be a travesty. Attacks in the night are only for cowardly people, those afraid of the light. Unfortunately, it is a reality that no one might ever be tried for this despicable act. But I promise you this. To all those who seek to harm this city. Who seek to harm me and other servants of this vibrant city, listen well: You may walk away today, but our fight is not over. One day, you will fall."

59

A CITY BY THE SEA

There once was a city by the sea where the streets hummed with power yet no one was free.
And on a ridge overlooking their home, a trio met on a meadow of stone.
All came for power they felt they were owed, none of them knowing how events would unfold.
They traded in violence and shouts and rage, but it simply revealed how each was caged.
And as nightfall reigned, the king walked away, the others defeated as the tree branches swayed.
Yet passion is persistent and victory elusive, so setbacks today are never conclusive.
Try as it might, the wind will blow, but the flame nonetheless continues to glow.

Two roads diverged in a wood, and I—

I took the one less traveled by,

And that has made all the difference.

—THE ROAD NOT TAKEN, *ROBERT FROST*

Two paths lay ahead, which one would you rather tread?

EPILOGUE I

STERLING'S PATH

Year 2050—Future Reality 1

Aldrix sits in the back seat of his Cadillac, Apollo steering smoothly through traffic.

They glide along the smooth asphalt on their way to see his son. Aster invited him to the seventy-fifth floor, hoping to gain insight from his father. Aldrix loves to be wanted, but he's glad the final decision is now someone else's problem.

As they turn onto Renlen boulevard, the golden tower comes into view, obscured somewhat by the haze in the air. Sterling looks out and recoils. Along the sidewalk, dozens of people gather.

The Droughties huddle together, their matted hair and smoke-tinged clothes only further proof of their inferiority.

"Apollo?"

"Yes, sir"

"Roll up the window."

The tint hides the masses from Sterling's sight, also obscuring the slums piled high on the hills in the distance. Aldrix takes a sip of water, the crystalline liquid filtered to perfection. He likes this new filter. It gives the water such a nice taste.

The car whizzes by the *Chronicle*'s building, still blaming him for the polluted air and poisoned sea. Though, he finds it classless to go about criticizing an old man for their problems. It isn't his fault that these Droughties decided to live in disaster-prone areas. His family's power has driven the city to be more vibrant than ever. He never thought he'd live to see so many incredible technological developments fueled by his creation.

Humans adapt. That's what they do. If the climate wants to change, so be it. Sterling will just pay more engineers to shield him from the impacts. The car slows to a halt, and Apollo opens Aldrix's door. He boards the elevator, and it rockets upward. When the doors glide open once more, the entire city is visible. Aldrix smiles. The view never gets old.

Those below can say what they wish, Aldrix thinks. *I did what it took to survive.*

Heavy is the head that wears the crown, yet the man who dons it is still king.

And after all these years, the Sterlings remain sovereign.

EPILOGUE II

EMERALD'S PATH

Year 2050—Future Reality 2

Emerald walks toward the looming skyscraper on her way to a meeting. All around her, green lanterns line the streets. People rush past her about their business. No one giving her a second look. They stare only at the beautiful banners that are all around them. Hung from streetlamps and posted over doorways.

As Emerald nears the building, she sees holograms dance around the entrance, an animated forest surrounded by soft music. Balloons are suspended over the gates. The city celebrates.

She remembers walking out of city hall disgraced but determined. How Sterling walked away, all the investigations and allegations dropped. She thinks back to Amelie's words: "Just because you don't have authority anymore doesn't mean you don't have power."

She thinks of the late nights building her new organization. Fielding calls, convincing everyone to the table. Business moguls, civil servants, climate experts. From their city and others. Together. She recalls how her palms sweated as new policies were voted in. How her heart swelled with smug satisfaction when Sterling refused to come to the table. How his rotten company was soon left behind.

Now Emerald stands before the glistening tower that pierces the clouds. It is not golden. It is a spire of glass with a single word glowing green from the pinnacle: Alteryn.

A tingle of pride shoots through her spine. She walks into the pristine lobby, and they wave her through the security scans. She shoots up the elevator.

She sits in the smooth lounge of Alteryn's penthouse floor, awaiting her summons from her host. It doesn't take long for the calm tone to sound and the glass office door to slide open. Emerald's jaw drops at the face that greets her.

Sierra Maamoun rises from behind her desk. She wears a plain white blouse with a bracelet filled with cobalt stones. She extends her hand. "Ms. Silva, it's nice to finally meet you. Happy Net-Zero Day."

Emerald clasps the hand of her late friend's daughter, and the two sit for a discussion of the distant past and coming future. Together, they look out the window at the streets and hills below. The green lanterns and banners all announcing the same thing:

Happy Net-Zero Day! Net-Zero Hooray! Five years, Net Zero!

Emerald's chest fills with satisfaction. Tearing her gaze from the sight below, her eyes land on the painting hung behind Sierra's desk. The mountainscape is filled with a raging storm, a single torch standing rebelliously against the snowcapped peaks. In the sky a promise is written and mismatched stars dance. Sierra notices her shift in attention, answering the question that hangs in the air, "My mom couldn't finish it, so my dad and I got it done."

Flashes of memories twirl through Emerald's mind as she glances between a painting from the past and the present sprawled out before her. She can't help but think about how far she's come. How long it's been.

How much she's learned, since her haven burned.

OUR HAVEN

In 2050, I will be fifty-two years old.

Over the coming decades, our collective narrative will not be as simple as two storylines.

We are not choosing between good or bad, this or that, Sterling or Emerald.

Reality is messy, and both the challenges and opportunities are infinite.

But there is a single commonality between all those potential roads:

They are all *ours* to choose.

HOW TO BE A FLAMEKEEPER

People often want easy answers for how to solve the Climate Crisis. I myself am no exception. Climate change is a systems-level issue, and so we need people within all sorts of systems to act. I recognize that personal action alone will not be enough. So, when thinking about a call to action, I struggled to think of something tangible to close with.

I was fortunate enough to have the opportunity to speak with a number of people, many of whom received mention in the subsequent pages. Whether directly told or indirectly said, each of them shared the diverse ways in which anyone can be involved in contributing to a green future where we reduce fifty-one billion to zero.

There is no definitive list I can provide, no single line of guidance, and no magic solutions. Climate Change is going to require everything we've got, so here is my single ask of you, dear reader:

Bring your talents into the climate conversation. Maybe you will paint a landscape that raises thousands of dollars for conservation. Maybe you will design a structure made entirely of solar panels. Maybe your musical talent will become the anthem of the climate movement. Maybe you will be the political representative who understands the systemic changes that are necessary. Whatever it is, we will need to use your unique skillset to transform society into the green future that we must achieve. You don't have to be a PhD to contribute to climate solutions. Individual action may seem fruitless, but not when done collectively or when used to spur grander shifts toward a greener world.

Whatever you do, we need it. We need artists to move people's hearts to action and engineers to revolutionize our global infrastructure. We need entrepreneurs who prioritize green initiatives in the corporate space and doctors who will alert society to the effects of climate on health. Said another way, while we certainly need Suzukas, we also need Emeralds, Ezras, Lucases, Nicks, and even environmentally conscious Sterlings. Most importantly, *we need you.*

We need you to drive systemic changes wherever you have leverage. This is not about guilt. It is not about demonizing others for eating meat or flying on planes. This is about building entirely new ecosystems that incentivize sustainable lifestyles around the globe while simultaneously lifting up those negatively impacted. Together we will build a future that avoids the worst of the climate crisis. I can't wait to live in that world.

CHALLENGE AND COMMUNITY

I stumbled upon an incredible diagram on the podcast, "How to Save a Planet," which seeks to assist anyone in determining how they can contribute to the climate movement. It asks listeners to identify three things 1) what brings you joy, 2) what you are good at, and 3) what needs doing. I have added one more: 4) what inspires others or has a systemic impact. Find where those four intersect for you, and you'll be on your way to saving the world.

On the next page, I invite you to draw, write a list, scribble, and doodle whatever will allow you to answer the four questions above. When you're done, having identified a way you can use your skills and passions, I have one final ask.

Take a photo of your personal climate action—diagram, list, or drawing. Then share it along with another photo of yourself online in which you are acting upon your chosen climate contribution. Tag it with #Ourhaven to see what others are doing!

Share with your friends how you're using your gifts to contribute your unique part to our world. If everyone does this, we will be a bit closer to a future like Emerald's.

MY CLIMATE CONTRIBUTION...

RESOURCES

For inspiration on how you can contribute, feel free to check out the following:

DATA AND RESEARCH

- Project Drawdown
- Oliver Wyman Climate Action Navigator
- The Intergovernmental Panel on Climate Change

PEOPLE AND CONVERSATIONS

- Kate Marvel (Climate Scientist, NASA)
  - Ted Talk: "Can clouds buy us more time to solve climate change?"
- Mary Anne Hitt (Senior Director of the Climate Imperative; Former Director of the Sierra Club)
- Greta Thunberg—Speech at Davos 2020

PODCASTS

- How to Save a Planet, *Gimlet Media*
- A Matter of Degrees

BOOKS

- An Indigenous Peoples' History of The United States, *Roxanne Dunbar-Ortiz*
- This Changes Everything: Capitalism vs. the Climate, *Naomi Klein*
- How to Avoid a Climate Disaster, *Bill Gates*
- All We Can Save, Dr. *Ayanna Elizabeth Johnson and Dr. Katherine K. Wilkinson*

ACKNOWLEDGMENTS

"I remember all the ways people have affected me; how our stories became memories; and if you were brazen enough to make one with me, you're in there somewhere."

TOMATOES, SHANE KOYCZAN

This project is the culmination of all of the memories, experiences, and people that have shaped my life so far. From the library at Complutense University to an apartment in São Paulo and the countless classrooms where I scribbled ideas frantically in the margins of notebooks, this project has been an adventure from the start. So thank you to everyone who has paved my road to this moment.

Mom, Dad, and Lindsey, thank you for your infinite love and support. Bonma and Bonpa, your love and wisdom are unmatched. Mother Gladys, thank you for always fueling my passion for reading and for being a wonderful teacher. Brooke Norman, thank you for spending a Saturday chasing the sun beneath an overcast sky.

And thank you to all the family members who have played a part in raising me into the person I am today.

There are also many friends who have been pivotal in this process, especially everyone on team Safehaven. You have all been my support system throughout this entire ordeal. Thank you:

André Amaral, for always diving into my dreams with me and selflessly sharing stories of your own. Ann Shaw, for constantly innovating toward a better tomorrow. Our world is better off because of visionaries like you. Anne Coyne, for somehow managing to keep a straight face when I told you my crazy book idea over bowls of ramen. And for your compassion at every step. Brianna Gist, for inspiring me with your spirit and blessing me with your laughter. Your grace and dignity are simply unparalleled. Merci. Cecilia Aguirre, for backstage laughter, mic room conversations, and life lessons. And for seeing something in a shy kid. Cira Mancuso, for writing a book so good it inspired me to write my own. For being the first in line for this book, but the last to leave the study hall with me. Felipe Lobo Koerich, for wit, class, and comments full of sass. You are an excellent editor and an even better friend. Looking forward to the day you rule the world. Grace Fox, your talent has always been spectacular, but your dedication to designing the best cover possible has been remarkable. It is a privilege to have a friend as fun and committed as you. Hannah Song, for encouraging me from the start and never letting me get too serious. Katie Anderson, for never hesitating to support a friend. Linda Wen, for reading this story way too many times, eating way too many crepes, and dreaming together about uncertain futures. Maya Nagarkatte, for your constant enthusiasm at every turn. Miyumi Aoki, for a lifetime of friendship and never letting me forget where I came from.

Abi Lovell, Beth Mallon, Cecil-Francis Brenninkmeijer, Hayley Grande, Jan Menafee, Lianna McFarlane-Connelly, Lindsay Lee, Pat Walsh, Paul Doherty, and Veronica Thomas, thank you all for your friendship and invaluable input over the course of this project.

To Stefanie Luthin, Randi Orlin, and Nickie Demakos, thank you so much for lending your artistic gifts and bringing these words to life for the first time.

Thank you to Savannah McIntosh and Kennedy Urban, who rallied behind someone they'd just met to make my dreams come true. You are both wonderful friends. I can't wait to see where we all go from here.

Thank you to Y.A.Zuch, Cheryl Johnson, Kenna Chic, and Jeanne Behm for being incredibly patient sensitivity readers and for giving your eye-opening perspectives on identities I do not claim.

To the team at New Degree Press, thank you. This has been a wild ride, but you guided me every step of the way. Eric Koester, Tom Toner, Leah Pickett, Shawna Quigley, Linda Berardelli, and Kaity Van Riper, I cannot thank you enough for your steadfast commitment to making this book the best it could be.

Special Thanks to...

Adam Nader, Alex Martino, Alex Skarzynski, Alexandra Chaidez, Alison Vinciguerra, Amanda Meegan, Amerisa Kyriazis, André Amaral, Andrew Johnston, Andrew Dolan, Angela Wong, Angela Valdivieso, Ann Heggans, Anna Kindler, Anne Coyne, Anne Paglia, Annie Shaw, Ashley Quint, Bella Weissman, Beth Mallon, Brendan Burke, Brendan

Shaw, Brett Treacy, Brianna Gist, Brigid Bendig, Brooke Norman, Bryan McDermott, Bryn Bogan, Bushra Shaikh, Carmen Lantigua, Carmen Wale, Carol Rutledge, Cecil-Francis Brenninkmeijer, Cecilia Aguirre, Charles Nolte, Chelsea Cohen, Cielo Aquino-Remington, Cira Mancuso, CJ Pospisil, Cole Tamondong, Colum Goebelbecker, Cristina Sciuto, Dan Silkman, Daniel Arenas, Daniel Buell, Daniel Wheelock, David Luckett, Dawn Kemp, Diego Velazquez Saloux, Divya Ganesan, Dotti Anita Taylor, Dwana Hirshman, Eileen Durkin, Eliza Lafferty, Elizabeth Donnelly, Ella Silvers, Ellie Boyle, Emily Erickson, Emily Jonsson, Emily Vitale, Emma Garvey, Emma Sculles, Eric Ellis, Eric Koester, Eric McDonald, Erica Harrell, Erika Kennedy, Ethan Young, Felipe Lobo Koerich, Frances R. Simmon, Gabriela Charlot, Gene White, Gia Ariola, Gladys Ross, Gordon Rutledge, Grace Fox, Grace Kim, Grace Rector, Gracie Tillotson, Graciela Llorente, Hanna Blankemeier, Hannah Song, Hayley Grande, Helen Savaiano, Isabella Falero, Jack Berson, Jacob Epstein, Jacqueline Gordon, Jalen Benjamin, James Owens, James Peters, Jan Menafee, Jane Hutton, Jane Patti, Janet Silvera, Jasmine Hoskins, Jeffrey D. Wray, Jen Golobic, Jenni Loo, Jeremy Atuobi, Jessica Belica, Jimmy Herdegen, Joey Fernandez, Joy Armstrong, Joyce Rutledge, Judith McDermott-Jeter, Judith Stockmon, Julia Hartnett, Julia Hyacinthe, Julia Jackson, Julie Blankemeier, Julie Griffin, Karen Baldwin, Kathleen Flanagan, Kathryn Paravano, Katie Anderson, Katy Schuller, Kelly Goonan, Kenetta Bailey, Kennedy Urban, Kia Dean, Kiara Gradilla, Kirby Crane, Kiren Chaudry, Krista Pospisil, Laura Ratlif, Lauren Levin, Lauren Wylie, Leo John Arnett, Leslie Davis, Leticia Chacón, Lexi Tiemann, Lia Gonzalez, Lianna McFarlane Connelly, Lily Tushman, Linda Wen, Lindsay Lee, Lindsay Pistorius, Lisa Fauntroy,

Lisa Green, Lisa McNeill, Lisa Morrow, Lora Galich, Loretta Singleton, Lydia Cole, Miyumi Aoki, Maeve Simon, Maggie Lyons, Maggie Taaffe, Marc Steward, Marco Rondinini, Mark Ausbrooks, Martha Chimienti, Mary Ellen Bottone, Mary Kate Jezuit, Mary Kate Vorisek, Matthew Alfano, Matthew Fisher, Maureen Lonergan, Maya Nagarkatte, Meena Morar, Megan Doherty, Michael Flynn, Michael Saxon, Michael Summey, Michelle Carter, Mikayla Swanson, Miles Jackson, Miriam Norman, Miro Ehrfeld, Miss Phyllis Wallace, Nadia Smith, Nichole J Simmon, Nickie Demakos, Nicole Nichols, Nina Onyemeziem, Nina Gordon, Noelani Garcia, Olivia Baldwin, Omari Collins, Owen Baldwin, Pat Walsh, Patt Malenfant, Philomena Harbaugh, Phyllis Rutledge, Ralph Nader, Ray Shiu, Rhea Gordon Williams, Richard Rutledge, Rodney Robinson, Rosa Gist, Ruth Winfree, Sabrina St-Onge Dhaliwal, Sandy Handan-Nader, Sara Mantich, Savannah McIntosh, Scott Smith, Sean and Zakia Datcher, Sonali Persaud, Spurgeon Robinson, Stefanie Luthin, Stephania Lopez, Stephen E Brown, Steven Reich, Sydney Lupo, Tara Maloney, Teresa J. Madden, Tessa Murray, Thomas Heggans, Jr., Tithi Patel, Tracy DuPree Davis, Virginia Connolly, Wakaha S. Sampei, Walter Evans, and Zoe Mendel.

A Final Note

A note of gratitude to you, dear reader. A story is only as good as the people who explore it. I hope this provoked your imagination and leads you to new adventures ahead.